CW00499780

20

About the author

Susan Parry began writing when her twin daughters were small, and she was working full time as a university professor at Imperial College. She now devotes her time to consultancy work, including forensic studies and archaeological investigations that form the basis for her writing. Her husband, Mark, is retired so they are now able to spend more time together in the family home in Swaledale, where the views from her house provide inspiration. Together they have walked many of the areas described in the books, accompanied by their Airedale terrier. Her grown up daughters, Elspeth and Alice both have careers in crime – on the right side of the law. Visit her website at www.SusanParry.co.uk.

By Susan Parry

Corpse Way
Death Cart
Grave Hand
Craven Scar
Purple Shroud
Frozen Ground
Grand Depart
Potent Poison
Stone Tomb

STONE TOMB

SUSAN PARRY

Viridian Publishing

First published in the United Kingdom in 2018 by
Viridian Publishing

Viridian Publishing
PO Box 594
Dorking
Surrey
RH4 9HU

www.viridian-publishing.co.uk
e-mail: enquiries@viridian-publishing.co.uk

ISBN 978-0-9567891-6-7

For Lyra

Chapter 1

'You and my boy should see more of each other. You *are* brothers,' said Shane, glancing in the rear view mirror and pulling into the outside lane.

The old van's engine was straining as they drew slowly alongside a wagon then gradually moved past it.

'Half-brothers,' muttered Alf.

'Aye, but you shared the same mother and that's important.'

Not important enough that you abandoned her without a penny, thought Alf.

'I know your dad don't like it but you're always welcome in our house.'

If Dad knew he was doing a job with Shane, he would be disappointed and saddened to think he had lied to him about where he was going. Dad was always so reasonable he'd never needed to pretend he was with his mates before. But he knew he wouldn't approve of any dealings with Shane Armstrong.

He continued, 'I know it still hurts him that my Jesse decided to come and live with me but I'm his father and the poor lad was only thirteen when your mother died. Those years living with Roy were difficult for him.'

Alf ignored him. They *were* difficult years; difficult for all three of them after Mum passed away. Dad coped – just. He could hardly remember his mother but recalled when Jesse ran away to his biological father, the times when he was brought back kicking and screaming and Dad's anguished expression. As he got older, Alf became aware of the reason why his father was so adamant that Jesse remained with them until he was sixteen: Shane Armstrong was a small-time criminal, not clever enough to organise anything himself but working for others in the area, avoiding prison only through his ability not to get caught.

The van swerved and suddenly they had left the dual carriageway and were travelling down a narrow lane. Shane took the bends at speed, assuring Alf that there would be nothing around at this time of night – even the pubs had been closed for a couple of hours.

Already Alf wished he hadn't been so quick to agree to his brother's request to accompany Shane on a bit of business.

'What's actually wrong with Jesse's leg?' he asked.

'Broke it.'

'How?'

'Tripped over or bashed it or something.'

'I thought he said something about a dog.'

'Maybe he tripped over a dog. Anyway I told him to ask you to cover for him.'

'*You* suggested me?'

He couldn't say exactly why but it made him feel worse that Shane had drawn him into working for him. It was as if he was scoring points over Dad, by enticing him into his shady world.

Shane was lighting a cigarette and offered one to Alf.

'I don't.'

'Of course you don't. Roy wouldn't allow it, would he?' He laughed. 'Jesse used to enjoy visiting me because I'd let him have the odd puff and a drink. Your Mum used to play hell about it.'

Alf opened his window and breathed in the fresh, cool air. He could smell the countryside even though it was too dark to see the fields.

Shane continued, 'She gave me a hard time over that.'

"A stroppy teenager" his dad's relatives called Jesse. *Takes after his father* they would say, *not like young Alfie.* The two men were such complete opposites it wasn't surprising that they didn't get along. Dad was such a straight, honest guy who cared about everyone, while Shane was just out for what he could get. Once Jesse moved in with Shane permanently, he became just like him.

Alf on the other hand had grown up like *his* dad, he supposed, or at least how his dad wanted him to be. But however commendable the desire to go to university was, there was the question of money. Which was what had got him into tonight's little escapade. Somehow Jesse had persuaded him that doing a night's work with Shane every so often would help the funds.

The winding lane seemed interminable. Shane had turned on some dreadful country and western song and was tapping away on the steering wheel in time to the music.

'I bet you missed your mum.'

He seemed to be waiting for a response but Alf ignored him.

'You know her and me got married young,' he continued, 'on account of her expecting Jesse. But we stuck it out for four years so it can't have been so bad, can it?'

Left her with a four year old kid to bring up by herself.

'She was a difficult woman. Always nagging me to better myself.' He opened the window to toss out his cigarette butt. 'In the end I couldn't take it and got out.'

Alf knew he'd gone off with the woman that managed a betting shop in Middlesborough but had had several unsuccessful liaisons since then. He was no catch with his long greasy hair and ridiculous earing. Although Dad was eight years his senior, he was much better turned out, not that he was interested in dating.

'Hope you like a bit of country music,' Shane said. 'Radio doesn't work and this is the only one I've got with me. I don't suppose it's your sort of thing, eh?'

'No.'

'So what d'you like? Paul Weller I reckon with that mod haircut!' He laughed.

The road had widened and they seemed to be gradually moving downhill.

'So where are we going?' Alf asked, not wanting to find out *why* – yet.

'That's for me to know and for you to find out. The less you know the better my lad.'

That did not sound good. Of course he knew there was a chance the job wasn't legal and he was already forming the suspicion that they were going to be poaching.

'We're going to be doing a bit of walking on rough ground so I hope those boots are strong.'

'Yes, Jesse told me. So where are we walking to?'

'Just through the woods. We'll have to be quiet mind, so once we're out of the van it's no talking.'

That will be a relief, thought Alf.

The music droned on and Shane continued to hum and tap until he took a right and finally they came to a stop.

'Remember what I said, not a sound.'

He gave Alf a head torch and told him to get out, shutting the door quietly then following him over a wall and down a track. It was wonderful to be out of the smoky atmosphere of the vehicle and into the fresh, cold night. It was so quiet Alf could hear Shane breathing heavily as he made his way into the woodland. By the light of the torch, he could see that Shane was carrying a shotgun, confirming his belief that they were after rabbits, although he didn't see why he would need his help.

Their torches bobbed and flashed around as they stepped over roots and rocks. They were following a track in the wood and Alf could detect the sound of a stream away to his left. Several times he nearly fell as he tripped on a root and once he walked into a tree. Finally, ahead of him, He saw Shane step off the track and start picking his way through the undergrowth.

'Stay where you are!' he instructed as the light gradually disappeared. About fifteen seconds later there was a metallic rattling and a shout.

'We've got one. We've only bloody got one!'

A light appeared in the direction of Shane's voice.

'Over here – come quickly!'

Alf moved cautiously in the direction of the light until he spotted Shane. He followed him into the undergrowth where he stopped by a large crate and peered in.

'Is it a dog?' Alf asked.

'No, it is not a dog. It's a fox. A bloody fox has taken the bait.' He didn't sound pleased.

The crate rattled as the animal shrank back from their torchlight. Alf could see it was trapped in the metal cage.

Shane was muttering that he should have brought the dogs. Now he'd need more rabbit for bait.

'I don't need you, Alf, my boy. You get yourself back to the van.' He chucked the keys at him.

He left the rattling of the cage behind as he went as quickly as he could back to the path. There was a loud shot, just one shot and after that the wood was quiet.

'I tell you, it wasn't there when I went down yesterday!' Amy was busy serving out the vegetables for the children.

'You probably didn't notice,' replied her husband, helping himself to roast potatoes.

She shook her head in exasperation. 'I certainly would have seen a great ginger fox lying by the path.'

'Was it all covered in blood?' her son asked with a grin.

'Don't talk with your mouth full, James!' She sat down and picked up her knife and fork. 'In fact that's why I stopped. It was so perfect lying there, you'd think it was asleep.'

'P'rhaps it was,' suggested Anna.

Amy wished she could agree with her young daughter but when she bent over the animal she could see it was lifeless.

'Probably natural causes,' suggested her husband, helping himself to gravy. 'No-one round here would be out shooting.'

He was right. The nearest farm was too far and the old farmer was too frail to be out with his gun these days.

'Anyway, I've got to get on after dinner; there's a guest arriving this evening.'

James sighed loudly. 'I thought you said there wasn't anyone coming until Thursday.'

Amy wished her son wouldn't make his disapproval of their bed and breakfast guests quite so obvious.

'Well he rang this morning and asked very nicely if he could stay and I said he could. It's only for a few nights he said.'

The meal was over quickly and she was left to clear up. James went off to play with his friends and Jeff was in the garden, where Anna was helping him clear a patch of nettles. Amy went to check on the guest room armed with some of her homemade biscuits in a little Kilner jar.

Mills had expected Phil to come over during the weekend. They hadn't made any specific plans but she'd suggested it and he seemed to agree; if he didn't arrive soon the weekend would be over. His phone line hadn't been connected yet and without a mobile signal there was no way to contact him. Would it be wrong to go to see what was up? Perhaps he was ill? He might need help. It was definitely essential she went over.

The drive from Mossy Bank across to Whaw was just a few miles over the tops. Phil had chosen to rent the same cottage he'd used when they'd met years ago and it hadn't really changed, apart from becoming more dilapidated. She could have asked him to stay with her in Swaledale but she didn't want to pressure him. He had seemed in quite a vulnerable state when she'd visited him in Paris at Christmas and he needed time to settle back in England.

The improvement in the weather had brought out the visitors and there were a number of cars parked at Surrender Bridge as she passed through. A few children were paddling in the stream at the water splash and two red-faced cyclists were struggling up the hill as she sped down into Arkengarthdale. Once she crossed Eskeleth Bridge towards Whaw the road seemed interminable, growing narrower and narrower as she climbed. She prayed she wasn't going to meet anything coming the other way.

Eventually she reached the tiny cottage, on its own in the middle of nowhere. It was a beautiful spot but leaving the car to walk down to the cottage she wondered how accessible it would be in snow. As she passed the front window she spotted Phil seated facing her. She waved. No response. His eyes were open but he wasn't seeing her, he was staring into the distance. She waved again but nothing. She leaned forward and tapped on the glass then stepped back as he jumped from his seat and stared rapidly around him.

'Who is it?' he shouted. 'What d'you want?' His face was drawn and he was frowning. She'd not seen him look so angry before.

She knocked very gently on the door and waited. Eventually a sheepish figure peered out at her.

'Hi Mills.' He stood without moving.

'Can I come in?'

'Yes.' He left the door, moving back into the tiny sitting room.

'Were you asleep?' Mills asked, hoping to cover his embarrassment at the outburst.

'I guess so.' He sat back down on the sofa.

Mills remained standing. 'I thought you might come over to mine. I could cook... or we could go out.'

She'd spent hours preparing a special lamb casserole recipe that she'd found on the internet for Saturday night and when he'd not appeared it became their potential Sunday lunch and now it could be their supper.

He hadn't replied.

'Or we could cook here if you've got something in?' Was she sounding desperate?

'To be honest, I'm not very hungry.'

'That's ok.'

They sat like strangers for a while until Mills could bear it no longer.

'How about a drink then? We could go to the pub and you can watch me eat.' Mentally she was putting the casserole in the freezer.

He grunted. 'I need a shower.'

'That's fine, I'll wait.'

He dragged himself from the sofa and disappeared upstairs. Soon she could hear the water running. She looked round at the worn brown furniture, the damp waterlines on the wallpaper and the dirty windows and told herself that *she* would get depressed in this environment. But she knew it wasn't his surroundings that were the cause of his demeanour. He'd spent five years examining the bones from mass graves in Colombia and last year on the site of a plane crash as the expert in identification of bodies. When she'd first met him he was the carefree osteoarchaeologist she was asked to assist on a case. That was nine years ago, just after she'd finished her PhD. She was never sure why he chose to go abroad and finish their relationship but it had happened. She was just glad that they had been able to renew their friendship – for that's what it was. The last year, working on the crash site had taken its toll and his return to England was supposed to get him back to his original occupation of working on archaeological bones.

'Sorry about earlier.' His hair stuck up in clumps where he'd dried it with a towel. The colour had returned to his face and he'd had a shave. It was the Phil she was used to, even down to the Radiohead T-shirt. 'I must have dropped off.'

'I thought we could walk down to the CB – my treat,' added Mills since he looked surprised.

It was a short walk beside the river, once they left the lane and took the footpath into the wood. It was a walk they had taken several times when they'd been together before. She knew he would relax once outside and his mood predictably lifted as they strolled along. Of course, in the past they would have been accompanied by Earl, Phil's beautiful lurcher, but she couldn't bring herself to mention him. It was too painful to remember how the dog had been poisoned while she was looking after him and how Phil had received the news while abroad.

It was too soon for the early diners and they sat near the bar surrounded by empty tables. Mills had noticed how Phil was more comfortable in the absence of crowds when they were in Paris. Several times they'd had to leave a café or a bar when it became too noisy. He would become restless and eventually quite agitated until Mills would suggest it was time to go. She could see the relief on his face, as if he couldn't admit it himself and was grateful for her rescuing him.

They were both drinking diet colas, Mills because she assumed she would have to drive home; it was work the next day and she would be leaving the cottage at seven as usual. She'd not seen Phil consume alcohol since he'd returned to England and she wondered if he was on medication that precluded it. A drug to calm his nerves perhaps? Whatever treatment he was getting, he needed something to occupy his time, to take his mind off the horrific scenes he'd witnessed over the past few years. He'd described the mass graves, the torture he could detect from the bones he'd observed, the small bodies he'd examined.

'So are you up to anything this week?' she asked, wanting to introduce her idea as naturally as possible.

He shook his head and looked around to avoid her gaze.

'I was thinking…' she hesitated, not wanting to sound as if she was trying to organise his life. 'I was wondering whether the National Park might have anything interesting going on.'

'What d'you mean?'

'Something archaeological but not involving, you know… bones.'

'Such as?' He sounded disinterested.

'I don't know but they're always digging something up, aren't they?' She knew she was beginning to sound almost wheedling and decided to give it a rest. 'They're taking orders now. Let's see what they've got on tonight.'

Phil definitely became more sociable once the food had arrived and Mills wondered what he'd been eating over the weekend. She'd taken him shopping when he'd moved in but that was a week ago and she'd expected that they would stock him up again when he came over.

'You'll need to get some form of transport soon, won't you?' she asked. 'Will you get another bike?'

She wasn't sure whether he'd passed a driving test for a car; he'd always been on a motorbike when she knew him.

'I suppose, although a pushbike would do for now.'

'Really? You do realise how hilly it is round here?'

'It'll do me good, help me get in shape.'

He concentrated on his meal until his plate was clean then ordered a pudding, while Mills had a coffee. The place was filling up and she was soon suggesting they set off back up the dale. The sun was still shining and it was warm, even through the woods.

'So shall I approach the National Park or have you been advised to avoid anything for now?' Mills asked when they reached his ramshackle home.

He didn't reply.

'Perhaps you could tidy up the cottage instead,' she said with a grin.

He looked round but ignored her. 'You could ask them,' he said with a shrug.

Chapter 2

Amy watched James drop his bike down in the garden before flinging the back door open. His face was streaked with dirt, his knees muddy.

'What *have* you been up to?' she asked.

'Nothing much. We went down to the river and played seals.'

'Seals?'

'You know, like the film "Navy Seals vs Zombies". I was a zombie.'

'When did you see that?'

'On YouTube. There's a trailer for it.'

Amy despaired. Was there anything this ten year-old missed? She made a mental note to check out the YouTube video and told her son to clean up before tea.

But he wanted to tell her about the fox.

'I took Olly to see it,' he said. 'He was well impressed!'

'Was he really?'

'He'd never seen a fox close up before.'

'They don't last long round here, love. Not when people keep chickens.'

'We had a good look at it and we found where he'd been shot.'

'Really?'

'Yeah, Olly found it, right between the eyes. Pow.' James pretended to fire a hand gun.

'It wouldn't be a little gun like that, son.'

Amy looked up as her husband appeared. 'That fox was shot, Jeff.'

'Right between the eyes!' James repeated.

'Must've been a good shot then, whoever it was. Surprised you didn't see that, it would've blown half its head off.' Jeff was addressing his wife.

'Yes,' said James with a grin. 'We saw it.'

'So who would've done that, then?' Amy asked.

Jeff shrugged. 'No-one round here.'

'Well I just hope it wasn't kids. I don't like youngsters playing around with guns.'

'Mum, all the farm boys have guns,' complained James. 'Olly goes rabbiting with his dad.'

'I'm sure he does but we aren't farmers and you aren't a farm boy, so don't even think about it,' warned Amy. 'Now go and wash but don't make the cloakroom dirty, we've got a guest remember.'

'When is he coming?' Jeff asked.

'He said he'd be here by six, so any time now. He might need a lift down to the pub.'

'Doesn't he have a car – or a bike?'

'No, he's on foot.'

'Then he can walk.'

'He could but I said we could ferry him if necessary. It's these little niceties that make the difference. Remember what they said on the course?'

'That was two days wasted,' grunted Jeff as he settled in his chair.

'I think it was very valuable and worth every penny. We knew what to expect and I've found the handbook very useful. Anyway, I don't know why you're settling yourself down; I need you to quickly change the bulb in the bedside lamp, the one nearest the door.'

Jeff sighed, struggled to his feet and left the room muttering under his breath. Amy went into the lounge for the third time that day to check it was in order for her guest. She straightened the pile of magazines and puffed up the cushions before standing back to admire the room. So far their first season was going well and she had no regrets about leaving Banbury to start afresh in the Dales, despite what the rest of the family felt. The kids would settle once they started school properly and Jeff, he just needed to get sorted out. He was a professional joiner but so far he'd only picked up a few bits of work for other people. She hadn't realised it would be quite so hard for him to find his feet.

She was roused by the door bell ringing and quickly removed her apron before rushing to welcome the new arrival. He wasn't her usual kind of clientele, as she liked to call them. He looked unkempt but she couldn't put her finger on it exactly. He was unshaven and there were tattoos creeping out from under his collar. His only luggage was a small rucksack. As she ushered him up to his room, they passed Jeff on the landing, where he gave her a thumbs up before running downstairs. Her guest admired the view and said what a lovely room it was. He was clearly impressed by the en suite which, Amy explained, had only been fitted that year. They chatted for a while, standing awkwardly beside the bed and he said to call him Len. Amy said she would leave him to get settled in.

'Here's a key for your room and the other one is for the front door. We like guests to feel free to come and go as they please.'

It was something they'd said on the course.

Her visitor was back early and Amy suggested he might like to watch television in the lounge. She took him a tray of tea and some parkin which he consumed in silence.

'Did you enjoy your meal, Len?' she asked and he replied it was a bit posher than he was used to.

'I came back along the footpath, like Jeff suggested,' he told her. 'It was interesting.'

'Why's that?' Amy asked.

He was smiling. 'I passed a chap with a gun,' he said. 'Well it's not something I come across in Sunderland – and if I did, I'd be really worried. I assume it was a gamekeeper?'

'Maybe, or someone rabbiting,' said Amy.

But as she collected the tea tray and left him alone, she puzzled over who it could have been at that time of the evening.

Mills went on to email as soon as she was back home. She wrote to Dave at the National Park asking whether he would like an extra pair of hands to work for him. Her message emphasised Phil's expertise, assuring him it wouldn't cost them anything. He could turn his hand to most things but wouldn't want to deal with bones or remains of any kind.

Just as she pressed send, the phone rang.

'Mills, it's Nina. I just wanted to catch up after your first weekend… you know… with Phil.'

Her friend was almost more excited than she was to have Phil back in the Dales. She had good reason to be fond of him since her husband owed him his life. Nine years ago Phil had saved Nige when he'd been left for dead in the snow by a man who was now serving a very long sentence for murder and attempted murder.

'Yes it was fine.'

'You must bring him over next weekend. I can do Sunday lunch. He hasn't met the children and Nige is really looking forward to see him again.'

'That would be good but he's quite, you know, tired at the moment. He's still recovering from all the dreadful things he's been working on.'

'I suppose he must be but he'll soon be his old self. After all he's used to digging up bodies and all that gory stuff.'

'I think it has affected him more than he realises, Nina.'

Her friend was a police officer and she'd had to deal with some serious cases but it couldn't compare with identifying body parts from a recent air crash and Mills told her so.

'I see. Sorry, I hadn't realised. Is he getting counselling?'

'I don't think so. I asked when I was in Paris but he said it wasn't necessary. Now he's back here it may not be on offer.'

'Then he should see his doctor.'

'I don't think he's even bothered to organise a GP yet but I'll mention it.' She was sure he would ignore her.

'I forgot to ask you, how's work now you're full-time at the university?'

'It's fine but summer term is always a bit hectic, especially with exams coming up.'

'But just think of the long summer holiday, Mills.' Nina was laughing.

'You know perfectly well that's a myth.'

'But everyone believes it. I'm always being asked how Nige is going to spent the long break and I have to tell them that he will be taking students on field trips and it's the only time he can do his own research.'

'But you'll have a family holiday?'

'Nige is threatening to take us all camping in Wales so the children can learn about their roots. It fills me with horror.'

'But if the weather is nice…'

'In Wales? Nige is always telling me how much it rains there. And he wants to visit all his aunts and uncles.'

'That's nice.'

'They all chatter amongst themselves in Welsh and Nige has to explain what's going on. You know he's teaching Rosie?'

'How's she getting on?'

'Quite well actually but now I don't know what he's telling her!'

'You need to learn it yourself or you may find the children speaking together without you being able to understand them. Imagine the mischief that could cause!'

Mills was at the university early for a Monday morning. She'd woken at five and instead of lying in bed worrying about Phil, she decided to make an early start. By eight, after coffee and a Danish pastry in the cafeteria, she was ready for the day.

Nige didn't arrive until nine-thirty, which was normal for him. He usually dropped the children off at school to let Nina get away early. As he pointed out, the university was much more flexible over hours than the constabulary. He finally appeared clutching a takeaway coffee and sank behind his desk with a groan. Mills still felt awkward taking up space in his domain but that was the deal and he hadn't complained. Students coming to see Nige still seemed surprised to see her there, which might have been avoided if the department had got round to adding her name to the plate on the door.

'Good weekend?' Mills asked.

'Yes, not bad actually. Nina was at home both days, which makes a change.'

'No big cases on then?'

'No, touch wood.' He knocked on the desk.

Lectures had finished and the exam season had begun. It was a busy time and Mills had her fair share of invigilating to do in the next few weeks but she also had some free time to work on her own research. It was the first time for some years that she was able to do so and there was definitely an expectation that she would be producing original work and publications in scientific journals. Because she was shared between the Archaeology and Forensics departments, there was pressure to carry out research in both their fields and it was still evolving. Secretly she had rather hoped that Phil might help her with the challenge.

'Nina said you're bringing Phil over next Sunday?' It was more a question than a statement.

'Yes.'

'That's good. We're looking forward to catching up with him again.'

When she explained that their friend needed to recuperate after his stressful work, Nige agreed and repeated what his wife had said about seeking counselling.

'I might try and mention it when I see him,' Mills offered but she was uncertain how she would broach the topic.

The morning passed quickly as she tried to come up with suitable research topics. Her PhD had been on bog bodies and in her last assignment she had exhumed a skeleton that turned out unexpectedly to be recently buried. She had been quite interested in the accurate ageing of skeletons after that, which was why she thought Phil could have helped her, as an expert osteoarchaeologist. But now it didn't seem such a good idea. She was saved any further head scratching as she was needed in the main hall at two to invigilate the third year forensic chemistry exam. She would need a quick sandwich first.

The cafeteria was quiet and Mills was pleased to be able to sit alone and look at her messages. To her surprise there was a missed call from Dave at the National Park and a voicemail. Mills checked the time and rang him.

'Mills, thanks for the message. I remember Phil – he helped us several times in the past, although I haven't seen him for quite a few years.'

Mills explained briefly where Phil had been and what he'd been doing. She was interrupted several times by Dave's expressions of surprise at what Phil had had to contend with.

'Anyway, he's back now and I just wondered...'

'I've discussed it with my colleagues and we do have something. You said he was living in Arkengarthdale?'

'Yes.'

'There's a nuclear observation post near Tan Hill. We want to investigate it before it deteriorates. Do you think he might be interested?'

'Yes of course,' she lied. She was sure she could get him interested. 'But what is a nuclear observation post?' she added.

'It's a Royal Observer Corp post for monitoring a nuclear attack, basically. It's an underground bunker and until the sixties it was manned on occasions when they were carrying out exercises. I'll send you the links to the websites about them. We've already covered a similar one at Grinton.'

Mills thanked him and finished her sandwich. She felt excited by the proposition and hoped Phil would be too. If only he would get his phone line sorted out she would be able to let him know. She sent him a message, in the hope that he was out and about somewhere where there was a mobile signal then ran to the main hall with a minute to spare.

The students were lined up or milling around in the corridors. Over fifty nervous faces watched her as she entered the main hall and shut the door firmly behind her. Her assistant, a PhD student she knew by sight, was distributing papers and calculators systematically along the lines. When everything was ready, he gave a nod to Mills and she propped open the door, instructing the students to come in and leave their coats, bags and electronic equipment on the tables at the back of the hall.

'Has everyone got their exam number?' she reminded them. Amazingly they all seemed to have remembered. 'Then you can sit anywhere but don't forget to number your answer book – and do not put your name!'

Anonymity was an essential part of the marking system at the university now. Each student was allocated a number so it should be impossible to know whose work one was marking. It was true that class work was generally printed from a computer now so it was unlikely the handwriting would provide a clue. Everything was being done to make the examination system as objective as possible.

Mills was now responsible for the next three hours. Her assistant was simply there to accompany examinees to the cloakroom if necessary or deal with any medical issues. She hoped there would be none of those. Just two students were eligible for extra time. There was one last instruction: to place their student ID card on the desk to prove who they were.

'So, you have three hours. I'll let you know when you have thirty minutes left – remember you mustn't leave the hall after that time. If you finish before that, you should leave your papers on your desk and go as quietly as you can. Right, turn over your papers please.'

She had been given the names of two students with dyslexia who would be given extra time, but she would be relieved of her duties after three hours so it wasn't her problem. She joined her assistant at the desk at the front of the hall and settled down for a long and tedious afternoon. She did not approve of colleagues who stalked up and down the rows distracting the candidates but sympathised with the desire to stretch one's legs. She had deliberately brought some paper and a pen in her bag so she could use the time to do some project planning.

The first fifteen minutes or so were always very quiet. It was drummed into the students that they should read the questions thoroughly and more than once before selecting which ones to answer. Then the heads would go down and the frantic writing would begin. Hopefully it would be an uneventful session.

The first hand went up at two-twenty. Mills stood, trying to avoid her chair making too much noise. She tiptoed down the middle row to a lad she had seen in her classes.

'Question three has got something missing,' he whispered.

A few heads turned. He thrust the question paper into her hand. She'd looked at the questions but most of them had meant little to her. She wasn't a chemist and that particular question was on fires, which definitely was not her subject.

'Are you sure?' she asked, playing for time.

'To calculate the time to flashover we need to use this equation.' He pointed to a long series of symbols called the "Babrauskas and Thomas formulas".

'OK.' She waited.

'But to do the calculation we need to know the ceiling height and it's not here.'

'Perhaps you're supposed to assume it?'

He looked puzzled.

There was nothing she could do. There was no way she was going to look for the missing information now. All she could suggest was that he uses a figure assuming a certain ceiling height – after all, it would show he knew what he was doing. The lad grunted and said he would leave it. As she moved towards the front of the hall another hand went up. In all, eight students queried the question. She was tempted to suggest a ceiling height for the question and announce it to everyone but what if they didn't actually need it for the calculation – she would be in trouble. When she told the PhD student what was happening, he offered to find Dr Cuthbert, who apparently was the fire forensics expert. She told him to stay put, they were bound to have their first toilet request soon and she'd need him to act as escort.

At last three hours was up. No-one had left early and the students were told to exit quietly while the candidates with extended time carried on. When the relief invigilator arrived, Mills took him into the corridor to explain about the query on question three of the paper.

'Typical of him,' he said.

'But the papers are checked before they're printed.' Mills knew the transcriptions of all papers were carefully reviewed for any typos.

'Which proves it was Colin's fault.'

There was nothing Mills could do but let the course administrator know what had happened. She walked back to the office to collect her laptop before wandering out into drizzling rain. It had been a bit of a rubbish day except for the news from the National Park and she decided she would turn off at Reeth to see if Phil was around. He hadn't replied to her message and she suspected he hadn't left the cottage all day.

On the way she tried to decide the best way to broach the subject of the bunker with Phil. If the site was near Tan Hill he would need some form of transport, even if it was a push bike, and it would have to be a topic that grabbed his imagination. She would offer to help but the aim was for him to have something of his own to work on, a reason for getting out of bed in the morning.

The roads were surprisingly empty on the way back up Swaledale and into Arkengarthdale, and, much to her relief, the lane was clear up to Phil's place. She pulled the car onto the narrow verge above the cottage, hoping the Mini wouldn't sink into the soggy ground. There was plenty of space for a car to pass but she wasn't sure if a tractor would make it without damage. She ran through the rain and straight inside, assuming Phil was home if the door was open. She called and looked round but there was no sign. She stepped back outside and looked up and down the lane. She called again but all she could hear was a pheasant in the woods below.

It was six-thirty; she would stay until seven. The kitchen was as grubby as it had been when he'd moved in a week ago. His dishes had added to the picture of neglect. She ran the hot tap but the water remained obstinately cold. She boiled a kettle and added it to the bowl with a generous squirt of the cheap washing up liquid. By the time the dishes were cleared, the surfaces cleaned and the crockery packed away, it was nearly seven. She checked the bathroom and gave the basin and loo a quick scrub. From there she went upstairs and was in the middle of removing the grubby blanket that constituted Phil's bedding when she heard the door slam.

'Mills? Is that you?'

'I'm up here!'

Footsteps on the stairs and he appeared, hair plastered on his damp face, his shorts and T-shirt dark with rain.

'What are you doing?' he shouted, coming across and wrenching the blanket from her hands.

'Cleaning… tidying… I was waiting… Where have you been? You're soaking wet.'

'Well it is raining!'

Suddenly he seemed to see the funny side of the situation and let go of the blanket. Mills let it fall to floor.

'The door was open, I didn't know where you were,' she explained.

'I went for a run.' He was pulling off his wet things and rooting through clothes piled on a chair by the bed. He was oblivious of her presence.

'I'll go downstairs,' she said. 'I've got some news.'

She waited in the tiny sitting room, regretting that she'd come at all. She could hear him moving about above her, while she rehearsed how she was going to broach the topic of the nuclear observation post. It went quiet upstairs for a few minutes and finally Phil appeared. He'd dried his hair with a towel by the look of it but he was at least dressed in a shirt and trousers that looked almost new.

'Did you say you were coming?' he asked, flopping down in the other chair.

'No but I left a message.'

'Still no connection; they say it will be another two weeks.'

Mills sighed. 'I came to tell you about some work in the National Park. I thought you might be interested.'

'Sure, I'm always happy to hear what you're up to.'

He was smiling. Was he winding her up?

'I meant that *you* might be interested in.'

'Me?'

She ignored him and continued to explain what she knew about the project. 'I need to get onto the internet sites that Dave suggested. We could do that tonight if you like?'

He stared at her but didn't say anything.

'Well, *I'll* look anyway,' she said pointedly.

A minute went by.

'Did you have a good run?' she asked, thinking that he looked exhausted.

'Yeah, good.'

'Did you go far?'

'About 15k. I aim to do it every day.'

So that was how he was spending his time. 'You must be starving!'

'Not really, I picked up a sandwich in Reeth.'

'You were in Reeth?'

'Yeah. It's a nice circular run, not too strenuous. I took the bag and got a few things.' He indicated a khaki rucksack flung down in the hall.

So you could have seen my message, thought Mills. She stood up. 'So long as you're ok, I'll go home to search for some information about the National Park project and give it to you some time.'

Phil followed her to the door and she heard him shout 'Thanks' as she climbed into the car. There was no way she was going to attempt to turn her Mini round so she set off down the narrow lane on the route through to Whaw, cursing under her breath.

Chapter 3

'Did you have a good day?' asked Amy.

Her guest was unpacking his rucksack in the hall. She looked at his boots disapprovingly.

'You can leave them downstairs – and I can take your flask and wash it out ready for the morning,' she offered. 'Did you enjoy your walk?'

He'd taken her advice and followed the path through Langthwaite that led up onto Fremington Edge, eventually dropping down into Reeth. He'd come back up following Arkle Beck.

'It was good weather until this afternoon but I didn't let the rain spoil my day. The views were grand from up on the top there. I need a shower now,' he declared.

'You won't want to be doing any more walking today then. If you want a lift into Reeth this evening, let me know,' Amy told him. 'There are plenty of places to eat.'

'Cheers – I'll think about it.' He picked up the rucksack and made for the stairs.

'Are you a bird-watcher?' Amy asked, indicating the binoculars round his neck.

'Well, amateur. I saw a number of species I don't normally get to see in Sunderland – curlews and lapwings.'

'That's what we like about it up here, the wildlife.' She was reminded of the fox she'd seen. 'The woods are full of creatures – foxes, rabbits, badgers…'

'Badgers? I'd like to see a badger.'

'Well, they say there are badgers in the wood as you go down towards Eskeleth Bridge. I've not seen them myself but that's what I've been told. My husband Jeff will probably be able to tell you.'

Amy took the thermos into the kitchen and rinsed it out, leaving it ready to fill in the morning. It was time to start preparing the meal for the family. The children were due back from their friends and Jeff would be out of the shed soon enough.

She was making the batter for toad-in-the-hole when her husband appeared.

'Been busy?' she asked.

His lack of employment was one thing but he spent most of his time pottering about when he could be looking for a job. He ignored her and opened the larder door to find a beer.

'I told Len that you'd give him a lift into Reeth,' she said. 'You'd best not have a drink yet.'

He shut the larder with a sigh and sat at the table.

'D'you know where in the woods the badgers live?' she asked him.

'The sett,' he corrected her. 'They live in a sett.'

'Ok, do you know where their sett is then?'

'Why do you ask?'

'Len says he hasn't ever seen one.'

James burst into the kitchen followed by Anna, talking excitedly about Olly's new computer game. Before Amy could quiz him about it, Jeff suggested a game of football and they all disappeared into the garden.

Dinner was almost ready when Len came to say he would walk down to the pub at Langthwaite. Amy repeated that her husband would take him to Reeth but he insisted he was fine and left. She was disappointed that she wouldn't be able to make her husband provide his taxi service – it was the only thing he contributed towards their hospitality venture.

Mills wanted to help Phil but she seemed unable to get through to him, so on the way home she'd decided to forget the offer from the National Park. She wasn't in the mood to cook and made beans on toast, comfort food that she resorted to when she felt rubbish. Not in the mood for watching TV, she checked her emails and came across some more links from Dave and was soon making notes on the Royal Observer Corps nuclear monitoring posts.

The underground monitoring station at Tan Hill had been opened in 1963 when the Cold War with the Soviet Union meant the threat of nuclear attack had been seen as a real possibility. Mills sat mesmerised by a series of films and videos from the time, describing how the underground bunkers would have been used to identify where a nuclear explosion had taken place and monitor the fall-out. Obviously she knew there had been a time when public service broadcasts and leaflets told everyone what to do in the case of a nuclear attack but this really brought it to life. A network of nearly sixteen hundred monitoring stations built underground and manned by ten thousand volunteers, just in case of a nuclear attack that never came.

The monitoring station at Tan Hill had been closed in 1991 when the Cold War ended and the Royal Observer Corps members were disbanded. As far as Mills could tell, nothing had been done with it since then. If the bunker had been left untouched there would be lots of interesting things in there, judging by the video showing the post in Cornwall owned by the National Trust and open to the public. What she could see was how small the space was – no bigger than her sitting room but longer and thinner, with the same low ceiling. Access was by a vertical iron ladder and Mills wondered whether it would still be useable after twenty-six years. She was certainly looking forward to finding out.

Whatever Phil decided, she definitely wanted to have a look and sent an email to Dave to confirm they would go ahead. She made herself a coffee then returned to the website to see what the observer corps volunteers were expected to do. It appeared they only manned the bunkers for practices, when three of them would be crammed into the tiny space fourteen feet below ground. The lid over the entrance would be sealed and they would stay there without running water or electrics for the length of the exercise. At least there was a chemical toilet, she noted.

She had to review the films several times before she grasped how the network of posts operated. In the event of an attack, each post would check to see the direction of the blast and its brightness, so people in the central control could pinpoint the origin from reports all over the country. The idea seemed to be that measurements of fall-out from the blast would allow the control centre to establish safe parts of the UK and the population would be able to escape the effects of fall-out. From what she understood of fall-out it sounded rather optimistic.

She devoured a chocolate bar, cursing Phil for being so difficult then immediately felt guilty. The poor guy was a mess and needed professional help, even Nina had said so. Well perhaps her friend could persuade him, if Mills could get him there for lunch on Sunday. If only she could talk to him but he was completely out of contact until his stupid phone line was connected.

As she threw the chocolate wrapper away she decided that what Phil needed was a dog. He'd been devoted to his lurcher when he lived in Arkengarthdale previously and if he wasn't working full-time it would be a perfect opportunity to take on a new pet – even better, a puppy. After scouring all the possible websites in the area she discovered that the RSPCA rehoming centre had a three year-old lurcher that was in need of a loving home. Mills resolved to talk Phil into a trip to Great Ayton at the weekend, certain he wouldn't be able to resist.

'It's after eleven and he's not back yet,' Amy told her husband when he came into the bedroom.

'Pub's just closing.'

'I hope he's not going to roll in drunk! I'm not keeping breakfast for him if he's up late.'

'He'll be fine.'

Jeff was struggling into his pyjamas. Amy noted his clothes were flung on the chair in the corner. The bed juddered as he clambered in beside her. She switched off the lamp and lay listening for the sound of the front door opening but all she could hear was the tick of the clock.

'He'll walk back on the road won't he?' she asked.

'Probably.'

'I wouldn't like to think of him on the footpath in the dark.'

'I expect he's got a torch.'

'He said he met a man with a gun last night.'

There was no response, just regular breathing that signified Jeff was asleep.

Amy lay alert for a while but she must have nodded off because now she could see it was ten past one. The clock face was illuminated by the light from the landing. She crept out to switch it off. Sighing, she went downstairs to deal with the hall light too but stopped on the bottom step. There were no boots down there. Had her guest really ignored her request and worn them upstairs? Irritated she snapped off the light switch and returned to the landing. His door was shut and she could hardly tackle him now but in the morning she would be having words.

'Still no sign of him,' complained Amy.

'Wait until the kids have gone,' said Jeff. 'He'll be sleeping off a heavy night.'

'Trust you to sympathise with him.' She was cooking bacon and sausage already. 'There's no way I'm keeping this hot for hours.'

'Stick it in the oven. It's his fault if it's a bit well done.'

Jeff clearly thought it was a joke. Amy chivvied the kids to get ready and they disappeared with their father, complaining it was too early to be dropped off. She finished cooking the "full English" that was described on her website, along with options of packed lunches and light refreshments in the evening, by which she meant her home-made parkin. She ate the cold toast that remained on the breakfast table and made a fresh pot of tea. She sat for a while listening to the news on the radio. Still there was no sound from upstairs. Eventually, at half-past eight, she decided to venture to the landing.

The guestroom door was firmly shut but daylight shone from under the door. She went up and listened. She knocked gently, then more loudly when there was no response. She banged harder, several times, and called his name. Nothing.

Back downstairs she thought about what she should do. They hadn't covered this on the course. What if he was ill – or worse? She would wait for Jeff to get back. It was his habit to drop the kids at school and go on to Reeth for the milk and a paper. Sometimes he would stop for a chat in the shops or with a neighbour, not that they knew many people yet. She waited, becoming more stressed as time passed.

'Why didn't you go in?' Jeff asked when he returned. 'He might have done a runner!'

Amy followed her husband up the stairs. He hammered on the door then warned that he would be coming in. Amy stood nervously while her husband ran down to find the master key. So what if he had died in the night? The course didn't tell you what to do then.

When Jeff finally unlocked the door they could see the room was empty. The bed hadn't been slept in and there was no sign of Len.

'He's done a bunk!' yelled Jeff.

'Hold on,' said Amy. 'He paid for three nights in advance – and look, he's left his rucksack.'

She emptied it onto the bed.

'Just underpants and a wash bag.'

'So did he stay last night?' Jeff asked.

'I don't think so, unless he remade the bed very neatly and I didn't hear him go this morning, or come back in the evening.'

'Did you see what he had with him when he went off yesterday?'

'No, he just popped his head round the door. D'you think something has happened to him?'

'More like he just decided to move on and didn't have the decency to tell us.' Jeff went back downstairs, leaving Amy wondering whether to change the bedding or wait to see if Len returned.

Mills was awake at five again. The sun was already streaming through the flimsy curtains. She got up to peer out across the fields where the sheep were already browsing. Exam time meant no lectures so there was little point in her rushing into the department early and she had a better idea. If she dropped in to see Phil, she could confirm that the nuclear observation post project was going ahead and arrange for them to meet Dave from the National Park at the site. She would also tell him about her idea for getting him a dog.

The road was empty and with the roof down she felt quite exhilarated as she made her way up the narrow road to Phil's. She ran down the track and banged on the door, determined to start their discussion in a positive way. A few minutes later her mood was deflated. There was no answer and either he wasn't responding or he was out. The door was locked so she wandered round to the back of the cottage but there was no sign of life. She sat in the car for a while then tried knocking again but eventually she gave up and drove away, after putting a scribbled note through the door: *Please ring me, I've got some news.*

As she drove to work Mills tried to decide whether Phil was at home or had been out so early in the morning. It seemed more probable that he was in but not answering the door. She felt foolish if he didn't want to speak to her but what if he was unwell? He clearly hadn't recovered from the stressful work he'd been doing, so what if he'd done something silly? By the time she was seated in the office she was getting wound up and called her friend for advice.

'... so I didn't know if I should call the police but that sounds a bit dramatic, doesn't it Nina?'

'We get calls all the time and ninety-nine percent of them come to nothing. Don't worry.'

'But there's no signal so I can't call him.'

'Do you seriously think that something has happened to him?'

Mills was beginning to feel silly. 'Sorry, Nina, I was panicking. I'm sure he was just out somewhere.' At six o'clock?

'Perhaps he went for a jog. It's a lovely morning and you said he goes running.'

'Of course, that's probably it.'

'There you are then! But perhaps you should ask him for a key.'

It was a logical suggestion but Mills was not confident enough in their relationship to make such a request.

Later that morning the departmental secretary brought in a bundle of papers. It was her marking from the forensics exam she'd invigilated. Around thirty separate answer books neatly piled in code number order. Only the course director and the administrative staff would know which student was responsible for which paper. Sometimes, on field trips or in laboratory sessions, there were occasions when students were making written notes but her course work was submitted electronically so the students' handwriting presented no clues for her.

Like everyone who'd set an exam question, she'd been required to produce a model answer to the question, listing the key components that should be addressed and the marks attached to them. It was a rigid system – if the components weren't there the marks couldn't be allocated, however good the response appeared. Mills knew she was spending far too long on each paper and calculated that at the rate she was working it would take her all week to mark the pile of papers in front of her. It was lucky she'd only been asked to set one question that year.

When Nige left the office at five, Mills had completed five papers. She was getting into the swing and was definitely becoming quicker but she decided to carry on for another hour or so. She was in the middle of paper number seven when her mobile buzzed. At first she ignored it, preferring to complete the marking for that student. It buzzed again a minute later, presumably when someone left a message, and she looked quickly to see that it was from Phil. *Been out what do you want?* She sent a reply, hoping he still had a signal, suggesting she could drop in later. It took an age before he replied but eventually a simple *Ok* came back.

By lunch-time Amy had decided to strip the room. If Len was too lazy to let her know his plans, he would lose his accommodation. During the business of tidying up she found some clothes he'd forgotten to take with him. She bundled them and his wash things into his rucksack and left it in the porch. If he came back for it she would give him a piece of her mind. The course had told them that there might be awkward guests but Amy thought they'd been very lucky so far, tapping the wooden stair rail as she passed.

She'd just settled down with a cup of tea when a neighbour rang to ask if she could take a family at short notice – two rooms for three nights, starting that evening. She said she would be delighted and began immediately to prepare the extra touches that made the difference. She would send Jeff out for more milk and she would bake a special cake that the children would like.

It was while she was getting the flour out of the pantry that there was a loud knock on the kitchen door and a man marched in. It was as if he owned the place, she told Jeff afterwards.

'Hi Carol!' the man had shouted then stopped in his tracks, his hand still holding the door handle.

'What do you want?' she asked, backing away.

He was scruffily dressed, his hair looked greasy and unkempt, and he was unshaven.

The man looked puzzled. 'Where's Carol?' he asked.

'Carol? Carol's not here.' Then it dawned. 'They left last year.'

Carol and Reg were the previous owners of the guest house. Clearly the man was confused. He went to leave then stopped and looked round the kitchen.

'Sorry… I thought… I'm sorry…'

'Is there something… I mean can *we* help?'

He pointed up the valley. 'I lived up there when Carol was here. She'd sometimes help. I'd better go.'

'Help with what?' Amy was curious now.

'If I ran out of milk or something….'

'Is that what you want?' Amy didn't have any to spare until Jeff came back and told him so. 'I'm Amy Bradby, we took over the business from Carol,' she explained carefully. 'Where is it you're living?'

'It's the old Keeper's Cottage.'

'But isn't that derelict?'

'Nearly.'

The man was peering at her coffee machine.

'What's your name?'

'Phil.'

'Well, Phil, it's nice to meet you.' She moved towards the door and he took the hint, wandering out and down the lane while Amy shut the door firmly behind him.

It had been awkward when Mills first arrived at the cottage. Phil didn't say where he'd been that morning and she didn't like to ask so she launched straight into her speech about the nuclear observation post. She hoped that he would be as interested as she was to investigate the site and research its use. Maybe, one day, it could even be opened to the public. He listened without interrupting her until she had nothing to add.

'…so I told him we would do it.' She waited for a response.

'We?'

'Well obviously you'll have more time than I will – won't you?' Was he frowning or just thinking how to respond?

He walked about as if trying to make up his mind. Eventually he said, 'What if I don't want to do it?'

'Why wouldn't you?'

Then he explained where he'd been at six o'clock. He was finding the cottage claustrophobic. He'd been used to roughing it when working in Colombia and he still found it very difficult to settle in confined accommodation. Last night had been warm and the cottage was too hot, so he'd decamped to the woods for the night.

'Are you serious?' Mills regretted her reaction immediately. Of course he was. He looked hurt. 'I mean, did you have a tent?'

He smiled. 'No, I just took my old sleeping bag and slept under the stars. It was great.' His expression changed. 'I don't think I can cope in a bunker of that size.'

'Well you wouldn't have to sleep in it!'

'I know. But I don't want to let anyone down.'

Mills sighed. She couldn't force him to take it on – there was no more to be said.

She changed the subject to hide her annoyance. 'You got a signal then?'

'What?'

'You saw my message. How did you get a signal?'

'I went out onto the tops and the phone suddenly burst into life. I'll know where to go now.'

It would be weeks before he got a line in this place, Mills thought.

'What about transport? Have you got that sorted yet?'

He shook his head. Yet another reason why the National Park project would not work, she thought.

'What about the bike?'

'Not done anything about it yet.'

Exasperated, Mills decided to leave before she said something she regretted. She had wanted to mention the dog but he seemed to be in such a negative mood she suspected even that idea would be rejected. He would have to sort his own life out.

'If you're going to visit this bunker, I don't mind having a look,' he said as she left.

Chapter 4

There had been three missed calls during the day and two text messages asking Alf to ring Jesse. Deciding it was time to confront his brother, he was sitting on his bed waiting anxiously for him to pick up.

Jesse didn't wait for Alf to speak. 'Listen, Dad needs you again tonight.'

'I can't do it.'

'What the… What d'you mean you can't do it?'

'I don't want to anymore.'

'Don't want to? You mean your old man won't let you!'

'It's not that.'

'No?'

'No, he doesn't…' he trailed off.

'He doesn't know? You haven't told him! So what's the problem?'

'I'm not happy with what Shane's doing.'

'Why? What did he do?' He sounded apprehensive.

'Catching foxes and… getting rid of them.'

'Well that's not illegal, is it? Foxes are vermin; he's doing a useful job.'

Alf had checked and he was right. 'Tell Shane I'm not coming.'

Suddenly his brother was serious. 'I could. But then he might let slip to Roy that you were out with him the other night.'

'What?'

'You heard. Dad will come for you at half ten.'

Alf thought about it and sighed. He didn't want to lie to his father again and felt trapped – like the poor fox.

'Ok.'

'Thanks a lot, Alf.' His half-brother sounded surprisingly grateful and relieved.

Downstairs his father was at the dining table with a pile of exercise books. He did his marking when he got home, before he cooked their evening meal. His grey hair was over his collar and soon Alf would have to remind him to get it cut. He glanced at his own reflection in the mirror over the fireplace and smoothed his fringe down.

'I won't be long,' his father called, without looking up. 'I've just got year eight's algebra to complete.'

Alf waited until he'd finished and was in the kitchen peeling potatoes before he announced he was thinking of going out again that night.

'You'll have something to eat before you go? I'm cooking sausages.'

Exams were over and there was no reason for Dad to be concerned if he wanted to go out with his mates. He actually said how he trusted him to be sensible.

'After all, if you do decide to go to university, I won't know what you're getting up to.'

'If I go to the University of North Yorkshire I could live at home.' It was the only way he could see he could afford it.

His father shrugged. They'd had this discussion so many times and every time Dad had come to the same conclusion: Alf should go away to university and be independent. But he didn't want to go. He couldn't leave Dad on his own. He didn't want to abandon his father.

It had taken three days but Mills finally finished marking the forensics exam papers and entered the results in a table against the candidate numbers. She took them back to the departmental office and handed them in to the course administrator.

'What happened about the question with the typo?' she asked.

The girl shrugged. 'Nothing. One student answered it but the rest just chose other questions.'

'Someone answered it? But how? Who?'

She pulled up a file on her computer monitor. 'Sara Pendleton.'

'Really?' Mills knew the girl and she wasn't the brightest kid on the block.

Seeing the list of names on the screen Mills asked if she could have a copy of the students' candidate numbers now that her marking was done.

'I'll email them. You'll be getting the full set of marks anyway, once I've calculated the results.'

Back at her desk Mills compared marks with the names of the students. As she worked through the alphabetical list the good scores and poor scores were pretty much predictable – except for one. Sara Pendleton had excelled in her own question, which was surprising – and suspicious since she often didn't appear and, when she did, she paid little interest in what was being taught. Mills would have predicted her getting fifty percent or less – not eighty-five. If Nige had been around she would have told him of her suspicions, although she wasn't sure what she thought had occurred. But in his absence she decided to speak to the course director about her concerns.

Dr Cuthbert was in the office next to that of the Head of Department. It was the arrangement for course directors to have access to the departmental administrators. Being given an office to themselves encouraged staff to take on these additional duties. Mills could see he was still there despite it being nearly six. She knocked politely and waited to be asked inside. He was sitting at his desk behind a pile of exam scripts.

The office was tidy compared to those of his colleagues. There was nothing to be seen except what was on his desk. He was equally neatly turned out, always dressed in suit and tie, which was exceptional in the department.

Mills waited for him to look up but he continued to concentrate on what he was reading.

'I wanted to talk about my exam question – well, the answers really,' she began.

He looked up with a confused expression, as if he'd been expecting someone else. 'Oh?'

'May I sit down?'

Mills took the chair facing him across the desk.

'What is it?' He seemed irritated by her presence and did little to hide it.

'I've finished marking my question on the third year forensic paper.'

'Good.' He leaned back in his chair. Mills noticed it was black leather and looked much more comfortable than her own computer chair.

'Yes but I have a concern about one of the students.'

'Poor marks?'

'No, quite the reverse. She has a very high mark, remarkably high.'

'Presumably she did her revision.'

'But it's much higher than predicted. I don't understand it.'

'So what are you suggesting?'

'I just thought you should know.'

He was looking back at the paper in front of him.

'Perhaps you should review your marking scheme; sometimes new lecturers are too generous with their marks.'

'The rest of the papers were in line with what I would have expected. It was only Sara Pendleton's that was questionable.'

He looked up sharply at the name and then relaxed into a smile.

'Ah, she's in my tutor group – I think you'll find she's been working pretty hard for the exams. Just shows how it pays off.'

Mills found it difficult to picture Sara Pendleton working hard on anything but decided to change the subject.

'The other thing I wanted to ask was about the question with the bit missing.'

It was the first time she'd raised the subject with him personally. He had set the question and she wanted to make it clear to him that there was nothing she could do about it during the exam.

He waved his hand as if brushing away her question. 'Just a silly administrative mistake. You don't need to worry about it. No-one answered it anyway.'

'But I thought…'

The door opened and Mills turned round. Sara Pendleton was hovering in the doorway, a strong flowery perfume filling the room. The silence was finally broken by Mills after Dr Cuthbert made no attempt to ask the student to wait outside until they had finished.

'I'll put my concern in writing,' she said, irritated by his lack of manners.

'Come in, Sara,' was all he said. 'We've finished, haven't we, Dr Sanderson?'

Mills went straight back to the office and considered what to do. She couldn't accuse the student of cheating without some evidence to back up her allegation. She would wait to see the outcome when all the marks were compiled. Meanwhile she was curious to know why Sara Pendleton had been going to see Colin Cuthbert in the evening now that teaching had finished and most students were busy revising or had gone away for the summer. As she passed the departmental office on the way out, she looked in to see Dr Cuthbert's door was closed but she could hear high-pitched laughter and assumed the student was still in there.

At home, Mills rang Nige to seek his advice but his response wasn't helpful.

'There's a list of things that constitute cheating, such as taking notes into the exam, that sort of thing, but you need evidence to prove it has taken place. It's a serious allegation, Mills. There's a formal procedure that includes setting up a panel to review the case and an appeals procedure for the accused. I don't think we've ever had a case in the department since I've been here.'

'But it doesn't make any sense that she could get such a high mark – she rarely turned up to my lectures and her course work is poor.'

'Well then, her overall marks will be more reflective of her capabilities, won't they?'

Mills reluctantly agreed that course work contributed a substantial part of the overall mark.

'My advice is to forget it. Now, more importantly, have you asked Phil about lunch on Sunday? Nina says she needs an answer.'

'I'm sure it'll be fine – if we're still speaking.'

'Surely it's not come to that already?' He sounded amused. 'Although you can both still come, even if you're not speaking.'

'It's not funny, Nige. Phil isn't well. I'm hoping you and Nina can persuade him to get professional help.'

It was becoming a routine for Alf to lie to his father. It was funny really because he assumed that his son had found a girlfriend and was too shy to talk about her.

'You enjoy yourself, son,' he'd said, giving him a fiver.

Never once did he ask why he was wearing boots and an anorak but waved him off saying he'd see him when he saw him.

Shane had sent him a text, threatening to come round to see Roy. It was a risk he didn't want to take so he gritted his teeth, hoping that the cage would be empty. He didn't bother to ask Shane why he did it. Presumably he was being well paid.

'How's Jesse's leg?' he shouted above the noise of the engine as they sped along the main road.

'Leg?'

'His bad leg.'

'Oh, getting better – gradually,' Shane added as an afterthought. 'What d'you think of the music? I found one of his earlier albums.'

Alf didn't reply. He wanted to make a careful note of the next turning off the road onto the narrow lane that led to the woods. He now had a pretty good impression of the route and planned to find his own way back at the weekend. He'd calculated it was about twenty-six miles, which was a long way but he could manage it if he took it slowly.

There was no need for instructions when they parked. Alf fitted the head torch, closed the van door quietly and followed Shane in silence. The route was familiar and he knew where to jump the beck and avoid the brambles. This time Shane didn't tell him to stay back. It seemed that neither of them expected to find anything; the difference being that Alf was hoping the cage would be empty and Shane was not. He cursed loudly and swiped at the undergrowth with his gun. The cage was empty except for the rabbit left as bait.

'This is no good!' he exclaimed. 'No effing good at all.'

'Perhaps all the foxes have gone,' suggested Alf as they made their way back to the road.

'Quiet!' ordered Shane. 'D'you want everyone to hear you?'

'If what you're doing is legal there shouldn't be a problem if people hear,' muttered Alf but Shane was well ahead and didn't respond.

Alf's plan was to locate the woodland first. He wanted to ask someone about what Shane was doing but he needed to know where it was. Someone must own the land and that person should be able to tell him.

'Saturday night,' Shane was saying as they drove back to Bishop Auckland. 'Last trip I'm afraid, mate.'

'Is Jesse's leg better then?'

'Yes, that's right. Jesse's leg's better.'

Mills had carefully planned the weekend from Friday evening through to late on Sunday. She would arrange for them to meet Dave at the bunker on Friday evening while it was still light. They'd be near "Tan Hill Inn" so naturally they would pop in there for a meal before she dropped Phil home. On Saturday they would go shopping in Darlington. She would suggest lunch in Yarm and casually drop into the conversation that there was a lurcher needing a home down the road in Great Ayton. Finally, on Sunday, they would have lunch with Nina and Nige, where they would persuade him to get counselling. All sorted.

Her plans were quickly undone when Phil finally responded to her voicemail on Friday morning. According to his text he was expecting a visitor who was bringing something from France so he would be busy on Friday and Saturday. He was looking forward to lunch with her friends on Sunday however and would meet her there.

Furious, she sent a message to Dave postponing their meeting and was about to message the rehoming centre when she stopped. To hell with it, she'd go herself. Phil needed a dog and she would get him one, although he didn't deserve it. Later, sitting alone watching television, she thought she might possibly keep the dog herself. Either way, that lurcher was getting a home.

Fortunately, Mills was due to spend the next day at the forensic lab in Harrogate. Her visits had been just once a fortnight since Christmas and she was feeling rather guilty about it. It was understood that she would continue to work there once she started full-time at the university but her first year of teaching had been full-on. The summer was her opportunity to rectify the situation and she also hoped it might present an opportunity to carry out some research.

Brenda greeted her with a cheery 'Hello pet!' and immediately suggested coffee.

'Wow, you're looking well,' said Mills. 'Have you put on weight?'

'I certainly have. I am officially two stone heavier than I was last year.'

'Well, you could afford to be.' That was when her boss was being treated for breast cancer and had become a shadow of her usual plump self. 'You look a lot better for it.' That was in part because she continued to wear the same clothes from before her illness and had begun to fill them out – a little.

Brenda suggested they went outside with their coffee, an excuse for her to have a cigarette.

'Where have you been, Mills?' she asked, pointedly. 'We've missed you.'

'Sorry. It's exam time and I've been down for invigilating several days a week. I only have one left next week.'

'That's good because I need your help with something that's come in.'

'What's that?'

'It's something rather different from the usual stuff. Donna is up to her eyes in bloods and DNAs and Tim is struggling through a large batch of soil samples. Now we've been asked to do a really off-the-wall piece of nonsense.'

'Is it police work?'

'No, it's a civil case – an argument between two men with more money than sense I would say.'

'How come?'

'This professor from a university in the States has published a paper purporting to be able to tell the difference between the bones of a native Indian and an American settler.'

'Sounds interesting.'

'They're museum pieces apparently; don't ask me how they got them. The trace elements in the bones are different because of the diet apparently.'

'Makes sense. There has been quite a lot of research done in that area – the geographical location can affect the composition of the bones and tissue at the trace element level.'

'So is it something you can do?'

'I don't see why not – at least we can analyse bone material easily, or rather Tim can, if he's not too busy. But if the American professor has already analysed the bones…'

'He has but another professor over here doesn't believe the results and has written a letter in the journal where the results were published disputing the data.'

'So he wants the bones reanalysed?'

'Yes.'

'Well that's not a problem if he can get some material and if we know what elements he wants – assuming we are set up for them.'

'Good, I'll give you his number and you can tell him the good news. Thanks, pet.'

She stamped on her discarded cigarette butt and led the way back inside.

Mills had to ring three times before she reached Professor Ross. He had a southern accent, rather posh, but despite a haughty air he was definitely pleased with the news that they could help him. He read out the list of elements under dispute and requested confirmation that Mills could provide analyses of sufficient quality to stand up in a court of law.

'This is a forensic laboratory with the appropriate accreditation and we have experience of giving expert witness evidence if required,' she reassured him.

'Well I hope you will be able to show his work to be what I believe it is – hogwash. Everyone knows that you can only show significant differences due to origin and diet using stable isotopes.'

Mills jotted that down on her notepad.

She asked him to email her the offending paper and spent the rest of the day familiarising herself with the contents. In her view the analyses the laboratory would have to do were not problematic but she went along to see the lab manager to get his agreement.

Glyn was at his desk sipping tea while he checked pages of data.

'Ah, the wanderer returns.'

Mills ignored his comment and smiled. 'How are you?' she asked amicably.

He sighed and waved at the pile of paper on his desk. 'I could do with someone to check the data and not have to do it *all* myself.'

It was one of her duties to help with checking that data had been transcribed correctly. It wasn't a difficult job but it was tedious and she could see why Glyn was cross with her.

'Give me the next folder,' she said. 'I'll do it now.' He passed it to her without comment. 'I did want to ask you something, Glyn.'

She told him about the request from Professor Ross and showed him the table in the paper that listed the elements in the two bone samples. The lab manager never appeared excited or interested in anything and merely nodded, saying, 'Tim can manage that if Donna helps him with the dissolution.'

It was that simple and Mills grinned as she carried the thick folder back to her desk for checking.

Brenda packed up early but before she left she asked after Phil.

'How's he getting on back in Yorkshire?'

Mills shrugged and put down her pen. 'He's not himself, that's for sure. He's distracted, unfocussed. I don't know…'

She went on to describe his moods and lack of interest in anything she suggested.

'Perhaps he just needs to chill out for a while, pet.'

'I thought he should get a dog.'

Brenda laughed loudly. 'You do, do you now? D'you think that will sort him out?'

She sat down on the edge of the desk. 'Phil has always been a complicated character ever since I've known him – which is a lot longer than you have. He needs his own space. Let him get acclimatised. After all, he's been away a long time.' She looked at her watch. 'Talking of which, I'd better get a wiggle on, it's my knitting class tonight.'

Mills picked up her pen and continued checking the files but every now and then she stopped to think about what Brenda had said. Maybe she should back off and leave Phil in peace.

'Well, that's an hour of my life I won't get back!'

DS Hazel Fuller threw down her handbag and collapsed into the chair in front of Ruby's desk.

'How come *you* don't have to deal with these time wasters?' she asked.

'I'm merely an unimportant researcher, that's why,' her colleague replied. 'Shall I make coffee?'

Hazel spent the next few minutes getting Linda Bailey's details into the system. There was no way she would be registering Chris Webb as missing at this stage, and she informed Ruby when she returned.

'She calls to say her partner hasn't contacted her. I ask you! How many times does that happen to a girl?'

'Do they live together?'

'Yes but he works away from home. He left on Monday and rang Wednesday to say he hoped to be home for the weekend. So it's six o'clock on Friday evening, he hasn't arrived yet and she starts panicking. He's probably stopped for a pint on the way back from wherever he's been.'

'Did you actually say that?'

'Of course not. I'm not completely heartless.'

'It's unusual for people not to keep in touch regularly these days though.'

'Is it?'

'Where is he working?'

'She doesn't know.'

'What does he do?'

'She seemed a bit vague on that too – something to do with animals, she said. They haven't been together long.'

Ruby took a packet of biscuits from her desk drawer and offered them to her colleague, who took two.

Hazel said, 'My ex would disappear for days, weeks even if the mood took him. I wouldn't hear from him until he reappeared as if nothing had happened.'

'I could do a check on this Chris Webb if you like – find out where he works.'

'Don't bother. He'll be back when he feels like it. I'm not wasting resources on the likes of him.'

Ruby was used to Hazel's abrasive manner and knew it didn't mean she didn't care. 'So, got anything exciting planned this weekend with your new man?' she asked as she closed down her computer and locked the desk drawers.

'He's taking me to some club in Newcastle.'

'Wow, that's cool.'

'Is it? I think I might be getting a little old for a night out clubbing.'

'What does Liam say?'

'You think I tell him what I'm doing in my spare time?' Ruby could see Hazel was serious.

'But he knows you're dating, right?'

'He knows there is someone but I don't introduce my dates to my son, especially when he's a bit younger than I am.'

More than a bit, thought Ruby. Hazel had admitted that he was closer in age to her son than to her, so he had to be at least ten years younger. Her colleague's series of unsuccessful liaisons was a constant source of gossip in the office, with Hazel often providing details of the final break-up. Her mood would always depend on the state of the current relationship and Ruby judged that things were not as rosy as they could be.

'Are you in on Monday?' she asked, thinking that by then the missing person would have to be registered if he hadn't turned up.

'No, I'm off until Tuesday.'

Ruby was relieved, it meant that DS Nina Featherstone would be on duty – and she would be bound to follow it up.

Chapter 5

Glyn wanted to lock up at five and so Mills reluctantly handed back the files with the checking unfinished and left the building. It was half past six when she caught up with the fish and chip van as it made progress along the dale and she stopped in Healaugh to queue for her supper.

She was eating her cod and chips out of its paper with her fingers, while she poured herself a glass of red and carried it through to the tiny sitting room. It was the end of a fairly unsuccessful week all round really. After a second glass she decided to go to the animal rescue website and view the picture of Harris, the lurcher. He looked similar to Earl, Phil's previous dog. Apparently he was a "lovely obedient animal with a gentle expression but a sense of fun – occasionally".

She followed the instructions to complete an application form, trying to imagine what Phil would answer to questions like *Do you have a garden?* and *How much exercise would you expect to give the dog?* The easiest bit was the answer to *Have you seen a dog or puppy on our website that you are interested in? If so please tell us the name.* She entered "Harris" with a flourish. All she had to do was sign the formt and email it to Great Ayton. Of course Phil should sign it really but in his negative frame of mind...

The application was submitted. She finished off the chips, which were now cold, and poured another glass of wine. At first, when Alex left, she had revelled in living alone again. The freedom to eat when she felt like it, watch telly programmes she wanted to see, go to bed early if she wished or stay up late without disturbing anyone. But now, if someone was actually concerned enough to ask, she would have to say that she missed the company, which was why she needed to talk to someone… anyone. She considered ringing Nina, but it was bedtime for the twins and she would be busy. She could call her father but he would quickly pass her on to her stepmother and Mills didn't feel sociable enough to hear about the problems of a yummy mummy in Canary Wharf. Fiona could complain about anything and often did. Her last visit to London had been a disaster because Fiona had taken advantage of her stay, leaving Flora with her while she went off to meet up with friends for coffee or lunch but ensuring she was back before Dad came home. Much as Mills liked little Flora – she refused to call her a half-sister since she was old enough to be her mother – there was a limit to her child-minding abilities and it all came to a head when Mills took Flora to the Surrey Docks Farm. Fiona had gone ballistic, accusing her of risking her daughter's life by petting the small furry animals. Mills had left the next day.

So Mills did what she always did when she had nothing better to do, she worked. What had the London professor said? "Origin could only be determined using stable isotopes" – whatever that meant. She poured another glass of wine and settled down to find out. She'd already made use of radiocarbon to date the bones of a skeleton, and she knew the decay of uranium and thorium isotopes could date rocks and fossils but that depended on the different decay rates of the radioactive isotopes of the elements, stable isotopes don't change, do they?

It was after midnight by the time she dragged herself to bed with her laptop. It was beginning to make sense. After all, she knew that environmental scientists used the fact that the ratio of lead isotopes varies depending on the origin of the lead so it was not inconceivable that other elements could also be used as fingerprints. The most useful stable isotopes for studying bone seemed to be those of nitrogen and carbon because they are in all foods and so absorbed into the body. Mills was even more enthusiastic when she discovered that these ratios were being used in forensic work to identify when the origin of a food like honey was being falsified. This was an area of research that would fulfil the demands of both the Forensic and Archaeology departments.

One more night in Shane's rattling van with his irritating country and western music and his perpetual smoking. Alf's father had commented on the fact that his clothes stank of smoke and asked whether it was him that was smoking. He wasn't sure that he was believed when he swore it was just his friends. One more evening to get through and then he vowed he would never see Shane again, whatever Jesse said.

It was pitch dark when they parked up. The night was clear but it was a new moon and they adjusted the head torches ready for the trek to the wire cage. Shane appeared to have given up on whatever he was looking for and remarked that it was the last time he was coming to this "God-forsaken place". However, as they neared their goal, Alf could hear a rattling noise. He stood still and concentrated. Possibly a grunting noise? Shane had gone on and he issued a sound of glee.

'That's more like it!'

Alf waited.

'Where are you?' Shane was shouting.

Alf walked forward quietly, keen to see what Shane was on about but scared of what he might find. In retrospect he admitted to himself that he had probably guessed what it was. It had been worrying him for days. After all, if it wasn't a fox he was after – which, judging by Shane's disappointment on the first night, he wasn't – it could only be what was struggling in the cage now. But even so he was still hoping it was another fox.

All he could see in the torchlight were flashes of white; the rest was too dark. Shane moved closer and there was the black and white head. For a second it could have been one of those sheepdogs but this wasn't barking or whining, it was making a sort of hissing growling sound.

Alf stood, waiting for a gunshot. It was what he'd guessed. Shane was being paid by a local farmer to catch and kill badgers.

'Go on then!' he shouted. 'Murderer!'

'Oh, I ain't going to kill him,' replied Shane. 'We're taking Mr Brock back home with us.'

Alf hadn't expected this. 'What are going to do with it?'

'Never you mind lad. Just help me with the cage.'

'No!'

'What d'you mean, no? You take the other side,' he ordered.

'No way! I'm not helping you take it away from here.'

He grabbed Shane's hand and tried to wrestle it off the handle of the crate but he was surprisingly strong and twisted his wrist back.

'Listen to me, laddie. You help me get this feller back to the van or you may regret what you're doing!'

Alf backed off, ran a few yards and waited. He turned off his head torch and held his breath.

'Come here you effing stupid kid!'

But there was nothing he could do. He wouldn't find him as he stepped slowly and carefully further away from Shane's voice, cursing and swearing at him all the time.

It seemed like hours before Shane stopped thrashing around in the undergrowth. Suddenly it went quiet and Alf had no idea what had happened. He didn't dare go back towards the cage but felt his way in the opposite direction until eventually he could see headlights moving along the lane. It might have been Shane but it didn't sound like the van. He waited until it had gone then made his way over the wall and started back towards the bridge. All the time he was expecting to hear Shane coming up behind him but all was quiet and he sneaked past the van and onto the road in the opposite direction to where they'd come from.

When he reached a village the pubs were closed and no-one was around. He passed through Reeth and onwards, unsure how best to find his way. Headlights, too big to be from Shane's van, appeared suddenly and he stuck out his thumb. Brakes squeaked and a window was lowered.

'In trouble, mate?'

Alf made up a story about being dumped by his girlfriend and the minibus driver was happy to take him as far as the A1, where he was going south.

'Been delivering school kids up here for their Duke of Edinburgh awards but my wife is expecting and I've just heard she's gone into labour. I'm hoping I'll be back in time to pick her up!'

He dropped Alf off at the Exelby services where he approached two guys in a van arguing over who was going to pay for the fuel. They were heading home to Durham after some gig in Leeds. They didn't ask any questions, just dropped him off in the middle of town and drove off, leaving Alf to kill a few hours in the bus station before the six-forty to Bishop Auckland.

Dad had already gone to the supermarket when he arrived home. Alf sometimes accompanied him on these Saturday morning outings but now he collapsed on the sofa without even taking off his jacket. He was woken by the sound of the front door opening and jumped up to help his father in with the bags.

'You made a night of it,' he said, putting the kettle on. 'Are you hungry? I've got bacon.'

Alf so wanted to confide in his father, tell him everything, but he was caught in a lie that he couldn't get out of now. All he could do was find his way back to see what had happened to the badger.

Mills woke late, her mind buzzing with fragments of a strange dream. She carried her laptop downstairs and made a large pot of tea while she re-read the notes she'd made before she'd fallen asleep. Out in the garden the sun had warmed the bench but a gentle breeze helped clear her head. She had wanted to take Phil to meet Harris this morning but now she would either have to go alone or admit it was a daft idea to adopt a lurcher on his behalf. He would be entertaining his friend today, the one who was bringing him something over from France. She'd initially assumed it was a man but now she realised that the reason he didn't suggest meeting this friend was because it was a woman – a girlfriend from Paris, probably. She had a good mind to drop in anyway, even though she knew it was a really stupid idea.

After a shower and some breakfast, sense prevailed. Mills checked the fridge and made a list, locked up the cottage and lowered the soft top on the Mini before heading to Darlington. She didn't need to go so far for groceries but she told herself she could look for some much-needed new clothes and it was on the way to Great Ayton; she might as well look in at the rehoming centre to see if Harris was still there. On the way through Arkengarthdale she passed the end of Phil's lane and looked up as if half-expecting to see him but it was clear. The road over to the A66 was usually quiet and today the only vehicles she passed were a convoy of MGs going in the other direction. Traffic increased as she joined the main road until she was nearing the turn off for Darlington. In a sudden change of plan she decided to do her shopping on the way back and continued towards Great Ayton, stopping only to put the postcode of the re-homing centre into the satnav.

She should have realised that the centre would not have processed her on-line application so quickly. The woman was very pleasant and helpful but there were lots of questions and it soon became blindingly obvious that she was not looking for a pet for herself but for a friend. It was not a good start. She was asked why only a lurcher would do and their concerns grew when she admitted that Earl, Phil's previous lurcher, had died as a result of being "kidnapped". Mills even thought it would help to explain about Phil's depression but somehow it came out all wrong. Eventually they advised her to bring Phil along so he could complete the application form himself.

'May I just see Harris?' she asked.

He was lying quietly in a kennel between a "staffy" called Billy and a greyhound called Betsy. When they approached he stood and stared with gentle brown eyes. His hair, his ears, everything – he was so like Earl it hurt. She thanked the woman and hurried out into the car park with a lump in her throat. She couldn't face shopping in town now and took the quieter route back via Northallerton, wiping away the tears every now and then as she relived the moment when they'd searched desperately for Earl and eventually found him almost lifeless in the stone outbuilding. She sighed. There was half a bought shepherd's pie in the fridge and a bottle of Prosecco she'd been saving for something special. She would pass the evening watching the box and go to bed early, hoping Sunday would be a better day.

'So what are you up to today, son?'

Alf was dressed early, ready to return to the woods to see what had happened to the badger. It wasn't surprising his dad knew he had something planned.

'I was going to go for a cycle ride – in the Dales'.

'Seriously? That's a fair trek.'

'I know but I want to get out.'

'Have you checked how far it is?'

'About thirty miles.'

His father whistled.

'I'd offer to come with you…' Alf held his breath. '…but I've got all these essays to correct.' He indicated the pile of papers at the end of the table.

'It would be great to have company but I'm happy to go alone, Dad, really.'

They smiled at each other and carried on eating their cereal.

'I can make bacon butties if you like, son.'

He shook his head. 'Toast is fine.'

While Alf finished off the toast, his father made cheese sandwiches and packed them in a carrier bag.

'I've popped an apple and some biscuits in as well. We don't want you getting hungry out there.'

'I can always get something on the way.'

'I know. Look, what if we stick your bike on the roof of the car and I take you over there?'

'There's no need.'

'I know but I've been thinking. I could sit in a nice spot with a view and do my marking. It would make a change. You can go off and have a good bike ride and then we could meet up for a bite to eat before we come home.'

'Ok.'

Alf didn't want to refuse the offer, which would save him hours of exertion. He decided how he could get close to his target without arousing suspicion. 'Tan Hill. The highest pub – we could eat there, Dad.'

'Right then, we'd better get going.'

In the car, Alf couldn't help but compare the journey with the trips he'd made with Shane. The smoke-free environment for a start. No music, just a bit of conversation now and again when they pointed out interesting things or discussed an item from the news. Alf's father was a careful driver and it took an hour to get to Reeth, where they stopped to buy cans of soft drinks and use the toilets. They arranged to meet up at the "Tan Hill Inn" in two and a half hours. Alf had said he would cycle the long way round via Keld but actually planned to go up Arkengarthdale, stopping off to search the woodland at Low Eskeleth. He pretended to adjust his saddle until the car disappeared up Swaledale then waited a few minutes before setting off.

The road over the bridge was familiar but once he had taken the turning he was confused. It looked so different in daylight. He dismounted and pushed the bike slowly along the lane, watching for tyre marks or footprints to indicate where they had stopped previously. It seemed a long way before he found the first signs of where it might have been – an indistinct track leading into the wood. He lifted his bike off the road for a few yards to where he could lay it down half-hidden under brambles, leaving his bag of sandwiches attached to the handlebars. Uncertain whether he was on the right path, he walked slowly deeper into the wood, hoping he was going in the right direction.

It took him three attempts to find the place. First time he ended up almost back on the road so he started again. This time he walked in a straight line regardless of the path and came out by the stream. He knew now that he had to veer to the right just as he had done in the dark and finally he recognised a thorn bush he had walked into on the very first visit. Now all he had to do was step into the undergrowth and the trap would be in front of him. Only of course it wasn't. The clearing where it had been was empty, the undergrowth smashed down where the trap had been set.

Alf stared helplessly. He'd had no plan. Perhaps he'd hoped the cage would still be there, something to prove that Shane had been at work. If it had been, he would have been tempted to show Dad, telling him everything. Disappointed, he stumbled back to sit by his bike, chewing on a sandwich and wondering what to do next. Clearly Shane had managed to get the badger and cage back to his van somehow – perhaps calling Jesse to help.

'I wondered who the bike belonged to!'

The man was standing with his hands on his hips, glaring down at him. Unsure whether he was expected to answer, Alf swallowed his mouthful and wiped his hands on his jeans.

'What are you up to, son?'

'Nothing.' Alf struggled to his feet, heart racing. The man was carrying a shotgun slung over his shoulder.

'I thought you might be looking for something.'

His expression was stern but the voice was calm. Alf wondered if he was a mate of Shane's but although the man's accent wasn't local, he wasn't a Geordie either.

'I just stopped to eat my lunch. I'm going now.'

'Have you been rummaging about down here before?'

'No sir.' He looked up at the man. He was younger than Shane or his dad and Alf was struck by his manner – sort of cool. 'I'm meeting my dad at Tan Hill,' he added, hoping it would add credibility to his story.

'You'd best be on your way then, lad.'

The man watched him as he packed up, dragged his bike out of the brambles and made his way unsteadily back to the road. His heart was still going too fast once he was on tarmac and he didn't dare look back as he made for the bridge. There he slowed to turn right and was nearly knocked off his bike by a motorcyclist racing past him and cutting across to go left towards Barnard Castle. He was covered by his helmet but Alf wondered if it was the man that had confronted him in the woods – if it was he was

- 66 -

definitely heading in the right direction for Bishop Auckland where Shane's cronies lived.

The ride up to the pub was tough but pedalling hard helped him to vent his anger at Shane and Jesse. If the man in the woods wasn't their mate, he certainly suspected Alf of being involved in what they'd been doing. What if he'd been an undercover policeman? He pedalled faster and harder as the hill became steeper. Alf wasn't the only cyclist going in that direction, he was overtaken by several dressed in Lycra and he felt like a real amateur in his jeans and T-shirt. The road seemed to go on for ever and he was ready to give up when finally the pub came into view.

His father was waiting outside with a drink in his hand. He waved when he spotted Alf.

'I expected you to come from the other way,' he said, laughing, as he led Alf inside. 'Quick, there's a table in the corner.'

Alf didn't have much of an appetite.

'You shouldn't have eaten the sandwiches,' his father said, tucking into his meat pie.

'Did you get your marking done?' Alf asked.

'Some of it. It was so pleasant I stopped off and had an ice-cream in Muker and took a stroll down to the river. I thought I would pass you at some stage but I must have missed you somewhere.'

Alf thought his father looked better for his relaxing day and told him so to change the subject.

'You know, I've really enjoyed it. We must come out here again sometime.'

Alf hoped he would never see the place again.

Chapter 6

Nina and Nige lived in a row of terraced houses built long before garages were needed. At the weekend cars lined the street on both sides and it was always a challenge to find a parking space. Mills cruised up and down twice before squeezing her Mini into a space that was only just big enough. It took three attempts before she was close enough to the kerb. It was a fair walk back up the street to their house.

'Come on in,' called Nina, opening the door before she had rung the bell. 'Phil is already here!'

'Is he?' Mills had wanted to talk to her friend about Phil before he appeared and had deliberately arrived early.

'He came on his new bike,' Nina explained.

'He *cycled*?'

'Motorbike, silly. Come in, they're probably still talking about it. Nige was out in the road admiring it for ages, green with envy.'

Mills could see the two of them sitting together out in the yard, drinking beer from bottles and chatting excitedly.

'It's so nice to see Phil again,' called Nina from the kitchen.

'How do you think he seems?' asked Mills when her friend reappeared with a glass of wine for her.

Nina considered for a moment. 'Fine, I think.'

Rosie and the twins came thundering down the stairs to greet Mills. Nina and Nige's daughter had just had her eighth birthday and Mills had brought her a present. The boys hung around while she opened it but lost interest when they saw it was a book and ran outside to bother their father. It wasn't long before the men came inside and Mills asked Phil when he'd bought the motorbike.

'A friend brought it over from Paris for me. He was getting rid of it and was too good a bargain to ignore.'

So presumably that was who had come to stay on Friday. Mills sat back and let him monopolise the conversation, after all Nina and Nige hadn't seen him for years and Phil seemed happier than she'd seen him for a long time – or was that due to the beer? She didn't know how many he'd had already but she counted several more before they finally sat down to eat. Mills was relieved that no-one asked Phil about his work abroad. Instead Nina provided topics of conversation that Nige picked up and ran with, including how he was teaching the children Welsh in preparation for their proposed holiday to meet members of his extended family.

After lunch the boys wanted to go to the playground and they all wandered along to the park a few streets away. While Nige and Phil pushed the swings and helped the little ones on the slide, Nina pointed to a seat in the shade.

'He seems just like his old self, doesn't he?' Nina said.

'He does today. Do you think he's drinking too much?'

'If he is, so is Nige.'

'He didn't tell me he was getting the bike.'

'Perhaps it was going to be a surprise.'

Mills didn't answer. She was watching Phil having fun pushing Rosie on the roundabout while she shouted for it to go faster.

'Maybe getting the bike has cheered him up,' Mills said.

'Exactly. Now he'll be independent again.'

'So he won't need me to ferry him about.'

'Exactly.' Nina was looking at her. 'You should be pleased. If he really is suffering from the trauma of seeing all those body parts at the crash site, he needs support and you're doing a brilliant job. You just need to avoid overthinking it – don't push him.'

'You don't think I should get the lurcher then?'

Nina laughed. 'Does he want a dog? Have you asked him?'

'Not yet. But I will.'

'I'm sure it will work out fine.'

'You do? I asked him about the nuclear bunker project and he said a big no.'

'That's a shame.'

'I'm going to look at it anyway. I don't want to let the National Park down.'

'Good for you!'

Mills wished she thought Nina meant that.

There were tears when Tomos and Owen had to leave the playground and they only agreed to come away when bribed with a visit to the sweet shop on the way home. Mills was left alone with Phil while the family went inside to choose sweets. They stood side by side staring at the display of magazines and toys in the window.

'It's great you've got transport again,' offered Mills.

He nodded. 'Yeah, it's good to have wheels.'

'You could go and look at the bunker now.'

'Yeah, I could. I was talking to Nige about it and he thinks it's a good idea.'

'Really?' Well, if *Nige* thinks it's a good idea… but Mills forced a smile. 'I'll let Dave know.'

'Dave?'

'At the National Park.'

'Ok.'

Heeding Nina's advice, she didn't go on to discuss Harris the lurcher.

Tomos and Owen had taken a real shine to Phil and insisted they play football in the yard. Mills took the opportunity to thank Nige for talking Phil into the bunker project and asked him what he thought about her idea for a research project that would satisfy both the Archaeology and Forensics departments.

'…you see using stable isotopes in bone identifies the person's diet. For example, strontium isotopes could show whether they come from a coastal environment or inland,' she explained.

'I know that's been used for certain historical burial sites but is it still relevant these days? Food comes from all over the world.'

'Yes but we drink water that's sourced locally and that has different strontium isotope ratios, depending on the location.'

'So is it used in modern forensics?'

'Exactly, that's what I want to work on – if it is, I can look at how reliable it is. The problem is that we don't have the right sort of instrument for doing stable isotopes with that accuracy.'

Nige went quiet for moment then grabbed his mobile and began looking something up.

'Geology must have one because I know they use strontium isotopes to date fossils and marine sediments. Yes, here it is – a thermal ionisation whatnot. It's some sort of exotic mass spectrometer.'

He showed her the description which she instantly recognised as a more sensitive version of the equipment used routinely at the forensic lab. If she was able to get access to Geology's equipment that would be perfect.

'So how are you going to look at modern bones if…'

Mills could see over Nige's shoulder that the football game was over and the boys were heading inside followed by Phil.

'…so I'll just have to wait for the examiners meeting to see what happens about Sara Pendleton.'

Nige looked puzzled.

'You two talking shop?' Phil asked as he came inside. 'Where's Nina?'

'I'm here in the kitchen,' she called. 'I'm making sandwiches for the kids then we can have a cup of tea.'

The time flew by as they chatted about the children and what Nige and Nina had been doing over the past few years. Everyone avoided asking Phil what he'd been up to, Mills noticed. Soon it was time for the boys to go to bed and Mills felt obliged to say she should go. Phil, however, leaned back on the sofa, showing no sign of moving when Mills said her goodbyes. Nina came out onto the street and gave her a hug.

'It's been lovely to see you both. Don't get too down, Mills. I am sure, in time, he will be back to his old self.'

Mills smiled and waved but she wished she shared her friend's optimism.

Amy was about to strip the beds ready for the new arrivals when the doorbell rang. It was quite usual for people to call on the off-chance there was a room free so she ran downstairs ready to politely tell them she was fully booked until the end of August. The young woman on the doorstep was skinny, her paleness accentuated by the oversized denim sundress that hung loosely off one shoulder. Out on the lane was a small car and Amy could see a child seat in the back.

'Can I help you?' Amy asked.

'Sorry to bother you Mrs Bradby…' she began.

'Were you looking for accommodation? I'm fully booked but I can give you the name…'

'No,' she interrupted. 'I want to know if Chris is here.'

'Chris?'

'Chris, my partner. Is he staying here? He had this address. I rang?'

'You did?'

'I spoke to a man, he said Chris wasn't here. But yours is one of the addresses he'd written down – that's why I came.'

Amy looked at the woman, more a girl really, and asked her to come in. She sat her down at the kitchen table and put the kettle on. She told her that there was no Chris booked in. But then the girl pushed a photograph across the table. It was a man smiling for the camera, a holiday snap, and there was no mistake, it was her guest, Len. She started to ask why she called him Chris but the girl interrupted, wanting to know where he was.

'I'm sorry, love. He left last Monday. He paid for three nights in cash but he'd planned to be here for the week. I didn't bother because the room was free until the weekend.'

'He said he'd be home on Friday night.'

The poor girl was hunched in the chair looking distraught. 'I went to the police,' she said, 'but they wouldn't do anything.'

Amy handed her the tissue box and put a mug of strong tea in front of her. She assumed they'd had a row.

'Was he taking a holiday, love?'

'No, he was working. He works away a lot, nights and stuff. That's why I didn't worry when he didn't text me. Sometimes he can't.'

'There's not a good signal round here.' Amy was curious. 'So what's his line of work then?'

'Animal welfare.'

'Right.' So that was why he was asking about the badgers. 'I'm sorry I can't help. All I can tell you is he left last Monday night and didn't come back. I've got his rucksack if you want to take it.'

While the girl finished her tea, Amy asked about her kiddie. She had a little girl, just over two years old, called Katie. Her own name was Linda.

'I'd better go,' she said at last.

The rucksack was still in the hall and Amy automatically gave the girl a hug as she handed it to her.

'You've got my number. Give me yours and I'll let you know if I hear anything.'

Amy jotted it down on the pad by the phone and opened the front door. She watched the car disappear down the lane, wondering what she would have done if her husband had disappeared.

That evening she discussed the visit with Jeff.

'Must've been her that rang a couple of times,' he said. 'I could hardly tell what she was saying – Newcastle accent?'

'Yes, just like Len. She had a child seat in her car and all. I felt sorry for her. D'you think he's abandoned her and the kiddie?'

'None of our business.' He was lying back with his eyes closed. 'Forget about him.'

'She took his rucksack anyway, so I suppose that's that. I just can't help thinking…' She stopped. He was asleep or pretending to be.

Amy wasn't surprised when the phone rang later in the evening. It was typical of prospective guests to ring at the most inconvenient times. They sometimes apologised but she always said there was no problem. Jeff would moan if he had to mute the television while she answered but that was the downside of being in the hospitality business.

But it wasn't a guest.

'I'm sorry to bother you again.' The accent was unmistakeable. The girl's voice was shaky. 'Linda?'

'Yes. I wanted you to know… I spoke to the police again. It was a different officer and she was much more helpful. She says Chris is officially a missing person now. They said I should let you know.'

'Of course, love.'

'They'll probably come to see you. That's why I…'

'Of course. Do you think… I mean I wondered…'

'He hasn't gone off somewhere. I told her. He wouldn't go without telling me. I said, he loves Katie so much. He can't have just… left.'

'Of course not. I see.'

'Anyway, she said they'd treat it as urgent – because he's been missing so long already.'

'Of course.' She instructed Linda to look after herself. Apparently her mum was with her, so she had support.

Amy was in tears when she told Jeff who it was.

'Don't get involved,' he said. 'If the police come, just say he left without telling us anything. We don't want to be messed up in it, do we?'

It was Tuesday before Mills could meet Dave and
Phil at the nuclear bunker. She arrived at the site long
before eleven o'clock and had been standing on the
empty moorland for some time, a breeze keeping her
cool in the bright sunshine. It had been quite easy to
spot the structure sticking out above ground but she'd
had to strike out across the boggy grassland once
she'd left the car at the side of the road. From her
vantage point she could watch for vehicles
approaching and eventually spotted a black Land
Rover slowing to a halt behind her Mini.

While Mills watched the National Park officer
picking his way across to her, she wondered if Phil
had forgotten or simply wouldn't turn up.

'Is this the first time you've been up here?' Dave
called as he reached her.

'Yes. You?'

'Yes.' He produced a set of keys and began fiddling
with the large rusty padlock on the entrance hatch.
'Let's see what we've got here.' After a few
expletives, he gave up, declaring that none of them
fitted.

Mills commented that the padlock was very rusty
and looked as though it had been there since the
sixties when the bunker was closed down. She pulled
at it and to her surprise the latch clicked open.

'How did you do that?' Dave asked with a laugh.

'It must've been unlocked or rusted through.'

Mills looked anxiously across at the road, hoping to
see Phil arrive. He was already ten minutes late. Dave
removed the padlock and pulled back the latch.

'Let's have a look, shall we?'

He began tugging on the hatch door but it seemed to be too heavy for him to lift on his own. Mills was about to offer to help when they were distracted by the sound of an engine. A motorbike had left the road and was making its way across the grass. Phil had arrived. They watched him dismount and leave his helmet with the bike. He was fifteen minutes late but there was no apology. Mills introduced him to Dave without comment.

'I've brought a head torch,' Phil said.

'Well,' said Dave, scratching his chin. 'The aim of today is to see if we can get in – I mean, open it up and have a look-see. You need to sign a risk assessment before you can go down.'

'Really?' Phil looked disappointed.

'We need to be sure there are no serious hazards: working in confined spaces, lone working, working at height.'

'At height?' Mills asked.

'Yes, you'll see.'

The two men struggled with the hatch door until it finally released, flying back and noisily slamming open. All three peered down into the space twenty feet below them. It was dark and very smelly. Dave produced a torch and shone the beam around below them. The light was reflected in a dark pool of water on the floor below. A vertical metal ladder attached to the side wall went all the way down to the bottom. Mills knew that beneath them was a small room and immediately she was reminded that Phil suffered from claustrophobia.

'So we're not going down today?' Mills asked, hoping they couldn't detect the relief in her voice.

'No. they'll finish off the paperwork and give you a copy, Phil. It will require two of you to be here when you're working, for safety, preferably someone up here when the other is below. There's no phone signal here and certainly nothing down there.'

Mills was anxious that Phil might change his mind before they were allowed to access the bunker.

'When *can* we go down?' she asked.

'I'm sure it will be ready by the end of the week. I'll just need a signature to show you've read the assessment.'

Phil helped him lower the lid down and Dave slipped the rusty padlock into position.

He looked at his watch. 'Do you guys want something to eat? We could go to the pub and I can tell you exactly what we want to get out of this.'

They travelled in their own vehicles to the "Tan Hill Inn" and ordered sandwiches. Mills noticed, approvingly, that Phil had a soft drink. The place was as busy as usual with tourists wanting to visit England's highest inn. While they waited for their food Dave enthusiastically described possible plans for the bunker.

'I'd really like to open it for visitors to see how it would have operated in the sixties,' he said. 'There's a bunker in Cumbria at Threlkeld which opened to the public earlier this year and it would be fascinating to have our own reconstruction for people who are interested. That's all in the future of course. For now we would like to examine what state it is in and make a proper study of it, like we did at Grinton.'

Mills had read about that particular archaeological examination while she was researching the bunkers and asked Dave how it had been investigated. Phil listened but didn't contribute to the discussion. When their sandwiches arrived the conversation waned until Dave asked Phil what he'd been up to since leaving

England. He didn't answer at first, having just taken a mouthful of food.

'Not really a conversation for over lunch!' she mumbled.

Phil looked at her sharply. Dave apologised unnecessarily.

'What about you, Dr Sanderson?'

Relieved, Mills launched into a long explanation of her lecturing duties at the university, divided equally between the Forensics and Archaeology departments.

'In fact I'm working on an interesting project which has a foot in both camps,' she continued. 'Stable isotopes. I'm going to use them to identify the origin of… of… well, remains.'

She looked over at Phil but he was busy finishing his food. If he'd heard he wasn't showing it.

'It sounds fascinating,' Dave said. 'I'm impressed. We might be asking you for help in the future then.'

Yes, thought Mills, *it does sound impressive – if I can bring it off.* But she wasn't at all confident she could.

As they were leaving, Dave told them to wait and went to the back of his Land Rover. He returned waving a large padlock.

'It's not new but I've got the key for it. Here you are.' He handed the key to Phil. 'I'll go and fit it now but you mustn't go down until I give you the go-ahead.'

They all went their separate ways after lunch, although Mills did tell Phil she would text him when the risk assessment came through. There was no point in going into work so she went back home to spend the afternoon researching the stable isotope studies that had been carried out on recent bodies.

Chapter 7

Despite Linda informing her that the police would be coming to see her, Amy didn't know who it was standing on her doorstep the following afternoon.

'I'm sorry, love, who did you say you were again?' she asked, wiping her hands on her apron.

Nina continued to hold out her ID. 'I'm Detective Sergeant Featherstone.'

Amy looked at the card and then at the woman. It was rare to see an Asian face in these parts and she had such lovely skin – and her hair was so black and shiny…

'It's a police matter,' the detective said.

'You must be here about the man that's missing,' Amy said, apologising and inviting her into the kitchen.

She insisted on making a cup of tea and brought out the shortbread biscuits she kept for her guests.

'It's silly, I was expecting someone in uniform,' Amy admitted, once they were both seated at the table.

'It's been passed to us because there's serious concern about Mr Webb's whereabouts.'

'That really is his name? Chris Webb? He called himself Len when he was here.'

'Did he give a surname?'

'Hardy, he said it was. Len Hardy. He's not been in touch with her then?'

'No and I understand he was staying here before he disappeared?' She was getting a notebook out of her bag. 'Can you tell me how he travelled here?'

'He said he was on foot. I assumed he was on a walking holiday.'

'You didn't see a car drop him off?'

'No.' Amy poured herself another cup of tea. 'He arrived Sunday night.'

'Did he book the room in advance?' The policewoman was writing everything down.

'He rang on Sunday morning and as I had the room empty I said he could stay until Friday, when I had a couple booked for a long weekend…'

'So he was due to stay until Friday?'

Amy felt uncomfortable at all the questions. 'No, he said he would *probably* stay for the week but gave me the money for three nights.'

'So he was thinking of staying at least until…' she was counting on her fingers, 'Wednesday?'

'Perhaps. I said he could stay until Friday.'

'Thank you.' She was turning to a new page. 'Now, can you tell me what he was doing when he was here?'

Amy had to think. 'He went to the pub for a meal on Sunday night and on Monday he went walking.'

'Which pub?'

'The "CB Inn", it's not far. He cut through the wood. Oh…' She had remembered something important.

'What is it?'

'He said he saw someone with a gun in the woods.'

'A gun?' The woman put her notebook down.

'It's not unusual in these parts,' Amy reassured her. 'I'd be worried if I saw a gun where I used to live but the gamekeepers and grouse shooters they all have guns round here.'

'Right, so you don't think it concerned him?'

'He did comment on it but I told him not to worry. Would you like more tea?'

'Thanks. You said he went walking on Monday?'

'Yes, up Fremington Edge. It was a route I'd suggested to him as it was a nice day. He said he'd enjoyed it.'

'So you saw him that evening?'

'Yes. He had a shower then went down to Langthwaite to eat. We offered to take him but he said no need. We like to help our guests as much as possible but my husband was pleased he didn't have to turn out. And that was the last we saw of him.'

'He didn't come back?'

'He wasn't back when we went to bed so I couldn't lock the front door and I had to leave the lights on. They were still on when I checked later but I thought he might've left them. It wasn't until the morning we found he wasn't in his room.'

'So you don't think he returned from Langthwaite?'

'No. I feel awful now. I was cross with him for going off without a word but now I think I should've done something, notified someone. They should teach you about that on the B&B course.'

The policewoman smiled sympathetically. 'You weren't to know.'

'But his rucksack was still here. When that girl came by on Saturday I was so upset.' She felt like crying now, if truth be told.

'Is there anything left in his room now?' The policewoman was putting her notebook away and closing her bag.

'Well, no. I had guests coming and so I changed the bed and put his rucksack in the hall. His wife took it when she came.'

'In that case, thank you for your help. I'll probably go to the places where he had his meals to see if any of the staff remember him.'

Amy gave her directions and watched her drive away. She was feeling quite shaky and went to sit down for a minute.

Nina had actually volunteered to visit the B&B where Chris Webb had been staying. She liked the Dales and was pleased to have the opportunity for a drive out there, even though it was late afternoon. It was very likely she would be appointed Family Liaison Officer if it turned out the missing person hadn't just decided to leave home or run off with another woman without telling Linda, poor girl. And there was a slim chance that she could catch up with Mills while she was in the area.

The girl behind the bar at the "CB" hadn't been on duty at the weekend but she was able to look at the booking sheet for the Sunday night.

'Hardy, you say?' she asked as her finger moved down the sheet. 'Yes. Table for one – it must have been between six-thirty and seven because a couple took the table over at eight o'clock.'

'So he was alone?' Nina checked.

'Apparently. He was given that table over there.' She pointed to the corner of the bar area.

Nina thanked her and went back to the car. It was too early to call Mills, she wouldn't be home from work yet, so she moved on to where Chris Webb had spent Monday evening.

There was nowhere to park in Langthwaite and Nina left her car as tidily as she could while an old man seated outside the "Red Lion" watched. When she approached the pub, he informed her that it was closed and wouldn't open until seven o'clock that evening. After a few moments of indecision, Nina returned to the car just as a tractor came down the hill towards her. She drove off quickly in the direction of Reeth, thinking it might be the perfect excuse to catch up with Mills.

She messaged Nige to let him know she would be home late and instructed him to give the kids their tea. Then she called Mills. She'd noticed how distant her friend and Phil had been on Sunday and wanted to find out what was wrong.

'Mills? I'm in Reeth. What time will you get home?'

'I'm here now. What are you doing there?'

'Just some police work. I'm in the "Buck", why don't you join me?'

Nina ordered a glass of lemonade and took it outside to wait. It wasn't often she had time to sit and enjoy a quiet moment. She retrieved her notebook and recorded what the girl in the "CB" had told her – he'd eaten alone. She needed to find out if it was the same on the Monday night: did he go to the "Red Lion" as he said he would and what time did he leave.

It wasn't long before she saw her friend's Mini drive past and a minute later Mills strolled up.

Her friend bought herself a small glass of beer and a bag of crisps for each of them. Once they were settled and had exchanged a few pleasantries, Nina asked her outright what was wrong.

'Wrong?'

'Don't look at me like that! You were hardly your usual jolly self on Sunday.'

Mills shrugged.

'On the other hand, Phil seemed very relaxed. Do you think he's getting better?' Nina asked.

'Don't ask me, I don't know what he's thinking.'

'He talked a lot to Nige on Sunday. He didn't tell me everything they spoke about but he did say that Phil has nightmares.'

Mills sipped her drink. 'Yes, he even sleeps out in the woods sometimes.'

'I noticed you arrived and left separately,' Nina tried again.

'He had his motorbike.'

'That's good, isn't it? He'll be able to get about now.'

'Yes, we visited the bunker up at Tan Hill this morning. He's got the key now. He's just got to wait for the risk assessment to be approved before going in.'

'Will you be working on it with him?'

'I doubt it.'

Nina folded her empty crisp packet carefully and finished her lemonade.

'You don't seem happy that he's doing so well. He's mobile, he's got work to do…'

'It's fine, Nina. Can we change the subject, please? What are you doing over here? It's a bit out of your way.'

'It's a misper. A man visiting Arkengarthdale has disappeared. I said I'd come to see where he was staying.'

'Was he on holiday?'

'No, he wasn't. He was working, which is a bit odd.'

'Why?'

'His partner couldn't really explain what he does.'

'Nothing new there. Can you explain what Nige does?'

'No but I know he's an academic working at the university. She wasn't sure what organisation he worked for.'

'Have they known each other long?'

'Not sure. She's got a toddler but... Anyway I'll need to talk to her again after I've visited the "Red Lion". The person I need to speak to isn't there until seven.'

'Plenty of time for us to catch up then.'

'We could call Phil,' Nina suggested.

'No! Anyway he still doesn't have a signal.'

'Ok, just us then.'

It had been like old times with Nina, before the children were born, a rare opportunity to chat – just the two of them. Her friend was more like an older sister, so sensible, so calm, and so well-groomed. There was no more mention of Phil and as she drove back, Mills reflected that she was lucky to have such a good friend.

At home, the cottage seemed empty and cold, despite the warm summer evening outside. There was nothing to do but return to the work she'd abandoned when Nina had called and come up with a research project fit for a university lecturer straddling two subject areas. By the evening she'd developed an approach she could put to the departments involved. She would do a feasibility study – a sort of literature survey – to identify how the archaeological research could be applied to modern forensic investigations, to demonstrate whether the science was robust enough to stand up in court. She would need support from the geology department if she was to do any analytical work on modern bones or teeth and that would have to come later. For now she would treat it as a desk study, and she had a reason for that: if Phil was going to help her, she needed to keep the project purely academic without any real body parts involved.

She turned off her laptop and went to the kitchen. The fridge was bare, except for a small piece of cheese and a wilted lettuce. She took a tin of tomatoes from the cupboard and boiled some water for pasta. This is becoming a habit, she thought, as she fried an onion and made a rather inferior sauce. She wondered what Phil was eating, if anything. She would've called him, if there was any point. Without a signal, he would receive her message a day or more later. Anyway, until the damned risk assessment came through she had no reason to get in touch.

The landlady of the "Red Lion" was behind the bar when Nina returned just after seven. She'd spotted a car park on the main road and walked down to the pub, enjoying the warm breeze. The tables outside were already filled with adults and children enjoying the last of the afternoon sun. Inside it was empty and surprisingly cool. She refused the offer of a drink but sat down at a table near the bar and asked the landlady if she could spare a few minutes to answer her questions. She came round and sat opposite Nina.

She passed a photograph of Chris Webb across the table for her. It was often the case that the picture produced by the family was either a very formal one taken at a wedding or a very informal one at a party. Linda had given her one she had taken on holiday. He was seated at a table beside the sea, with a big grin, raising a pint glass in salute. After deliberating for a while the landlady felt sure it was the man who had eaten there the previous week.

'It was about a week ago – I don't remember which day but it was quiet. Vegetarian, he said.'

'Was he alone?'

'Yes but he was chatting to a few of the locals.'

'Would you be able to give me their names?'

'Probably. Is he in trouble?'

'No, he's been reported missing. We're just trying to trace his movements on Monday night.'

She gave Nina the names of three men who were there when Webb came into the bar. Two lived in the village and she gave Nina their addresses, the third one, called Phil, was from further up the dale but she didn't know exactly where.

'He's only just moved back here,' she said. 'He's been living abroad, in...'

'France?' offered Nina.

The woman looked startled.

Nina apologised. 'I think I know who you mean.' She paused. 'Can you remember what time Mr Webb left?'

She thought for a moment then shook her head. 'No. It wasn't early. He was here most of the evening but he wasn't the last to go.'

'Did you see him leave? Was he alone?'

'I don't remember, sorry.'

'Please don't be. You've been very helpful. Thank you.' She stood up. 'Perhaps I could call you if there is anything else that occurs to me?'

She could feel the families watching her as she walked over the bridge to the main road where her car was parked. Was it the fact she was dressed in a suit and was wearing heels or because she was a lone woman visiting a pub in the evening? She smiled to herself. Who was she kidding?

Back in the car she rang her friend again.

'Mills, how do I get in touch with Phil?'

'You could send a text or email. He won't get it until he's out and about though. No phone line yet.'

'So where does he live? It can't be far away.'

Her friend gave her a detailed description of how to get to the cottage from Langthwaite.

'But you're not going dressed like that?' Mills asked.

'Like what?'

'In your heels? You'll break your ankle if you attempt to go down his track – or your neck!'

'Fair enough. I'll just have to come back in hiking boots.'

'Send him a text if it's not urgent.'

Mills was right, thought Nina. She would report what she'd found tomorrow morning before deciding when to interview the three men seen with Webb in the pub.

In the car she called Nige, who assured her everything was under control. The kids had been fed. It was bath-time now and they would be fast asleep by the time she walked through the front door, he promised. She smiled as she started the engine and set the satnav to "Home".

As it turned out, it was not as Nige had predicted. There were shrieks coming from the bathroom and Rosie, who was in her pyjamas, shrugged.

'They're giving him a hard time, Mum. You'd better go and sort them out. It took Dad ages to get tea ready.'

The boys invariably became over-excited when Nige was bathing them. There were too many hi-jinks and not enough washing. As she climbed the stairs the whoops got louder and they were calling out to her.

'It sounds like you're having fun,' she said, peering round the door.

Nige had a blob of soap bubbles on the end of his nose.

'Dad's been blowing bubbles with his nose!' shouted Tomos excitedly.

'Has he indeed?' she said, pulling off her jacket and rolling up her sleeves. 'Perhaps Daddy should go downstairs while I get you to bed!'

Nige clambered to his feet and gave her a kiss, deliberately wiping the bubbles onto her face.

'Very funny. Off you go. I'll be down in ten.'

She carefully shut the door before lifting the boys out and drying them. Not until they'd cleaned their teeth did she allow them out into their bedroom. She had to put on her strict face, as they called it, to get them into bed and read them the shortest story she could find. Even so, she was still finishing the last page when Rosie came in to say goodnight.

It was a recent change in the routine for Rosie to eat with them in the evening. The boys had their tea early and were usually in bed by seven but now she was older, Rosie's bed-time had gone to eight o' clock. Tonight it was late and their daughter was keen to go to bed to read a new book she'd borrowed from the school library, so Nina and Nige were left alone to clear the dishes.

'I saw Mills today,' Nina said when they were sitting quietly watching the television. 'I'm worried about her. She didn't seem herself and you saw how she and Phil were on Sunday.'

'What d'you mean?'

'They ignored each other, didn't they?'

'I didn't notice. They seemed all right to me.'

'They hardly spoke – well, she hardly spoke. He was lively enough.'

'Yes.'

'Anyway, I'll be talking to Phil. Police business.'

'Right.' Nige began flicking through the channels.

'Are you listening, Nige?'

'Yes.'

'I was thinking that Mills doesn't have many friends, does she? I mean she's living in that tiny village. I've never heard her talk about any friends apart from her next-door neighbour. She's old enough to be her mother though. Does she have friends in the department?'

'Me.'

'Other than you, idiot. What about in the Forensic bit?'

'No… and soon she might have even fewer.'

'What d'you mean?'

'She'll make enemies in Forensics if she's not careful. You know what she's like. Doesn't know when to keep her head down and keep out of trouble.'

'Perhaps you should warn her,' Nina said.

Chapter 8

The meeting to discuss the missing man didn't last long. Ruby's checks had given no leads. His phone was turned off, he hadn't used any cards and had contacted no-one. However she had established that he worked as an animal welfare officer, receiving a salary from the RSPCA. The DI asked Nina, as an experienced family liaison officer, to visit Webb's partner again to fill in some more background.

'She says he was working,' said Hazel.

'The woman running the B&B thought he was on holiday,' Nina responded. 'I can ask her again, I've got to see Phil Freedman in Arkengarthdale anyway.'

'Isn't that...?'

'Yes. He's back in the country,' explained Nina. 'He may have spoken to Webb in the pub the night he disappeared.'

Once they were back in the office, Hazel insisted on discussing Phil Freedman.

'That man saved Nige's life,' she told Ruby. 'Didn't he, Nina? He's quite a catch wouldn't you say?'

Nina laughed. 'You know he and Mills were together – before he went abroad.'

'Of course. So how is that working out now he's back?'

'It's complicated.'

'When isn't it?'

Hazel had been asked to meet Chris Webb's line manager and set off for Leeds, saying she might be some time if they had dogs and cats to drool over. Ruby was at her desk with a list of contacts and phone numbers to check. Nina planned to interview

Linda Bailey before lunch and drive over to Arkengarthdale in the afternoon. With luck she would be home in time to bath the boys and wash their hair – something Nige tended to avoid if at all possible.

Her previous encounter with Linda Bailey had been at the local police station and Nina wanted to meet the girl in her own surroundings. She'd shared the flat with Chris Webb so it was an opportunity to assess the family arrangements and find out a bit more about the missing man.

As she was parking outside the block, Nina spotted Linda coming down the street, carrying a loaded shopping bag.

'I was dropping Katie off at nursery so I popped into the supermarket on the way back. I hope I haven't kept you waiting?'

Nina shook her head and locked the car, following her to the nearest block of flats.

'The lift isn't working but we're only on the second floor,' she explained.

The stairs were dark and smelly but they were soon in an open walkway with a series of identical front doors, every one painted white but dirty and peeling. Linda struggled with the key while holding her shopping bag but eventually they were inside. The contrast was startling. They were immediately in a room that was bright and clean and tidy. Linda took the groceries into a tiny kitchen and offered Nina tea or coffee, telling her to sit down. When she came through with the drinks, they were in cups and saucers on a tray with a plate of biscuits, sugar bowl and milk jug.

The girl's attitude had changed since they last met. Then she was tearful, a rather pathetic character who didn't seem to know what to do. She'd had her daughter with her and they clung together. Now she was subtly different in her demeanour, her dress, everything. Perhaps these were her work clothes and maybe it was easier with Katie safely at nursery. Whatever it was, it made Nina's life a lot easier.

'I've been thinking about Chris,' Linda began. 'I know we haven't been together long but he's a really steady guy, you know? He's not the sort to leave without saying.'

'You said you'd not had a row and nothing was worrying him.'

'Nothing more than usual. We're careful with our money – it doesn't stretch far, as you can see. Sometimes it gets a bit, you know…'

'What about his family? Do you have contact with his parents or siblings?'

Her face changed. 'No, he says they're not close. I haven't met them.' She sounded wistful.

'How long have you known him, Linda?'

'Six months.'

'So Katie…'

'No, she's not his. That was someone else.'

'Do you see the father?'

'No way! We don't have contact.'

'Does Katie?'

'No.'

She offered Nina a biscuit. 'He's not to come anywhere near us.'

Nina looked up. 'A court order?'

'Yes.'

She made a note to find the details. Clearly Katie's father was not a nice man.

'So, Linda, does Chris have a computer, a tablet, anything that he's left here?'

'Yes his laptop is here. But I don't know the password.'

'No problem. I'll take it and we can check it out.'

'You think he's got some double life, don't you?'

'Look, I...'

'It's ok, I understand. I'm beginning to believe it myself. It's the most rational explanation, isn't it? I looked it up. A quarter of a million people go missing every year.'

'But the majority appear very quickly.'

'I know. What I'm saying is that I accept that he's left me. It's difficult to admit when you think you can trust the person.'

'Let me know if there's anything that confirms your suspicions but meanwhile we'll try to find out more about his movements.'

'I found this list with the names of B&Bs in the Dales. When I rang them they said they hadn't seen him but the woman in Whaw told me he used a different name.'

'Yes, Len Hardy.'

'I've got it here.' She opened a drawer and gave Nina a sheet of paper. 'Shouldn't they be contacted again to ask for Len Hardy this time?'

'I'll do that, Linda. And this afternoon I'm going to visit someone who spoke to Chris the night he disappeared.'

Nina left feeling sorry for the girl. Clearly the flat was hers. She'd probably moved to the estate when she separated from Katie's father and she'd known Chris Webb just six months. He could only have moved in a few months ago and now he was gone. There was probably no crime to pursue. Although few people would go without their laptop, she thought, as she placed it carefully on the passenger seat beside her.

The day was getting warmer and she switched on the air conditioning as she set off for the Dales. Phil had confirmed he would be around to see her late morning and she wanted to ensure she caught him at home. She hadn't explained the reason for her visit and was rehearsing what she would say when they met.

'Sorry, Phil, this is an official visit.'

He was outside the house, working on his motorbike.

'I wondered why you wanted to come here. I didn't think it was to view my dilapidated living conditions.'

She followed him into the dark hall, unable to see where she was treading. There was a crash as she knocked something over. She had expected at least the offer of coffee or tea but he sat down and looked expectantly at her. The place was a mess but Nina reminded herself that he was living alone and generally men weren't house-proud, it was something she'd learned from Nige. The room smelled of smoke but the fireplace looked as though it hadn't been used for years. She noticed a packet of tobacco and some cigarette papers on the mantelpiece.

'I didn't know you smoked,' she said.

He didn't answer but gave her a cheeky grin.

Best not ask. 'Right then,' she began, 'I'll come straight to the point. I'm investigating a missing person. No reason to think anything serious has happened to him but he's been away from his address for over a week now.'

Phil was listening.

'So,' she went on, 'he was at the "Red Lion" last Monday, the nineteenth of June, and the landlady remembers you were there.'

'If she says so.' He looked uncertain.

'She does. Do you remember this man?'

She showed him the photograph. He studied it for some time and then handed it back.

'Could be.'

'Could be what?'

'Could be that he was in the "Red Lion" when I was there.'

'Did you speak to him?'

'Possibly.'

'She says you did.'

'If she says so, then I probably did.'

Much as Nina liked Phil she was becoming irritated.

'*Do* you remember him?'

'Not really.'

'Did he leave before or after you?'

'I don't recall. I'm sorry but I really don't remember. To be honest I don't remember much from day to day at the moment.'

'Phil, can I make myself a cup of tea?'

The smell of rotting food pervaded the kitchen as she moved the stacked dishes from the sink to fill the kettle and wash a couple of mugs. The sink was stained brown and she was tempted to roll up her sleeves and set to work. Somehow she controlled her instincts and carried two mugs of black tea back into the cramped room. Phil sat motionless where she'd left him.

'Thanks.' He took the mug from her.

They sat sipping their tea in silence for a while.

'I think you're finding it quite hard to adjust to life back in the Dales,' Nina suggested.

'It's not the place, it's me,' he said, leaning forward to put the mug on the floor in front of him. 'I haven't felt right since before I got here.'

Nina waited for him to continue but he was silent. 'What d'you think the problem is?'

'I can't sleep.'

'You should see the doctor. He could give you something.'

'No – when I sleep I get these nightmares. I see things that happened out in Colombia and, more recently, the air crash victims in Switzerland. It's too vivid. I believe what I'm seeing. I'd rather not sleep.'

'You need help Phil.' Nina knew she was taking a risk. He could resent her intrusion into his private problems. 'You need to see a professional.'

'Post-traumatic stress, you mean?' He looked annoyed. 'I'm not stupid, Nina. I know I'm not right but I'm not going to some shrink.'

'Have you talked to Mills?'

'Why should I?'

Nina considered for a moment. 'Because she cares about you – as a friend. We all do.'

His expression seemed to soften. 'I appreciate that, I really do. But I need time to adjust. It'll sort itself out in time.'

'You know in the force we're offered counselling for all sorts of reasons such as road traffic accidents. It's no disgrace to seek help.'

He ignored her.

'Anyway, I'd better be off soon. But I could wash the mugs out.'

She went into the kitchen and turned on the hot tap to begin washing the dirty dishes. He had followed her.

'There's no hot water,' he said. 'It runs off the Raeburn but I can't get it to light.'

'You should get it fixed.' She hoped her voice sounded cheery. 'What you need is a housekeeper!'

But he'd already left the kitchen and she followed him to the front door. Now her eyes were accustomed to the dark interior she could see what she'd knocked over in the hall – a shotgun. Not daring to move it in case it was loaded, she left it lying across the bottom of the stairs. He was already back outside tinkering with his motorbike.

That evening she rang Mills to see if she could persuade Phil to get help but her friend was surprisingly negative to the suggestion that they contact Catterick Camp.

'The army must have people to help staff with PTSD.'

'I'm sure they do, Nina, but he won't go.'

It was the last Wednesday in the month and time for another staff meeting in the Forensics Department. Mills would have preferred to avoid it but that was not an option. Her absence would be noticed and remarked on, no doubt. It wasn't as if she ever had anything to contribute as a very junior part-time lecturer in a department full of senior academics who liked the sound of their own voices. Others had arrived earlier to partake of the free tea and biscuits but Mills knew few of the staff and waited until the last minute to arrive, squeezing herself at a corner of the Board Room table just as the Head asked for silence.

There were a number of announcements regarding the summer vacation period when many went off to work elsewhere on collaborative ventures at home and abroad. Administrative matters went on for half an hour and there was much discussion over the new sexual harassment and bullying policy being rolled out across the university. Successful grant holders were congratulated and the admissions tutor gave a presentation on numbers for the next academic year – it seemed the classes were going to be larger than ever and everyone groaned.

Finally they reached the item on examination results. The Head thanked everyone for getting their marking done in time and announced that the marks were better than last year's. He asked Dr Cuthbert to hand out the summary of final figures to be approved at the Board of Examiners meeting on the following Wednesday. It took a while for the papers to reach the end of the table where Mills was seated. While the discussion started on the results of the first year students, she turned to the page with marks for the final year and scanned down the list.

She gasped when she found the name and looked up quickly to see if anyone had noticed. They were busy discussing the arrangements for the resits. Sara Pendleton, who skipped lectures and copied other students' coursework, had achieved an overall score of seventy-three percent, equivalent to a first class degree. It was unbelievable and Mills could hardly wait to get back to the office to tell Nige. She studied the breakdown of marks, which were consistently high across the board. She knew they couldn't have been falsified because she'd given Sara top marks herself. There must be another explanation.

But Nige couldn't offer any suggestions. 'Unless she actually cheated in the exam…'

'She didn't. I was there. I would've seen. No, it's something to do with Colin Cuthbert, I'm convinced.'

'You'd better be very sure before you accuse him of being complicit,' warned Nige. 'You'll make yourself extremely unpopular.'

'I'm sure you're right.' Mills sank back in her chair. 'So how can I prove it, Nige?'

He shrugged. 'Are you thinking that he's been feeding her the answers?'

'There's no other way she could get such high marks.'

'Does he get all the papers back after the exam, before they're circulated for marking?'

'Yes.'

'So they could get swapped between the exam and when you receive them?'

'Yes.' Mills saw where he was going. 'So she could answer the questions at her leisure, using notes or even copying bits from the other papers?'

'It's a thought – but only if you believe Cuthbert is helping her.'

'I don't see I can prove that.'

'Is there anything that happened in the exam that could help identify whether the paper was completed at the time?'

'Not really. Except the question with the bit missing that Cuthbert set. She answered it although it was incomplete. But I've already asked him how come she got marks for that and he effectively told me to mind my own business.'

'Well, there you are then. That's the weak link. You have to find a way of bringing that to the

Board's attention at the Examiners' meeting next week.'

'Yeah, right and how do I do that, Nige?'

'My advice is to forget it Mills. Don't make waves. The potential consequences really aren't worth it.'

Sara Pendleton had answered six questions in the forensics examination. Apart from the one Mills had set and that of Dr Cuthbert's, there were four more, all gaining equally high marks. Mills pondered over the spreadsheet long after Nige had left the office that afternoon. The questions had been set by four other members of the department: two young male lecturers, one slightly older female senior lecturer and an old male professor. She decided to approach the lecturers and senior lecturer about the student's remarkable change in competence to see if they were as concerned as she was.

The email she wrote simply pointed out that she had been surprised, even incredulous, that Sara Pendleton had attained such high grades in the examination and wondered if they had similar concerns. She put the three names at the top of the email and pressed "send", praying that at least one of them would agree with her.

Next morning Mills was anxious to get to the office to see whether she'd had a reply to her email and she didn't have long to wait. As she turned into the car park she spotted Colin Cuthbert by the main gate deep in conversation with one of the young lecturers she'd contacted. She was locking the car and heading for the building when she was stopped in her tracks.

'What the bloody hell d'you think you're playing at?'

Mills turned to see what was going on.

Cuthbert emerged from between the cars and was approaching, still shouting. 'Who are you accusing of cheating, you stuck up little bitch?'

Mills was too shocked to speak.

'Spreading rumours! What are you trying to do, eh? No-one is interested in your lies young lady, I can tell you that now. I can have you thrown out of here, do you understand? I can make it so difficult for you that you'll be glad to leave forensics for good.'

Mills was speechless. She walked quickly through the entrance and straight into the ladies' cloakroom where she stood by the basins, shaking. She was crying because she was angry, angry with him and angry with herself for not standing up to him. She'd been there for several minutes when the door was opened partially and a face peered round.

'Is everything all right?' It was the Head's personal assistant, Emma.

She nodded and smiled at the woman, who quickly disappeared back into the corridor, shutting the door gently behind her. It was a long time before Mills felt she could leave without the risk of seeing Cuthbert again but eventually she splashed her face with cold water and dried it with a paper towel. She looked a mess and she wasn't staying in the same building as that man. She walked straight out to the car and set off for Harrogate.

When Mills arrived at Yardley Forensics, Brenda took one look at her and pulled her towards the tea room.

'You look in need of a strong black coffee,' she said. 'Have you been out on the town?'

Mills had to smile. 'No, no chance.'

Brenda waited until they were back in the office before she asked Mills again what was wrong.

'Are you not well, pet?'

Mills shook her head. 'No, I'm not ill but I am sick – sick to death of Dr Colin Cuthbert.'

'Who's he when he's at home?'

'He's the course director for the third year forensics class and he's responsible for their examination results.'

'So?'

'So there's a student who hasn't achieved more than fifty-five percent in any of her course work who is suddenly getting top grades for her written exam and he won't do anything about it.'

'You think she cheated?'

'I'm sure she did.'

'Perhaps she got someone else to sit the exam.'

'No, I saw her – I was invigilating.'

'How then?'

'I think Dr Cuthbert gave her the answers either before or after she sat the exam.'

'Really? That's…'

'Cheating, yes.'

Mills told her how Cuthbert had confronted her in the car park.

'It sounds suspiciously like he's hiding something.'

'I really don't know what to do about it, Brenda.'

'It's obvious, pet. You go right to the top. Speak to the Head and let him know what's been going on.' She headed towards her office then stopped and turned back. 'Meanwhile, to change the subject, Tim's given me the bone analyses for Professor Ross. I need you to go through them and write up the results as soon as possible. I'd like to send the report off this afternoon.'

'No pressure then.'

'It will take your mind off other things, pet.'

It was true, once she got stuck into processing the data she forgot her troubles and was totally absorbed in her work. The results for the bones were actually not dissimilar to the figures published by the American professor but the range of numbers varied enormously, suggesting they could not be used to provide definitive information on origin. She wrote a report highlighting the negative aspects of the analyses and prepared a table, comparing their results with that of the American.

Brenda was waiting impatiently and grabbed the report as it was coming off the printer, page by page. As soon as she had the complete document she ran into her office and there was silence for about five minutes.

'Excellent!' She strode through the door, with a broad grin on her face. 'Good girl. The professor will be delighted.'

'It seems to show that trace element data may not be reliable for identifying the origin of a body.'

'True – which is a shame, I suppose. However, on this occasion we will have a happy customer. Would you like to email a copy of this to him? I'm going home now. I'll see you next week.'

Mills sent the results off then went to congratulate Tim on a nice piece of work. She wanted to know more about stable isotope ratio measurements and was hoping he would have had some experience of the technique, since his background was in geochemistry.

'I haven't worked on it myself,' he told her, 'but there was a post-doc in my department at Nottingham whose thesis was around stable elements in teeth and he was working at the NERC Isotope Geosciences Laboratory.'

'Where's that?'

'It's part of the British Geological Survey, I think.'

Mills hurried back to the office and went on the internet to find out more. It seemed she could apply to make use of their facilities, although she would have to wait some time to find out if she'd been accepted and it would have to be in the right area of research – archaeology not modern forensics. But if she was successful she would be able to get high quality data, from a laboratory away from Colin Cuthbert.

It was six-thirty when she quickly checked her emails and found a message from the Yorkshire Dales National Park. The approved risk assessment was attached and permission was given to go ahead. They might be able to get into the bunker at the weekend, if that was convenient.

Chapter 9

Nina was asking Ruby to see what she could find out about Linda Bailey's ex-husband when Hazel put her head round the door.

'The meeting is about to start, Mitch is getting in a strop!'

The cramped conference room was nearly full and they edged their way to the last empty chairs at the table. Mitch was the officer in charge of the investigation as it was now considered sufficiently serious for the DI to take over.

'Hazel, will you tell us about your chat with Webb's employer?'

'Not much to say really,' she began. 'He's part of what they call the Special Operations Unit.'

'Undercover work,' Mitch added. 'What was he working on?'

'They weren't specific. He has several cases, including dog fighting, fox hunting and poisoning wildlife.'

'So why was he in the Dales?'

'It's not clear. He had a fairly free rein to work as he saw fit. He last made contact with the office a couple of days before he disappeared. He was due to go in the following Monday for a meeting with his bosses.'

'We were involved in an operation on raptor poisoning in Arkengarthdale a few years ago,' offered Nina. 'There was a prosecution but it failed through lack of evidence. That was discovered by an RSPB officer I believe.'

Mitch ignored her. 'Do they think he was onto something in the Dales, Hazel?'

Mitch was always the same but Nina wasn't going to be put off. 'The owner of the B&B where he was staying said he appeared to be on holiday but his partner thought he was working.'

'Did she provide any further insights?' he asked.

'She's only known him a few months so she hasn't met his family and couldn't help with friends and associates. I collected his laptop to see if it helps.'

'I'm running through phone contacts, and I'm checking out her ex,' added Ruby.

'What's the connection?' demanded the DI.

'I just thought it might relevant,' Nina said.

'More importantly, does Webb have an ex?' he asked.

Nina was about to admit she hadn't checked but Ruby put a hand on her arm. 'No, he isn't married and has no children of his own, although obviously he was acting as a sort of step-dad to Katie,' she said.

'Katie?' Mitch asked.

'Her daughter,' Nina replied. 'She's two years old.'

He looked irritated. 'Have we checked whether anyone saw Webb the night he went missing?'

Nina nodded. 'I've interviewed the men who spoke with him at the "Red Lion" that night and they can't recollect anything significant. No-one remembers what time he left but it must have been around ten from what the landlady says. She seems to be our best witness so far.'

He sighed audibly. 'Did he stay anywhere else in the Dales?'

'No,' Hazel replied. 'He'd jotted down a list of places but his partner checked and only got a response from the one in Arkengarthdale.'

Nina tried to speak but Mitch was already making for the door. The meeting was over.

Back in the office Ruby asked if she should be checking on dog-fighting and fox hunting in the area.

'You can but my bet is still on him deciding that life with a two year-old that wasn't his was a tad too much,' said Hazel.

'Linda says he dotes on her,' Nina said.

'She would, wouldn't she? I used to think Liam was sweet at that age but his father was long gone by then.'

'By the way,' said Ruby, 'I've already checked up on Linda Bailey's ex-husband and father of her daughter. He sounds a right piece of work.'

'Why didn't you say at the meeting?' asked Hazel.

'The DI didn't seem interested.'

Nina nodded. 'He was more concerned with Chris Webb's relationships. So what did you find out?'

'A temporary Restraining Order was granted in May two years ago, just before Katie was born. The judge entered a final order in July when he didn't turn up to court. He was ordered to receive professional domestic violence counselling – I think that says it all.'

'Well done for finding that, it couldn't have been easy,' said Nina.

Ruby grinned. 'Actually it was simple because Linda Bailey made a 999 call in May last year when he violated the order. He went to the flat, drunk, demanding to see his daughter on her birthday.'

'Nice,' said Hazel. 'Sounds as though we should speak to him. Perhaps he's cottoned on that Webb is shacking up with his ex and has taken matters into his own hands. Do you have an address?'

'We know where he was living last year.'

'Great, give me the details and I'll take a trip to…?'

'Berwick.'

'You'd better take someone with you,' suggested Nina.

Mills had taken Brenda's advice to see the Head of Department. It seemed such a sensible plan when her boss suggested it but now she was outside Professor Cole's office, her resolve was waning.

His personal assistant gave her a warm smile and said she would see if he would be able to give her a few minutes. She emerged from his office looking a little flustered, ushering her towards the door, whispering that he was *very* busy. She was hardly inside the large office when he asked her what she wanted. Mills had been rehearsing her reply.

'I'm concerned that a final year student has been cheating in the examination.'

He sighed. 'Just as I feared. Dr Cuthbert has been to see me about your accusations. He is clearly not convinced by your arguments and unless you have some evidence to show me, there is nothing I can do.'

Mills wanted to ask him what evidence he expected her to come back with but he was already picking up a file.

'I have a meeting,' he announced and brushed past her. In the outer office he stopped and turned to face her. 'This isn't the first time that you've challenged a more senior member of my department. Last time your contretemps with Professor Green resulted in your suspension I seem to remember.'

Mills blushed as she recalled the court case that proved the man was incompetent. 'But *he* had to leave the university in the end,' she mumbled.

He glared at her. 'Dr Sanderson, I do not want a repeat of that performance thank you. Dealing with examination misconduct is the business of Dr

Cuthbert.' He looked at her quizzically. 'I gave you a chance in this department because Dr Featherstone gave you an excellent reference. He said you were a good scientist and I took the risk. However, if you continue to cause trouble it might not stop at suspension from the university.' He turned and marched out before she could think of a response.

As Mills left the outer office, Emma called after her.

'I saw what happened yesterday, Dr Sanderson. Just let me know if I can help.'

Back in the office, Nige listened until she had finished describing her meeting with the Head, including his remarks about Nige being the reason he took the risk of employing her.

'Well, that's nonsense,' he said. 'They were practically biting my hand off to have you with experience of working in a forensics laboratory.'

'Do you think I should raise a complaint?' she asked him.

'Against Cuthbert or the Head?' he asked, laughing.

'Both probably.' She could see why he was amused.

'I know what Nina would say.'

'What?'

'Keep your head down.'

'That's not like her.'

'Don't you believe it! She always plays it quiet and well-behaved. Never create waves, not in the force. She's had to put up with a lot in the past you know: bullying, groping, jokes, racial slurs…'

'Awful.'

'It was but never improved by raising it with a senior officer.'

'I thought it was best to raise it at the examiners meeting.'

'You are joking, aren't you?'

'No.'

'I wouldn't if I was you, honestly. Let it go, Mills. It won't do you any favours.'

Nige began working on his computer. Mills went to her desk on the other side of the cramped office, seated with her back to him.

'Nina is worried about Phil,' Nige said after a while.

'I know.'

'She said she's been looking to see where he could get help.'

'Really?' She tried to sound concerned.

'There's a place in Catterick…'

'He won't go.'

'She thought you could persuade him.'

'No.'

Mills made a half-hearted attempt to deal with her emails but was on the verge of giving up when a message came through from Dave.

'Yes!'

'What's that?' asked Nige. 'Nobel prize or the National Lottery?'

'The National Park. Dave's definitely going to let us in the bunker tomorrow.'

Mills sent a message to Phil before settling down to finish her presentation for a meeting on forensic archaeology she was attending in Rome in August. At lunch time she went down for a quick sandwich before leaving to give Phil the good news in person. The cafeteria was surprisingly busy considering that the exams were over. Most of the students had drifted away but she recognised some of the third years at a crowded table in the centre of the hall. After paying for her food she went over to the end of the table where two sensible girls from her class were seated.

'D'you mind if I join you?' she asked without waiting for an answer.

They looked surprised but responded politely.

'I won't interrupt your lunch but I just wanted to ask you something.' Mills had surprised herself. She looked up and down the long table to check that Sara Pendleton wasn't present. 'I was looking for Sara but she doesn't seem to be around.'

The girls exchanged glances before one said, 'She's gone away for the weekend. She'll be back for the vivas.'

'Oh, that's a shame. I wanted to congratulate her on her excellent marks in the exams.' It was inappropriate but she couldn't help herself.

The girls looked at each other again and then back at Mills but didn't respond.

'Yes,' she went on, 'top marks out of the entire class in the written exam.'

'No way!'

'Honestly?'

Clearly they were as surprised as she had been.

Mills couldn't stop. 'Yes. I was really impressed. She must've worked really hard after the end of lectures.'

They were both giggling.

'Yeah right.'

The other student tried to shut her up but she wasn't having any of it.

'She's on my floor in halls and the number of evenings she was in her room you can count on one hand.'

'Perhaps she was in the library,' Mills suggested.

'No, she wasn't.'

She wouldn't say more but her expression indicated she knew exactly where Sara was. Mills could guess but she was done. She wished them a good summer vacation, picked up her lunch bag and went straight to her car.

She enjoyed the drive to see Phil. It was Friday and tomorrow they were going to start work on the bunker together – if Phil was in the right mood. It was sunny and the forecast was good. Perhaps he might agree to go out to eat that evening.

Of course, it was too good to be true. As she picked her way down to the cottage she could see he wasn't around. The door was shut, there was no sign of his bike and when she called out there was no response. She was not going to even try the door after the way he reacted last time. She scribbled a note on the back of an old shopping list and shoved it under the heavy knocker on the front door. *Dave and I will be at the bunker at 10.30 tomorrow – be there or call me!* It seemed the best approach.

When Hazel had finally got through to Linda's ex-husband she was intrigued. His voice was smooth and well-educated, despite a slight Geordie burr to it. He sounded very pleasant and had agreed to meet her at his home in Berwick that afternoon. She was equally surprised to find he lived in a big detached house on the outskirts of town. The front door swung open as she parked her car on the gravel drive and she saw that Jason Bailey was older than expected – forty-five, fifty even.

'Come in,' he said. 'I've just got in myself. Would you like tea or a coffee perhaps?'

Hazel followed him into the kitchen – one of those spacious ones with a central island and large range stove. He must have sensed she was eyeing it enviously because he smiled.

'It's only been done a few months,' he said. 'We decided it needed freshening up.'

'We?'

'My mother and I. She said she was sorry to miss you, it's her bridge afternoon.'

He gave her a mug of tea and pushed the milk jug towards her. They sat, either side of the worktop facing each other.

'You know why I'm here?' Hazel asked.

'I can guess,' said Bailey. 'But I haven't seen Linda for over a year and I haven't been south of Berwick for several months.'

'It concerns a missing person investigation. Linda's partner, Chris Webb.'

'Never heard of him.'

'You've not met him?'

'No, how would I? I can't go to see my own daughter.'

Hazel knew that wasn't strictly true. He had visitation rights, under supervision, but hadn't asked to see Katie in the past year.

'Did you know that Linda has a partner?'

'No, but it's not a big deal.'

'And he's now a missing person.'

'I'm not surprised if he's done a runner. To be honest she's a very difficult woman to live with, a fantasist. Perhaps she was telling lies about his behaviour like she did with me.'

'I think the court found you guilty of domestic violence, didn't they?' Hazel couldn't resist.

Bailey reddened and she thought he was provoked but he deliberately sipped his tea for a few seconds before replying.

'I didn't do any of those things that she accused me of. I told you, she's a fantasist. To be honest, life with her was intolerable and it's been a relief to be away from it all.' He smiled and offered Hazel a biscuit. She took it and placed it on the worktop in front of her.

'Are you saying that you have never met or even seen Chris Webb?'

'Is that his name? No.'

'And you didn't know that your ex-wife was in a relationship?'

'No.'

She ate the biscuit slowly and finished her tea before asking him her final question.

'Did you attend the anger management course that the court ordered?'

She was hoping her question would irritate him but his reaction surprised her. He smiled and nodded. 'Of course I did. And it was very useful. It taught me that I am easily riled and that I shouldn't have risen to the taunts when they were hurled at me.' He seemed to be waiting for her to say something.

'Really?'

'Yes. I realise now that my wife was a very manipulative woman and I should have dealt with her abuse differently.'

'Abuse?'

'Oh yes. Not usually physical but I think you'd call her behaviour mental abuse. Anyway, it's over now and I've rebuilt my life.' He looked around. 'I'm happy here.'

'With your mother?'

'Yes, she was right – she never approved of Linda. Didn't like her from the off. Nearly didn't come to the wedding. Anyway she was soon proven right. Linda's behaviour deteriorated soon after we were married; to be honest I was surprised to find that her baby was mine, the way she behaved.'

Jason Bailey showed her to the door and walked down the drive with her. He watched her back out through the gate before returning to the house. Hazel watched the door shut behind him as she drove slowly before pulling to the kerb out of sight of the house. She wanted to think. It seemed that the man may have had some excuse for behaving the way he did. If so, there was no reason for him to lie. He certainly didn't seem the jealous type and he hadn't been to the house for over a year so how would he know about Chris Webb's existence?

Chapter 10

Since there had been no call from Phil, Mills assumed she would see him at the bunker. So far there was no sign, although it was another ten minutes before the allotted meeting time. The morning was dull and dark clouds were approaching from the west. It was disappointing, she thought, but it wouldn't matter if it was wet once they were underground. Already she could feel a few light raindrops in the breeze.

Dave appeared, wearing a waterproof jacket and carrying a large torch, just as the rain became more persistent. Mills wished she had come better prepared.

'Is Phil coming?' Dave asked as soon as he was within range.

I hope so, thought Mills. 'Yes,' she replied cheerfully.

'Looks like the rain's settling in.'

'Yes, let's hope he's here soon.'

Dave was working on the metal door when Mills spotted Phil dragging his motorbike bike off the road and making his way towards them. He removed his crash helmet and left the bike a few yards away.

'Hi, am I late?' he asked Dave, smiling at Mills. His mood seemed abnormally ebullient. Not his usual self at all.

'No, mate. On time. Give us a hand with this.' He was still struggling with the door. Together they flung it open and peered down into the bunker.

'Damn!' said Dave. 'I've left my hard hat in the Land Rover.'

They watched him marching over the heather towards the road.

'I wonder if *we* were supposed to bring hard hats.' Mills said. 'He didn't say.'

'I'll be fine.' His voice sounded strange. 'Absolutely fine.'

Before she could stop him Phil had stepped onto the top rung of the ladder and was lowering himself down.

'Wait!' Mills called but he'd disappeared.

She leant over as far as she dared and called to him. 'Have you got a torch? There's no light down there!'

His voice sounded far away although he was only twenty feet below her.

'It's light enough.'

She could hear him cursing as he reached the bottom.

'Is it very wet down there?'

'Yes! It's over my boots.'

She could hear him splashing about and then a shriek. Not a high pitched female sort of shriek but a long deep shriek that only a man could make.

'Phil?'

Silence. She called again but nothing. She looked down at the road where Dave was leaning into his car. Grabbing hold of the ladder she put her foot on the first rung. It slipped off. She replaced it and carefully positioned her other foot alongside. Her heart was pounding.

'Phil, answer me!'

Nothing. She began to descend slowly. The metal ladder attached to the wall went down vertically and each rung was thin and slippery. She clung to the side rails and kept moving, wishing she would reach the bottom. There was no sound coming from the bunker. Finally she could feel the cold water covering her boots and she felt gingerly for the solid ground before releasing her tight grip from the ladder. The muddy water stank.

'Phil?'

She was turning round slowly in the confined space, feeling her way on the walls until she was facing the opening into the bunker. It was dark and she had no idea what she was expecting to find. She'd seen the plan of the room, it wasn't large. If Phil had collapsed he should be in the middle of it.

'Mills! Phil! Are you down there?' Dave was shining a flashlight around from the top.

'Shine it down here, Dave,' Mills instructed. 'It's Phil. I think he must've collapsed or something.'

It was a powerful light and she could see that she was in water halfway up her calves. The light didn't reach the inner room but was enough for her to make out a figure on the floor, leaning against the wall, near the entrance. She called Phil's name and moved towards him, taking his arm and shaking him. She could feel a pulse and he seemed to be breathing so she let go and waded back to the bottom of the ladder. Looking up she could see Dave's worried face.

'He's unconscious but otherwise ok,' she called to Dave.

'I'll get help,' he called. 'Are you all right?'

'Yes but please hurry. He may have internal injuries. And throw me the torch before you go.'

She missed it as it fell with a splash but it continued to work despite the soaking. Dave disappeared and she turned to go back to Phil. Now she had light she could see his eyes were closed. She moved the torch from his face to his chest, his arms and legs then stopped. Those weren't his leather trousers and boots. As she moved closer she realised that Phil was lying across another person, a body that was almost completely under the murky water. Horrified, without thinking of any physical damage it might cause him in consequence, she began dragging Phil through the entrance and towards the ladder. She propped him half-seated against the wall and called his name, willing him to open his eyes.

'Please Phil, please wake up. We have to get out of here.'

She shone the torch back into the room at the body. She could only see the soles of two large boots but she didn't want to move any closer. What if it was still alive? She told herself it was impossible but she had to know so she edged towards the boots and shone the torch along the legs and up to the head. The body was lying face down in the water, there was no way it would be breathing, she told herself. She bent down to touch the arm and a hand floated to the surface. It was as cold as ice.

She moved rapidly back to Phil and cradled his head in her arm. He felt warm compared to the thing in there but he was getting colder. She felt a slight movement against her arm and shone the torch in his face. He blinked then started to breathe quickly and heavily. Soon he was fighting to get up and struggling to get away from her.

'Stop it Phil!'

She'd seen a panic attack before and knew she had to quieten him down before he damaged himself or her.

'We're going to get out of here now,' she said in as calm a voice as she could muster. 'Dave is getting help but we can do this together can't we?'

She stood up and attempted to help him to his feet, praying he hadn't broken anything. His breathing was rapid but he wasn't struggling now.

'How does that feel?' she asked gently.

She supported his weight as he attempted to stand, balancing himself against the wall.

'Does that feel better?'

He didn't speak to her but she kept talking softly, reassuringly, until he was propped up at the bottom of the ladder.

'Shall we try going up?' she asked him, uncertain whether it was a wise move. She desperately wanted to get back above ground herself.

'Give me a minute,' Phil gasped.

'It'll be easier when we're out in the open.'

'I know but I just...' he stopped to take another breath. 'Everything's spinning.'

'Ok, ok, we'll stay here until you feel better.'

She continued to talk to him, reassuring him that everything was going to be fine. After a few minutes Mills heard Dave calling down to her.

'Help is on its way.'

Mills told him that Phil had come round and they just wanted to get up into the air again. She persuaded Phil to go up the ladder first. She would support him if he felt insecure, she said, although she didn't know exactly how that would work. He stood hanging onto the rungs, looking up at Dave.

'Coming up,' he said and began the ascent.

Progress was slow but steady. Once Phil was on the rungs above water, Mills followed. Dave helped him out and made sure he was safe before offering a hand to Mills.

'What happened?' he asked her.

She shook her head. It wasn't as if she knew exactly what had occurred. He may have tripped and fallen over the body but she suspected that Phil had blacked out when he found it down there. She didn't want to say. She told Dave about the body lying in the water and after some questions he went off to contact the police, telling her to stay with Phil until the ambulance arrived.

She began to shiver, it was raining heavily and they were already soaked with cold, muddy water. Phil appeared to be dozing, passing in and out of consciousness but that seemed preferable in the circumstances. Time passed slowly with nothing to think about apart from the body submerged in the stinking water below.

Dave was back before any signs of the emergency services and he covered Phil in a blanket he had brought from the Land Rover before quizzing Mills about exactly what she'd seen. The police arrived first, two young officers in uniform. One went down to confirm what Mills had told them while the other asked Dave about the bunker: when had it last been open, was it locked at all times and who'd been down there? Dave confirmed it hadn't been used for years but recently they'd opened the door and Phil had the key for the new padlock.

'So did he unlock it today?'

Dave looked puzzled. 'No, actually it wasn't locked, was it Mills?'

She hadn't noticed and told them so.

The officer emerged from the bunker shaking his trouser legs to remove the excess water and took his colleague to one side. They were in conversation for some minutes before coming over.

'We'll be staying here until we get CID support. I presume your colleague here will be waiting for the paramedics?'

'Yes, he's still in a bad way.'

'They'll be a while yet. Do you think you could get him somewhere out of this rain?'

Dave looked at Mills. 'I can drive him to the "Tan Hill" if he feels up to it.'

So Mills cajoled Phil to a standing position and between them, they moved him slowly across the rough ground to the Land Rover. It was as if Phil was sleep walking when they instructed him to climb into the passenger seat. Mills followed in her car and they threw themselves on the hospitality of the highest pub in England.

When Mills was recounting the events to Nina that evening, she said it was like a dream – or rather a nightmare. Eventually the ambulance arrived and Phil was examined. It was decided that he should be taken in for X-rays to ensure he hadn't damaged anything. Mills took one of the paramedics to one side and explained that Phil appeared to be under stress after his work abroad and he made some notes. She followed the ambulance to Darlington and waited with him in X-ray. By then he was clearly exhausted and it was decided to keep him in overnight for observation. That was when she had driven to Nina's and broken down in tears.

Mills woke to the sound of loud whispers and when she opened her eyes she saw three small faces peering at her.

'I said you'd woken her up!' scolded Rosie, ushering the boys away.

'Is she awake?'

Mills smiled across at Nina. 'Yes. What time is it?'

'Nearly eleven.'

'What?'

She pushed the duvet away and leapt off the sofa. She was wearing a pair of Nina's pyjamas and looked around for her clothes.

'I washed your stuff – it's all dry except your jeans and jacket but you can borrow mine.'

'You are kidding, Nina. You're at least a size smaller than me.'

'Don't worry, I've got a pair I bought when I had the boys.'

Mills felt better after a cup of tea and a shower. The trousers had an elasticated waist and fitted except for the length of the legs. She turned up the bottoms and went downstairs.

Her friend surveyed her approvingly. 'Sit down and I'll get you some breakfast. How does a bacon sandwich sound?'

'Great but I must get to the hospital to see Phil.'

'He's on a ward. They wouldn't tell me any more than that – not being a relative. They won't let you in until visiting time so you might as well eat – you haven't had anything apart from the soup last night.'

Mills agreed to sit down and be waited on. Nige arrived back from the supermarket and they ate together with the kids. It was a long way from the horror of the previous day. Nige waited until the children had gone off to play before quizzing Mills about what exactly had happened down in the bunker. Nina had reprimanded him for his questions last night, allowing Mills to rest and recover from the ordeal.

'I rang Ruby this morning,' announced Nina. 'She didn't know much except that the post mortem is being carried out today. I assume she'll be working on identification of the body. At present all she knows is that it's a male, clothed but with no documents on him.'

Mills could see the boots, feel the hand. 'He can't have been there too long. The body was in good condition.' The phrase sounded strange as she said it; clinical and remote.

'How long d'you think?' Nige asked. He was animated, apparently excited by the discussion.

'Nige! Mills doesn't need to keep going over it.'

But she did. She wanted to make sense of what she had experienced.

'He was lying on his front. The water was up to here.' She pointed to her shin. 'His face was covered in filthy dirty water.' She was looking at the corpse now, seeing it in the torchlight. 'But I could see his hair, it was short and dark.'

'How was he dressed?' Nina asked, leaning forward.

Mills looked again at the picture in her head. It wasn't a shirt or a T-shirt. It was clear of the water, thick. A waterproof jacket perhaps; it was difficult to tell. 'Not sure, maybe an anorak. And big boots. He was lying straight out as if he'd fallen flat on his face.'

'Someone exploring the bunker who'd slipped and fell in the water?'

'I don't think so, Nige.' Mills had been thinking about it. 'The door was shut. It may not have been padlocked but the hatch door was closed. Someone shut that door with him inside.'

'I don't understand why the bunker wasn't locked,' Nina said, pouring Mills another tea.

She explained how when they first visited the site the old padlock wasn't working and they'd assumed it had rusted through.

'Dave found a replacement and gave the key to Phil, ready for when we had permission to go down.'

'So meanwhile the bunker remained firmly locked?' Nina asked.

'I guess so.'

'For how long?'

'Just four days.'

What Mills didn't mention, what had been worrying her, was that Dave thought the bunker was unlocked when he arrived – and only Phil had a key.

'When was the last time you visited Grandad?' Alf asked, once they were in the car.

'About a month ago,' his father replied. 'He seemed fine – the same old Stan, busy in his garden this time of year.'

'Does he still go out in the evening to pick the slugs off his lettuces?'

'I expect so. He used to pay you for them, didn't he?'

'Only in sweets.'

'You were small then.'

They fell silent and Alf guessed they were both thinking about the time when he and his half-brother spent most of the summer holidays with Nan and Grandad – Jesse's paternal grandparents. Right up to the year when Mum was having chemotherapy. Alf supposed his father thought it was for the best but it meant he saw little of her that summer when she died. That was when he was four and for several summers after that he would go to the cottage in Brough where Nan would spoil him and Grandad would take him fishing nearly every day. Jesse didn't come with him after that but went to stay with Shane until he finally went to live with his father permanently.

'Does Jesse ever visit Grandad?' Alf asked.

His father didn't answer immediately and Alf waited.

'It's difficult when family fall out. Nan didn't approve of Shane's lifestyle and refused to see him after he left your Mum but they wanted to keep in touch with their grandson. They wanted to see Jesse and have him stay with them but once he was living with his father all contact stopped.'

'They wouldn't let him?'

'I don't know, son. It was probably Shane that put a stop to it.'

'Is that why you still go to see Grandad?'

'He's a nice old guy and my dad passed away a long time ago. I think of him as family. I owe them a lot. He found it hard when Nan died.'

Alf remembered. He was ten and they wouldn't let him go to the funeral. He didn't go to stay in Brough after that because Dad said that it wasn't fair on Grandad and since then he only met him once a year at Christmas. It was Dad's idea to visit him, suddenly suggesting it on the spur of the moment. A quick phone call and it was agreed, they would take him out for Sunday lunch.

The front garden of the terraced house looked as well-cared for as it always did and the front step was as clean as Nan always kept it. The door opened almost as soon as they knocked and Grandad stood with his cap on, as if prepared to leave.

'I'm not quite ready I'm afraid. I've just got to turn off the radio,' he said.

They followed him into the neat room where the theme tune to "The Archers" was playing loudly.

'I always try to catch up on a Sunday,' he explained as he pressed the off button on a very modern looking radio. 'It's my new digital radio,' he added. 'Roy, take the lad out to see the soft fruit while I get my jacket,' he instructed. 'The apples are going to be good this year. And you can take some strawberries back when you go.'

Alf followed his father to the tidy kitchen, through the conservatory and out into the garden. Loud music was playing next-door and the smoke from a barbeque drifted from the other direction. Apart from a tiny patch of lawn, the rest of the long garden was a vegetable plot. There were straight rows of beans and lettuces, large courgette plants in the corner and a mesh cage to keep the birds off his redcurrants, gooseberries and raspberries. Alf knew every crop that Grandad grew because he had helped him sow, weed and collect most of them in the past. How excited he'd been to pick the gooseberries and help Nan make a pie with them. He hadn't tasted one since.

'*We* should grow some vegetables and fruit,' he announced.

'And who would do the digging and weeding?' his father asked good-naturedly.

'I would.'

'But you'd be away at college, remember?'

Alf was saved by the old man appearing at the back door, declaring he was ready if they were. After some discussion, at Grandad's suggestion, they drove down Mallerstang to the Moorcock Inn.

It was the first time Alf had sat in a pub with Grandad and they marked the occasion by wishing each other good health and clinking glasses. Once they'd ordered their meals the atmosphere relaxed and Alf sat back, happy to listen to the two older men chatting about the weather and local news until something made him sit up and pay attention.

'We had a nice trip up to the "Tan Hill Inn", didn't we, son?'

'Tan Hill?' Grandad put down his pint. 'Have you heard about the body they found over that way?'

'No.'

'That was up near Tan Hill.'

'We were there last week, weren't we Dad?'

'Yes but there was nothing about it on the news.'

'It was only discovered yesterday,' explained the old man. 'I heard it from one of the mountain rescue lads. They were brought in to recover the body because it was underground.'

'A caver?' asked Alf.

'No, no, no. It was in the Observer Corps bunker.'

Neither Alf nor his father had heard of the place and received a long explanation of how they were constructed.

'Was that in the war?' Alf asked.

'No, lad. This is during the Cold War, in the sixties, when we thought Russia was going to use nuclear weapons on us.'

'How come you know so much about it, Stan?'

'I was a member of the Royal Observer Corps. I used to spend tours of duty manning the post during the exercises. Two of us would be down there for hours. It was cold but it was important work at the time.'

'So they don't use these posts now?' Roy asked.

'No, shut down a long time ago. That's why I wondered how a body came to be down there.'

'Was it very old?' Alf asked, trying to dismiss the image of a rotting corpse as the girl approached their table with their lunch.

'No, the lad said it was quite normal except for the face which had been shot off.'

'I think we should change the subject now,' said Roy quietly, looking at his plate.

Nina had offered to take Mills to the hospital in Darlington on the pretext that she knew the way and where to park. Visiting was from one-thirty and the smell of lunch became stronger as they made their way to the ward. Mills had been dreading what state Phil would be in and was surprised to see him dressed and sitting beside his bed. He was wearing a white T-shirt and a pair of jogging bottoms, presumably provided by the hospital.

'They said I can go this afternoon,' he announced as soon as they arrived. 'I need to get my bike.'

'Are you sure?' asked Nina. 'Have they discharged you?'

'They just wanted to keep an eye on me overnight. They said I could go but someone had to be with me.'

'I'll be back in a minute.' Nina excused herself and left the ward.

Mills assumed she was going to check on Phil's story. She perched on the edge of the bed and asked him how he felt, wondering how much he had actually seen in the bunker.

'A bit fuzzy but that's probably because of the bang on my head.'

'Is that what they said?'

'They couldn't find anything wrong with me.'

'Do you remember much of what happened down there?'

'Not really. I told them I get a bit of claustrophobia in tight places and they said it was probably a panic attack.'

While they waited for Nina to return, Mills looked round the ward and studied the patients. She enquired about the nurses, the doctors and the food. He replied in monosyllables. Finally Nina returned to announce that she had agreed someone would be with him for another twenty-four hours and on that basis he could come back with her.

'What about your clothes?' Mills asked.

'My leather jacket is in this bag. My boots are nearly dry. They said I could have these.' He pointed at the trousers and T-shirt. 'Apparently the owner no longer needs them,' he said with a grin.

It took a while to get the paperwork in order before they walked slowly to the car. Phil was in the front passenger seat and Mills behind him, wondering how to persuade him to stay with her in the cottage. She needn't have bothered. When they arrived at Nina's, her friend told Phil she'd informed the hospital he would be staying with her until the following day but he'd have to spend the night on the sofa. He seemed happy to comply and soon he and Nige were ensconced in the yard with a bottle of beer each.

'Nige can take him over to collect his bike tomorrow,' she told Mills.

'I'd best be off then.'

Mills felt disappointed and rejected. It wasn't her friend's fault – she was being her usual kind and helpful self. She knew Phil would enjoy Nige's company and she wouldn't have to cope with his moods.

'Mills,' Nina called as she was leaving. 'I spoke to the ward sister. She says that Phil is being referred to the clinic in Catterick Camp. They cope with military staff affected by PTSD.'

'I hope he goes.'

'He will, we'll make sure of it. Nige will persuade him – he listens to him.'

Mills was sceptical.

'And remember, Phil saved Nige's life – so now it's his turn to repay the favour.'

Chapter 11

'They had to get the Swaledale mountain rescue to help retrieve the body,' Ruby told Nina. 'The post mortem is being held this morning and they hope to report by lunch-time.' She lowered her voice. 'They say his face was blown away.'

'Shot?'

'Yes.'

'That will make ID difficult.'

'Tell me about it.'

'But there will be dental evidence to identify him.'

'Only if you know which dentist to contact.'

'True.'

Hazel came in and asked Ruby to fetch some coffees. As soon as their researcher was out of the room, she asked, 'Is it right... that Phil Freedman is staying with you?'

'Last night. Nige is taking him home this morning.'

'Then you're off the case, Mitch says so. This murder, it's not looking good, Nina. I know he's a mate but...'

'What d'you mean?'

'He had a key to the bunker where the body was found.'

'So?'

'He's been arrested for murder before.'

'Hazel, that was years ago. It was a mistake. He was released.'

'I know but it doesn't change what it looks like. We'll wait for a time of death but my money is on it being recent.'

Nina could hardly bear to wait. She went to the kitchen and asked Ruby to let her know when the results of the PM were in.

'I'll be busy with the missing person case so I won't be working on the identification with you,' Nina explained.

Back in the office she finished telephoning all the addresses on Chris Webb's accommodation list. Finally she spoke to the owner of a B&B in Barnard Castle who recognised Len Hardy's name. He had stayed for three nights immediately before arriving in Arkengarthdale. She jumped at the chance to get out of the office but before she left she reminded Ruby to contact her the moment any results came through from the PM or Forensics.

The satnav took her to a neat row of houses on Galgate, where she was welcomed by a friendly middle-aged woman who offered her tea and cake in her kitchen. Glenda had her visitors' book open ready on the table, indicating the entry for the seventeenth of June. It was simply signed by a Len Hardy and the words "Very nice".

Nina explained why she was enquiring about him and asked if she could give her any information gleaned from his stay.

'I remember him well,' Glenda said. 'He didn't want a cooked breakfast. That was unusual. Just cereal and toast, he said.'

'Did he say what he was doing here?'

'No and I don't pry. He struck me as the outdoor type so I assumed he was hiking.'

'Did he have a car?'

She thought for a moment. 'I honestly don't know. It's not something that concerns me, love. He didn't have a bike or he would've wanted to keep it somewhere safe – I've got a shed at the back they use. He wasn't any trouble, you hardly noticed he was here.'

'Was anyone else staying that he might have talked to?'

She consulted the book. 'A family with three small children. I think he tried to keep out of their way.'

'Where would he have eaten in the evening?'

'Anywhere in town. He didn't say.'

Nina left Glenda her card and stepped into the street. Her phone indicated there were numerous places he could have eaten in the town and the chances of anyone remembering him or providing any useful information was almost nil. She was about to start the car when her phone rang.

'Nina, it's Ruby. The results are back. He was shot in the face at close range with a shotgun.' Her voice changed as she began to pick out sections from the report. 'They think he was killed elsewhere then dragged across the moor... his body was arranged to look as though he had fallen where he was found but there are no fractures to suggest that is what happened. Nothing to help with the identification – no operations or abnormalities. Apparently he was pretty fit...'

'How old?'

'Estimated twenty-five to thirty-five.'

'Time of death?'

'They say it's difficult but one to two weeks. Definitely not more than three but not less than a day or two. They say that's based on the water temperature in the bunker – something to do with waxing?'

'Thanks Ruby – and can you not mention to Hazel that I asked, it's just that...'

'I know, Nina. She told me you weren't on the case. I'll keep you up to speed.'

'Thanks.'

Nina sat in the car and repeated "one to two weeks; not less than a day or two." It was a wide window that included the time when the rusty old padlock wasn't locked through to when the new padlock was fitted and Phil had the key. She picked up her phone.

'Mills? It's Nina.'

'Hi. Is it Phil? How is he?'

'Fine as far as I know. Nige was taking him back this morning. Listen, I've got a question for you: did Phil have the only key to the new padlock on the bunker?'

'Why?'

'Just tell me, Mills.'

'I don't know. I could ask Dave.'

'Please do, it's important.'

'Why?'

'Why do you think?'

She pressed the red button before Mills could ask her anything else. She was smart, she'd work it out.

Mills waited in the office for Nige to appear, reluctant to go to the cafeteria in case she missed him. She couldn't wait to hear how Phil was and when she heard someone outside she jumped up to face the door.

'I was on my way to lunch and I thought I'd drop these in personally.' The Head's assistant handed her a thick set of papers. 'You might want some time to go through them.'

She smiled at Mills, hovering, waiting for a response.

'Thank you, Emma.'

Mills wasn't sure what they were but repeated several words of gratitude and the woman finally left. When she inspected the paperwork she realised the significance – they were the documents for the examiners meeting on Wednesday. Their delivery was a tacit gesture of support for Mills after her confrontation with Cuthbert and the Head. It was too late to repeat her thanks but if she followed her ally to the cafeteria she could thank her properly – and get something to eat.

As it turned out she didn't catch Emma but returned with a sandwich, by which time Nige was back.

'Is he all right? Is he at home? Is he going to be able to cope on his own?' Mills asked.

Nige held up his hands to stop her barrage of questions.

'He's back in the cottage. He seems ok.'

'What about milk and bread?'

'We sorted all that. I took him to the big supermarket at Catterick. We went round and loaded him up with food.'

Nina had instructed Nige to go shopping with Phil. She'd given him a list of things he would need but Phil had argued that he had plenty of supplies of everyday necessities and it had been quite an ordeal persuading him that he needed to stock up "in case he didn't feel like going out". That's what Nina had said.

'She'd put "ready meals" on the list and I found the frozen section but Phil said the freezer bit of his fridge was iced up. When we found the chilled meals which are quick to heat up, he tells me he doesn't have a microwave. Anyway there is an oven apparently so we put a few in the trolley. We filled the rest with crisps and beer.'

'Nige!'

'Only kidding, although he needs a few beers to cheer him up.'

'It sounds as though he's in a better state than he was on Saturday.'

'He's not in a good place, Mills. I could tell when we were in the shop that he was getting more and more agitated. He was commenting on the men in uniform. The camouflage seemed to upset him.' Nige sighed. 'I've always thought of him as such a strong guy, you know, the sort of person you could rely on in an emergency. I kind of looked up to him with the work he was doing abroad. There's no way I could've done any of that.'

'It's the work that's made him how he is, unfortunately. Hopefully the clinic will be able to help him. Did you talk to him about that?'

'Nina said to tell him he should go. He seemed to agree. Perhaps you should tell him too.'

'I don't think he'll listen to me.'

'Of course he will. I told him that you'd be dropping in.' Nige began tapping his keyboard.

'Did you?' Mills had decided not to visit unless she was invited but if Nige had said she would. 'I might go on the way home.'

'Good idea,' he said under his breath. He was concentrating on his computer monitor.

'Was the cottage… well, tidy?'

He looked up. 'Tidy?' He considered the question. 'Not really – bit of a tip to be honest.'

Now she had his attention again, she had one more question. 'Nina asked me whether Phil's key was the only one to the bunker. D'you think the police will have to question him?'

'I suppose they're bound to want a statement if he found the body. I'm surprised they haven't seen him already.'

'Hmm.' She was worried that an interview with the police might seriously affect Phil's mental health.

Nina pretended to concentrate on typing up her reports but was listening to every conversation and phone call to glean as much information as she could on the body in the bunker. Ruby received a call and immediately told Hazel that hair samples had been taken for DNA. Later, Mitch came in to see Hazel and although they were talking in low voices, she could tell that they were linking the missing person investigation with the murder. As soon as her colleague was out of the room, Nina asked Ruby if that was the case.

'The timescales fit and the description, for what it's worth. It's easily tested using a DNA sample from Chris Webb's home. Forensics are going over to collect a hairbrush or toothbrush or a hair from his clothing. It won't be long before it's confirmed – or proved wrong.'

Nina stared at her computer screen without looking at it. Phil Freedman lived near the crime scene, he found the body, he had a key to the bunker and he'd spoken to the victim the night he disappeared. Worse still, if the body was that of Chris Webb, she would be taken off that case too until they eliminated Phil from their list of suspects. In fact, she would no longer have contact with Linda Bailey because the poor girl would be in the middle of the murder enquiry.

*

For her own piece of mind Nina needed to talk to Phil and convince herself of his innocence. And that was how she came to be sitting in his cottage that afternoon when Mills arrived, carrying a large plastic bag bearing the logo of a local supermarket. As Nina helped her unload it in the kitchen, Mills asked her what she was doing there.

'Don't worry, it's not police business – quite the reverse. I'm being kept off the case.'

'Why?'

'Because I'm a friend of Phil's.'

Mills looked puzzled. 'Just because he found the body?'

'It isn't as simple as that, Mills.'

There was a sound at the doorway and Phil walked in slowly.

'We're just going to make a cup of tea,' said Nina.

'There are plenty of teabags,' he said. 'Nige made me buy a huge boxful. I told him I already had a load.'

'That's my fault,' Nina admitted. 'I told him to stock you up with everything.'

He shuffled out slowly, his shoulders were hunched and Mills looked at her friend.

'He seems really low.'

'Depression is a common symptom of PTSD.'

Nina looked towards the door. 'Is that gun still in the hall?' she asked and went out to look.

'Well?' asked Mills.

'No, it's gone.'

'Maybe it's locked away somewhere safe.'

Nina said. 'I'll check with him before I go.'

Her visit had been a waste of time. She'd only had a short time alone with Phil and had found it very difficult to communicate with him. He'd been asleep when she arrived and she wondered if the hospital had given him something that made him drowsy. She scrubbed at the mugs in the sink until the brown rings had almost disappeared then made the tea. When she carried the mugs through, Mills was sitting opposite Phil and an awkward silence filled the room. They sat sipping their hot drinks for several minutes before Mills asked Nina what she knew of the case.

'I know I shouldn't ask you but I just wondered if they've identified the body yet.'

'Not yet.' At least she could answer that honestly.

She glanced cautiously at Phil but he didn't even seem to be listening.

'Phil, did Nige ask you about the clinic?'

He shrugged.

'Have they given you an appointment?'

He hesitated. 'I think so.'

'When is it?' asked Mills. 'I can drive you there if you want.'

'I can get there on my own, I'm not a child.' He replied quietly but coldly.

She looked hurt.

After a long silence Mills announced she had to get home, telling Nina she'd be in touch.

When she'd gone, Nina couldn't stop herself. 'That was a bit harsh, Phil.'

'What?'

'The way you rejected her offer of a lift to the clinic. She only wanted to help.'

He took a deep breath and exhaled before replying. 'I just can't do it at the moment, Nina. It's too difficult. Nothing feels right. It's so much effort just to be me. I can't be what other people want me to be as well. I'm sorry.'

Nina wanted to say she understood but she didn't. She wasn't even sure what he couldn't do at the moment – the clinic? She didn't want to leave him alone but he seemed to be getting very tired.

'Before I go, Phil. Just one thing – the gun. You had one, out there in the hall. I'm not asking about licences and things, I'm not on duty now, but *please* tell me you've got it locked away safely.'

'Gun? You're mistaken, Nina, I don't own a gun.'

As she left Phil's cottage behind, Nina realised she was passing the B&B where Chris Webb had stayed before he disappeared. No-one had said she should stop working on the case, yet, and there was something she wanted to ask. When she'd spoken to the owner before, she'd mentioned Webb meeting a man with a gun in the woods. At the time it didn't seem important and Mrs Bradby had dismissed him as a gamekeeper. If it was turning into a murder investigation that sort of intelligence could be very relevant. What troubled Nina was that Phil had a gun but denied it.

The woman was in an apron, her hands covered in flour. 'Oh hello, come in. I thought you'd be back when I heard the news.'

Nina didn't respond but followed her into the kitchen.

'I said to Jeff, there'll be a lot more questions now.'

'Why's that?'

'With the body they found up at that nuclear bunker place.'

'You know about that?'

'News travels fast round here. The mountain rescue was called out to recover the body and we know someone who was on the team. His dad used to work down there in the old days, I remember him telling my husband all about it. Jeff is interested in all that cold war stuff – films and books about Russian spies and the nuclear threat.'

'Mrs Bradby…'

'Amy, please.'

'I'm actually here about Mr Webb and his movements while he was staying here.'

'Do they think it's him that they found dead?'

'I don't have anything to do with that investigation so I can't say.'

Nina could tell that anything she asked would be assumed to be relevant to the murder and wished she hadn't called in but now she was here…'Just one thing I wanted to check with you. In your statement you said Mr Webb met a man in the woods on the night he arrived.'

'Yes. He commented on it because he was carrying a gun.'

'Did he say what sort of gun?'

'Do they think that was the weapon?'

'Amy, please understand I have no information about the body they found in the bunker. I am here to report on the missing person case. So, please do you know what sort of gun it was?'

'No.'

Amy looked offended despite Nina's efforts to maintain a friendly approach.

'Do you know who might be able to confirm whether a gamekeeper was about that night?'

She sniffed. 'The estate, I suppose.'

Nina thanked her and rose to go. 'I will let you know when there is any news regarding Mr Webb,' she offered on her way out and Amy responded with a curt "thank you".

Chapter 12

Everything was moving inexorably towards the body being that of Chris Webb. The DNA pattern from the body was established and a sample of Webb's hair had been obtained for comparison – the results would be in within a few hours. Assuming there was a match, the investigation would start moving fast and Mitch had already asked for Nina's report from the missing person enquiry. She was typing up the last few details while listening to Hazel and Ruby's conversation.

'Ask Forensics for DNA or any other evidence that might belong to the assailant and get them to check with the database.'

Nina knew Phil's DNA would have been taken when he was arrested after an ex-girlfriend planted false evidence on a murder victim. But that was over three years ago so it would have been destroyed. She wanted to tell them that Phil had been lying across the guy so if they did find anything it would mean nothing. But she kept typing.

'Have they got evidence from the gunshot wound?' Hazel was asking.

'Shotgun pellets at close range. The samples are being analysed in preparation for a match if they find the assailant.'

Nina waited until she was alone before ringing Mills, asking her to search Phil's cottage for the missing gun and, more importantly, any cartridges.

'Are you serious? After yesterday? I don't think I'd be welcome there, do you?'

'He was tired, Mills. He said he was sorry afterwards,' she lied.

'I'm not going round there again, Nina.'

'He's not well. Nige and I will help him however we can but I need you to do just this one thing.'

'I don't mind if he's not there.'

'Well, obviously you can't search when he's in. Nige is going to make sure he gets to his clinic appointment. We'll let you know when that is and you can go then.'

Mills agreed reluctantly and put the phone down.

'That was your wife,' she told Nige. 'She wants me to take over her detective duties now.'

'What?'

'Nothing.' It suddenly occurred to Mills that she maybe wasn't to tell him.

'She said you're taking Phil for his appointment.'

'Yes. I rang the clinic. It's on Friday afternoon at two o'clock.'

'Oh.' She hoped she sounded disinterested and went back to searching for articles on post-traumatic stress disorder on the internet.

It was when Mills was leaving that afternoon that Nige asked if she would be in the following morning.

'Yes.'

'Is it the examiners' meeting?'

Mills looked at him as it dawned. 'Tomorrow, yes – and I haven't looked at the results yet!'

She gathered up the papers and almost ran to the car. She would have to go through them that evening. All the way home she was considering how best to approach the meeting the next day. It would be embarrassing to raise her concerns in front of all the other staff in the department but how else could she communicate them to the External Examiner?

The message on the answer machine was from her father, asking her to call. He said it was nothing urgent so she deleted it and put the kettle on. After a quick cup of tea and a hastily made ham sandwich she settled down to work through the file of examination marks and coursework evaluations. She was sure no-one else would bother to look at the pages and pages of numbers but she wanted to be sure of her facts. She moved rapidly through the first and second year figures, highlighting the columns against Pendleton, Sara. The marks were abysmal and only rectified by retakes of the written exams in both years. She put them to one side and opened the final results for the third year students, highlighting Sara Pendleton's scores in yellow. As required, she'd answered six questions and gained top marks in all of them, including the one Mills had set. The column for question five stood out because it was empty except for her one result. Eighty percent for a question that no-one else had attempted, the one with missing information set by Colin Cuthbert.

The next page contained the results for coursework. It was the first time she'd seen all the marks and they told a very different story. When Mills looked back, Sara's marks were comparable to those from previous years and there was nothing odd about them. She remembered how appalled she'd been at the brevity of Sara's essay on forensic analysis; the girl had clearly done no background reading but simply regurgitated the notes Mills had given the class. So she turned to the next page to see the final scores.

It was the first time she'd been privy to the amalgamated marks combining coursework and exam results in the formula used by the department that favoured examinations. At first she perused the names and their grades, which in most cases represented their abilities very well. Borderline cases were highlighted in red and these would be the candidates for a viva. There was one possible fail, two borderline upper second and three heading for a first. Sara Pendleton was one of them. How could she possibly be a candidate for a first! It was madness of course and the External Examiner would soon see that. Ok, so she really deserves a third not a second class degree but at least some justice will be served. There was no point in fighting the system.

Eventually, feeling rather better about the whole thing, she rang her father, concerned since he never usually wanted to chat.

'Millie? I'm glad you're in. Working late? I thought you'd be in by six.'

'You said it wasn't important.'

'No, it's not. Not really. I just wondered whether Fiona might have called you.'

'Fiona?' His wife hadn't called her since the argument in London. 'No, why?'

'I just thought she might have... you know... said something.'

Was she going to apologise or did Dad want *her* to?

'Look, I don't mind talking to her if she's there,' she offered.

'I'm afraid she's not.' Her father's voice was strangely thoughtful.

'Oh well, another time.'

'I mean she's not here, Millie.'

'So where is she?'

'That's the thing – I don't know.'

'What? She's disappeared?'

'No, not exactly. No, she hasn't disappeared, don't be silly. She went off.'

'She's left you? What about Flora?' Suddenly Mills realised that as much as she disliked her father's wife, she couldn't bear the thought of him losing Flora.

'Hang on a minute. Slow down Millie. She went off in a huff and took Flora and an overnight bag.'

In that case she'll be back, thought Mills. Fiona wouldn't last long with a small bag of clothes, unless she bought new stuff – that was certainly a possibility.

'So where is she now?' Mills asked.

'I don't know. I haven't heard from her and she isn't answering my calls. I thought she might've rung you.'

'No and I don't think she would, Dad. Listen, she won't be far away. She'll be at one of her posh friends. Check out the ones with children.'

'I don't have their numbers. I don't know where to start.'

'Ask Agnes, the nannies will all know each other.'

'Ah, that's the point rather. She left – a couple of weeks ago actually. That was what the row was about. Fi was getting stressed about getting another nanny and I suggested she could look after Flora herself. It didn't go down well, I'm afraid.'

Mills was speechless.

'Are you still there, Millie?'

'Yes, Dad, I'm still here. Look, I'll have a think and text you if I can suggest anyone. Meanwhile, why don't you check the credit card, she's bound to have bought clothes and stuff for her and Flora.' She noted that he didn't suggest she ring Fiona herself.

Mills chose her outfit carefully next morning and dressed in her only smart skirt and jacket, discarding the white blouse for a pink short-sleeved top to avoid looking too formal. She stood in front of the mirror and tried pinning her hair back but it flopped heavily back into position as it always did, skimming her shoulders and telling her she needed a cut.

She grabbed a piece of toast, stuffed the papers into her bag and slammed the door. She'd already made herself late by messing about with her hair and now the traffic was building up so she arrived with just ten minutes to spare. A quick visit to the "ladies" and she ran up the stairs to the Board Room where her colleagues were already helping themselves to coffee and biscuits. One or two colleagues smiled but no-one spoke to her and she sat at the end of the table furthest from where the Head and his personal assistant had already established themselves. To her surprise, Emma gave Mills a small almost imperceptible wave of the hand and smiled. Mills assumed the smart middle-aged woman on the other side of the Head was the External Examiner. Colin Cuthbert confirmed it by moving over and offering her a coffee. He looked so pleased with himself in his stupid bow tie and corduroy jacket.

Members of staff were soon ordered to take their seats and the Head began chairing the meeting in a very formal way, introducing the External Examiner, Professor Elsa Gray, by listing her impressive credentials. Once he had finished embarrassing their guest with his praise, he started on the agenda. The first year results were approved with two students required to retake one exam paper each. All of the second year students had passed, which apparently was a first. Eventually they reached the final results. Mills looked across at Dr Cuthbert who, as course director, would be presenting the outcomes of the vivas before the results were approved.

Cuthbert coughed nervously. 'Professor Gray was not able to sit in on the vivas this year due to an unfortunate mix-up with dates.'

Mills wondered who had been on the panel but no-one asked and *she* wasn't going to. The Head's assistant was passing round the paper bearing the final marks.

'As you can see, all of those interviewed passed with flying colours.'

The sheets hadn't reached her end of the table yet. He was reading out the names of those students with firsts. Just as she received the final results she heard the name Sara Pendleton. A quick check confirmed that the girl had been awarded a first-class degree in Forensic Science.

'May I ask a question?' Mills could feel her face burning as everyone in the room was staring down the table at her.

'You have a question, Dr Sanderson?' The Head asked irritably.

'I wondered who was on the panel for the viva?'

'It was myself and Dr Cuthbert. Normally Professor Gray would attend but in the circumstances…'

Emma was rifling through her papers. 'Except for Miss Pendleton's viva, of course,' she reminded him. 'You had to leave for a meeting before hers.'

There was an awkward silence. Mills was compiling her thoughts when a woman put her hand up further down the table.

'You also have a question, Dr Riley?'

Mills recognised the senior lecturer that she'd sent the email to… the message that had put Cuthbert into such a spin.

'I shared some of my colleague's concerns regarding Sara's remarkably high results,' she began. 'So I was interested to learn she was down for a first. However, I see that the course work is running at a more typical level.'

'Clearly she excels under examination conditions.' Cuthbert looked smug.

'That may well be,' she went on, 'but isn't it a requirement that the standard is consistent across all forms of assessment? I don't think that can be said of Miss Pendleton's course work.'

Everyone was looking at each other. This was the first year that Dr Cuthbert had been responsible for the final year course. Had he missed something?

'Perhaps Emma could advise us,' the Head said. 'Meanwhile this might be a good time for a comfort break.'

Several people left the room and Mills joined the queue to refill her cup. The only conversations were being held in low whispers. Cuthbert had disappeared and so had Professor Cole, leaving just the Head's assistant and the External Examiner at the end of the table. Dr Riley was heading in their direction.

'Margaret!' Professor Gray was standing up.

'Hi, Elsa.'

The two women hugged.

From their conversation, it appeared they had been researchers together somewhere. Unfortunately for Mills it was her turn with the coffee machine and there was no longer an excuse to listen in but, hopefully, Dr Riley would have their External Examiner's ear. She watched as both women academics turned to consult Emma and an animated conversation followed. At one stage they all turned to look at Mills and she wondered whether she should join them but just then the Head returned – with Colin Cuthbert in tow. Margaret Riley went back to her seat and further discussions took place between the Head, Professor Gray, Dr Cuthbert and Emma. At one point, from where Mills was sitting, things appeared to become quite heated until the professor raised her hand and spoke for some time. When she'd finished everyone nodded and the Head called the meeting to order.

The rest of the proceedings were very brief. The Head simply said, 'Ladies and gentlemen, it appears we have not been following the regulations to the letter. The issues only affect our final year students but it means we will be running the vivas again this afternoon with our External Examiner present. It also means that unfortunately Miss Pendleton is not eligible for a first and will be awarded a second class degree – a lower second – based on her performance. Thank you.'

And that was that. People started filing out and Dr Riley was gone before Mills reached the door. She went to her office still in a daze.

Nige was waiting. 'How did it go?' he asked.

'It was weird. She sort of lost out on a technicality.'

Mills explained what had happened and Nige nodded. 'That's the way it works here. You don't get graded on your average marks if one part is too low. It doesn't normally cause a problem because most students get consistent marks and it's unlikely you'd be brilliant in one area and hopeless in the other. The rule is designed more for people who are good at coursework where there is greater risk of getting help from someone else. That's why we have written examinations. It should work unless someone cheats in the exam.'

'As in this case.'

'So what happens to Colin Cuthbert?'

'Nothing, they just think he's an idiot not a cheating womaniser.'

'The university wouldn't call him a womaniser – he's taken advantage of an impressionable student, using his power to get sexual favours. He could be dismissed.'

Mills shrugged. 'What can I do? I'm insignificant compared to him.'

'I'd talk to Sara Pendleton. *She* must be feeling pretty cheated now.'

Mills sat for several minutes deciding what to do. Nige was right, it wasn't just Sara's fault that she'd got into the situation. The university had a policy to deal with exactly these circumstances. They might not believe a student but they would believe her if Mills backed her up. Sara was probably on her way home now – in tears. She sent the girl a sympathetic email suggesting she might like to come and talk to her about her supervisor, in confidence.

As soon as Nige had left the office, Mills picked up the phone. She was counting on the fact that Fiona wouldn't recognise the number and she was right.

'Hello?'

'Fiona, it's Mills. How are you?' She hoped her breezy manner would fool her and it did. So far, so good.

'Mills!'

Mills could tell she was putting on a cheery front.

'I can't get hold of Dad and I want to let you know I'll be down this weekend.'

It was a ploy she'd thought up overnight, a perfect way to get them talking again.

'I've got a meeting in London on Friday,' she lied. 'So I thought it's a great opportunity to see you all!'

There was a pause at the other end so Mills carried on. 'Is Dad there?'

'No – he's… he's… out at the moment.'

'How's Flora?'

'She's fine.' She sounded distracted. 'Look, Mills, I'll get your father to ring you tonight, yes?'

'Yes. But it's ok to stay over, isn't it?'

'It's… I mean… Look, I'll get him to ring you, all right?'

There was no more to say. Mills could feel her discomfort and, although she was enjoying it, there was nothing more to do but wait to hear from Dad that evening.

Mills hadn't expected such a rapid response from Sara Pendleton. Just half an hour after she'd sent the email, the girl appeared at the open door and called her name. She seemed to be slightly unsteady on her feet and Mills assumed that she'd been drowning her sorrows.

'Well, I'm here,' she announced. 'What did you want to talk about?'

She wandered into the office and sat down. She crossed her legs, exposing a vast expanse of thigh. She looked faintly amused, as if she was going to enjoy whatever came next.

'I was sorry to learn that your marks were re-categorised,' Mills began.

'Are you? Are you really, Dr Sanderson?'

Mills was already regretting asking to meet her.

'Yes because I think you've been led up the garden path by a certain senior colleague.'

That sounded a bit pompous, she thought.

'Led up more than the garden path, if you ask me,' she replied with a laugh. 'That man is a piece of work.'

'Dr Cuthbert?'

'Colin? Yes.' She went on to use expletives that she'd never heard a woman use before. It went on and on until the girl began to transform from an angry fishwife into a tearful adolescent. It was disturbing to witness. Mills pulled out the tissue box and waited until she'd calmed down.

'I wouldn't mind...' she wailed between bouts of crying. 'I wouldn't mind but he said it would be fine. That nobody would be interested and it was what I deserved.'

'Deserved?' Mills assumed she meant for the sexual favours.

'He said that someone with my disadvantaged background deserved help and he did help – at first. He gave me extra tutorials.' She looked indignantly at Mills. 'All above board. He helped me with my work but it wasn't going very well and I was going to quit. And then... then...' She started crying again.

'What happened then, Sara?'

She made a loud sob. 'Then he took me out for a meal and we got pissed. I went back to his and woke up next morning in his flat. It was then he suggested that he helped me get a good degree.'

'So it was his suggestion?'

She looked surprised. 'Well, yes. I didn't know you could do that, did I? He said he could help me get good marks in the exam.' She laughed. 'I told him – that wasn't going to happen but he explained it all and it made sense. I didn't know there were answers all written out for me.'

'Did he prepare them for you?'

'Oh no, they were answers he collected from everyone else.'

Like me, Mills thought.

'So all you had to do was read the answers and make sure you produced them in the exam.'

'It wasn't easy, you know. I had to work hard to remember them all.'

Mills smiled at the thought.

'And did you have anything more to do with Dr Cuthbert?'

The tough Sara Pendleton from Essex was back now. 'You don't think he did all that for nothing do you!'

Mills didn't know how to ask the question delicately and left further details of how the girl paid Cuthbert back.

'So where does this leave you now?' Mills asked, hoping Sara would make a complaint.

She shrugged. 'Dunno. With a Desmond I suppose.'

Mills recognised the slang for a two-two degree. 'You wouldn't be thinking of raising a complaint?'

'Is that why you brought me in here, to cover his back? You're all the same, you lot!' She leapt to her feet and made for the door.

'No! Quite the opposite,' called Mills. 'I think you should inform the Head.'

Chapter 13

'Mum, mum come and see!'

Amy was getting the tea ready and told her son to be quiet.

'But it's that man that came to stay!'

'What man?'

She came through, drying her hands and stood at the doorway.

'He's gone now,' said James.

The reporter was talking to a policeman and she turned to go back into the kitchen when she heard the name Chris Webb. It rang a bell but she couldn't remember where. It wasn't until there was mention of a partner Linda and a little girl that the penny dropped. She'd been right all along – it *was* her guest that they'd found down in that bunker place. When Jeff came in, she told James to turn the television off and go upstairs to wash his hands so she could give her husband the news.

'I said he was trouble,' was all he said before sitting down at his place, waiting for his tea.

'It's awful,' said Amy. 'When you think about that poor young girl and her toddler. How must they be dealing with the news that he will never be coming home. I must write to her… or ring… No, I'll send a condolence card. Do you think that would be all right?'

Her husband sighed. 'Are we getting something to eat tonight?'

Amy went into the hall. 'Anna! James! Tea-time!'

She'd found that sometimes it was best to just bite her tongue and ignore it but later that evening, when Jeff was out at darts, she switched to the BBC news channel and saw the face that her son had recognised. Chris was his real name, she knew that. But she didn't know he was an undercover animal welfare officer – the policewoman hadn't told her that. She'd been more interested in the man with the gun that her Len Hardy had seen when he was in the woods. Was that the man who killed him? As she told Jeff later, it made her blood run cold to think there might be a murderer out there in the woods behind the house.

'Have you seen the news?'

Alf was busy in the kitchen. 'What?'

His father came in with a newspaper.

'I heard it on the radio on the way home so I picked up a Northern Echo. The body Grandad was talking about. I thought there might be more detail.'

He shook the paper open and folded it in two. 'Here. "Body found in disused nuclear bunker." There's a photo from the air – I suppose it's a crime scene so they won't let people near. You can't see much, there's a tent over it.'

Alf was busily peeling and slicing.

'What's that?' Roy asked.

'I'm making chips.'

'There's a packet in the freezer.'

'These are sweet potato chips. They're better for you.'

His father laughed. 'You sound like your mother.'

He continued to read the newspaper article aloud. There was little information on what had happened to the body but they'd identified him as Chris Webb, a RSPCA officer operating in the area. He was working under an assumed name: Len Hardy. The police were asking anyone who had met him in the last few weeks in the course of his stay in the Dales to get in touch.

There was a photograph of him and phone number to contact the police.

'Well,' his father said, refolding the paper neatly and putting it on the table, 'it doesn't mention that he was shot, like Grandad said. They must be keeping quiet about that.'

Alf wiped his hands and took the paper to look more closely at the photograph. It was of a youngish man smiling, with a glass in his hand. His heart had missed a beat when he heard the man was an animal welfare officer but, no, it wasn't anyone he'd seen.

'So what are we having with these exotic chips, son?'

'Fishcakes.'

'And baked beans?'

'No. I thought we'd have green beans for a change.'

'Where did they come from?'

'I bought them in the market when I was in town.'

'Well, that sounds grand. I must get you to make our tea more often.'

'I don't mind, Dad. I like doing it. I thought I might like to train in a kitchen somewhere.'

But his father wasn't listening. He was already unpacking exercise books from his briefcase onto the dining room table and preparing to mark them.

After they'd eaten and cleared away, Alf went to his bedroom and searched on the internet for more news about the murdered man. Various local papers had the story about how Chris Webb was found. There was an interview with his partner and they said there was a little girl who would miss her daddy. The police didn't have any leads but were looking at possible connections with animal welfare issues in the area. The RSPCA wouldn't be drawn on why he was in the Dales but one site highlighted past events where birds of prey had been targeted and a dog-fighting ring had been uncovered. There was no mention of badger-baiting but Alf knew it was another thing that should have been on the list.

Roy called him down later because the local news had picked up the story and the television reporter was standing outside the "Tan Hill Inn". He simply stated where the body of Chris Webb had been found and gave a brief account of what the nuclear bunker had been used for. Then they moved to an interview with a senior police officer in uniform who asked for the public's help with any sightings of the man in the last two weeks. The same photograph of the man came up on the screen with the phone number to ring.

Roy commented that it was a shame they couldn't help, since they'd been in the area just a week after the man had gone missing. Alf agreed but didn't tell his father he'd been even closer a couple of nights either side of the man's disappearance. He didn't want to admit to himself even the slightest possibility that Shane might have come across him but he couldn't ignore the fact that the man was an animal welfare officer.

Mills sighed as she unlocked the car and a blast of hot air greeted her. It had been a long and trying day. She still wasn't even sure whether she'd persuaded Sara to raise an official complaint about Colin Cuthbert's behaviour. Once she'd calmed down the girl had pointed out, quite sensibly, that the department might not believe her and assume she was making it all up to get back at her tutor. Mills had argued that there must be emails or texts from him that proved what he was up to. Apparently they'd been careful not to exchange personal messages but she still had copies of the model answers that he had given her.

'That's good,' said Mills.

'They'll say I pinched them.'

'Maybe but I don't see how you could have got hold of them all. Are they paper copies?'

'No, electronic. He sent…'

'He sent them by email?'

Sara grinned. 'Yes. There was no message but they came from his email.'

'There you are then.'

She still expressed concern at making it all public and Mills suggested she went home and thought about it. Meanwhile she would send Sara the form for initiating a complaint. The girl even thanked her before she left.

Mills was keen to get home, have a long shower and a cold beer but when she walked through her front door into the cool of the cottage, the red light on the answer machine was blinking.

'Dad?'

'Millie? Good you're in.' He sounded harassed.

'What's happened?'

'Nothing bad. No, quite the opposite. Fiona rang me last night. She says you're coming down this weekend.'

'Ok.' Mills waited to see what effect the announcement had made.

'So she said she would come back if you're here.'

'Good.'

'Yes, good but she's only coming back while you're down.'

'Right, Dad. Listen to me. This is your chance to make amends for your disgraceful behaviour to her.'

Mills tried to keep from laughing. 'This is what you do – are you listening?'

'Yes, yes.'

'Ok. I'll tell her I'm arriving on Friday so she'll be there that evening. Arrange a babysitter and book that fancy restaurant where you proposed to her.'

'I'll never get a table at such short notice!' There was panic in his voice.

'Do you want to save your marriage?' Mills was enjoying herself.

'Of course.'

'Right then. Next you must contact the nanny agency and arrange for two or three nannies to come for interview on Saturday. Before you say it – I know it's short notice. Have you got that?'

'Yes.'

Mills had yet another idea. 'Finally, book something for Sunday that the two of you can do with Flora, as a family.'

'What?'

'I don't know but it must be expensive and you must have already bought the tickets so she can't refuse. Something like going on the London Eye.'

'We've done it.'

'A boat trip, Kew Gardens, the seaside, hot air ballooning, horse-riding. I don't know but I am sure you'll think of something.'

'But what about you?'

Mills was exasperated. 'It's not about me, Dad. It's about you and your wife.'

'Will you be there on Friday to babysit?'

'No, Dad, I won't be down on Friday or Saturday or Sunday.' It was time to come clean. 'I told Fiona I would be there so she was embarrassed into pretending to be at home with you. It seems to have worked so don't spoil the surprise – please.'

There was a pause while he digested the information.

'Thank you, Millie, I think I understand. This is my window of opportunity, as they say.'

'Yes, don't blow it.'

Mills left a message for Fiona, saying she would arrive on Friday by about five then went up to shower, smiling at the thought of her poor father panicking over the instructions she'd given him.

Nina was cooking supper while Nige dealt with the children. Their daughter was helping him bath the boys upstairs and she could hear the screams as hair-washing began. It was Nina's turn to cook that evening but she'd arrived home later than expected and so supper was running behind schedule.

It had been bedlam at the office now that the "body in the bunker", as the press dubbed it, had been identified as Chris Webb. She'd handed her report to Mitch and asked if she would continue contact with Linda Bailey. Her DI wasn't sure – he'd have to talk to his boss, so she was waiting to hear. It seemed that her connection with Phil Freedman was the elephant in the room and until Mills could put her mind at rest, Nina was particularly anxious about the gun that Phil denied owning. Her report that the murdered man had seen a man with a gun in the woods was being raised as very relevant to the enquiry. She'd overheard Hazel talking to Ruby about a police appeal for information regarding the man seen in the woods on the night before Chris Webb disappeared.

'Have you heard from Phil?' Nina asked her husband while they were eating.

'No.'

'Have you rung him?'

'No.'

'Are you going to see him?'

'On Friday, when I take him to the clinic.'

'That might be too late.' Nina took her plate to the kitchen and returned with a pot of yoghurt for Rosie.

'What d'you mean "too late"?' asked Nige.

'Nothing.'

She cleared his plate and began loading the dishwasher. For all she knew, Phil would be called in for questioning before then.

While Nige went up to settle the boys and see that Rosie brushed her teeth, Nina rang Mills – just for a chat, she said. She told her that her missing person was the man she'd seen in the bunker and it might be difficult for Phil.

'Hopefully the clinic will help,' said Mills.

'I didn't mean that, Mills. I mean he might become a suspect.'

'What? That's ridiculous!'

'I know but he found the body, didn't he? He had the key to the bunker. *And* he denies having a gun when I know he had it.'

Mills didn't answer immediately. 'You may have been mistaken.'

'Really?'

'I'll look on Friday when Nige …'

'That's why I rang. It might be too late then.'

'What d'you expect me to do, Nina?' Her friend sounded tense.

'Sorry. I don't know. I just worry about what will happen if they know Phil has a gun.'

She explained about the appeal for the man with a gun in the woods.

'That could be anyone.'

'But who?'

'A gamekeeper? A poacher?'

'A poacher's not going to come forward to the police are they?'

'Maybe not but someone might. Why not wait until they broadcast this appeal?'

Mills then changed the subject completely by telling her friend about her father's predicament with Fiona. By the end of their call, Nina was laughing aloud and when he came downstairs, Nige commented that it was nice to see her smiling for a change.

The DI was in uniform the next morning. Ruby told Nina that he was doing a briefing with the press at ten o'clock.

'It's about the gunman you reported him seeing.'

'He wasn't a gunman,' argued Nina. 'He was a man with a gun. I know that would raise concerns in Darlington or even Northallerton but it is perfectly normal in the Dales. For heaven's sake they even have shops where you can buy them.'

Ruby shrugged. 'The boss seems to think it's key to the investigation. After all, the victim *was* shot in the face and the gunman could have been waiting for him in the woods the night he was killed.'

'Do they know if he died the night he disappeared?'

'It fits with the estimated time of death of up to three weeks.'

Nina switched on her computer and stared at the screen, doing the calculation. He went missing on Monday the nineteenth of June and they found him on Saturday the first of July. That was twelve days. It fitted. An email popped up from Mitch saying it was no longer necessary for her to act as family liaison for Linda Bailey. His excuse was that they could find someone "more local" but she suspected other motives. So when Hazel returned from attending the press briefing, Nina tackled her about the family liaison role. Her friend looked surprised that she'd asked.

'You do know that Phil Freedman is a potential suspect?'

'Yes but…'

'You're too involved, Nina. No point in arguing with Mitch, he won't budge.'

With everyone concentrating on the Webb case, Nina was at a loose end and decided to use the time putting her mind at rest. She didn't believe the Phil she knew was capable of such violence but he was under stress. She could at least try to ascertain whether there was any possible motive before he was pulled in for questioning.

The spell of humid weather had continued overnight and Nina switched the air conditioning on full and sat waiting for the car to cool down. It was some minutes before the stickiness was replaced by a gentle breeze across her face. She called Phil's number but it rang and rang with no opportunity to leave a message. She thought about abandoning the idea but decided to risk a visit. If he wasn't there she'd take a walk in the woods where the gunman was supposed to have been waiting for Chris Webb.

There was no answer at Phil's cottage and the front door was firmly locked. Nina went round to the back but there was no other entrance and the windows looked as though they hadn't been opened for years. There was a well-trodden track disappearing from the rear, presumably towards the river. She followed it downhill until she reached an opening in the stone wall that led her into woodland. There was no phone signal so she wished she'd brought a map with her. She knew the B&B was north of the pub where Webb had eaten and assumed that she was between the two. She turned left and followed the river downstream, fairly certain she would eventually meet the road back to the A66.

It was no cooler in the shade, in fact it felt even more humid. Soon Nina had beads of sweat forming on her forehead as she negotiated the roots and rocks on the path. She could just see a stream to her right, through the trees and undergrowth. She found herself listening to every sound and looking around and behind her. Ahead the path veered away from the river and she took a last look before turning down it. There was a movement beyond the trees and she caught a glimpse of a figure standing, his back to her. Nina stopped, watching him turn and start walking towards her.

'Phil?'

He froze for a second then strode towards her.

'Hi Nina, were you looking for *me*?'

'Er, yes. The house was empty so I assumed you might be…'

He stood waiting for her to finish.

'So, Phil, how are you?'

She followed him as he retraced her steps back towards the cottage.

'I'm ok.'

They didn't speak again until he'd unlocked the front door and she'd followed him inside.

'Do you spend much time down in the woods?' Nina asked casually when they were seated.

'I suppose I do.'

'I expect there are rabbits.'

'Yes.'

'Nothing wrong with a bit of rabbiting,' she suggested.

He looked at her doubtfully.

'It's ok to shoot rabbits, Phil,' she reassured him.

He looked shamefaced.

'That's not a problem Phil. It's not *the* problem. Look, can I have a glass of water?'

Phil almost smiled. 'Sorry, would you like tea? I've forgotten how to play the host.'

She went into the kitchen and made two mugs of tea. She searched for milk but there was nothing in the fridge.

'Black I'm afraid,' she said when she handed the mug to him.

'I'm used to it,' he replied, without apology.

Nina had made up her mind to be frank with her friend and explained that he would be on a list of possible suspects because he had the key to the bunker. Also, few people would know the place existed. The fact he had a gun would not help, since Webb was shot in the face. He didn't look unduly alarmed when Nina had finished.

'I hate to say it of my colleagues but the fact someone was accused of murder in the past…'

Phil sat up as if to protest.

Nina held up a hand. 'I know. I know it's irrelevant but it won't be helpful. You need to be aware and when they question you, and I'm sure they will, you need to be *completely* honest.'

'Of course.'

'No pretending you don't have a shotgun?'

'No, of course not.' He leaned back looking all in.

Nina confirmed the arrangements for his visit to the clinic the following day and checked he didn't need anything before leaving.

He walked up to the road with her and a thought occurred as she got into the car.

'Phil, do you ever see anyone in the woods with a gun? Someone else rabbiting?'

He scratched his head. 'No, it's pretty quiet down there generally.'

Her clothes were sticking to her as she turned the car and drove off with all the windows down. She was coming out of Stang forest when a police car passed her, going in the opposite direction. She recognised the driver and bit her lip, she had a horrible feeling they were on their way to pick Phil up for questioning.

Chapter 14

Alf knew he was taking a risk contacting the police but he was pretty sure that the man with the gun who had threatened him in the woods had nothing to do with Shane. So he punched in the numbers that had been given out on Twitter and spoke to a woman who took his name. Then, while he was going round the supermarket, they rang back and asked him to give a statement. That was awkward. He told her he could come to the local police station later – he didn't want them coming to the house and spooking Dad.

Alf didn't know what to expect at the station but they were polite and asked if he wanted some water to drink, which was good because his mouth had suddenly gone very dry. It took a long time to make a note of his address and age before they asked him what he'd seen. He explained he was out for a cycle ride with his Dad and had stopped in the wood to eat his lunch. He didn't want to say why he was really there because he wasn't going to talk about Shane and the badger, he wasn't stupid.

'So was your father with you at the time?' the woman officer asked, writing on a large pad.

Alf explained that his dad was in the car and they were meeting up at the pub. She made more notes.

'So would you say this man threatened you?'

He tried to remember what the man had said.

'He asked what I was doing. He thought I was looking for something – asked if I'd been before. I said I hadn't and he said I should be going.'

'But he definitely had a gun?'

'Yes over his shoulder.'

She asked him to describe it. It was a shotgun, he was certain.

'He didn't threaten you with it?'

'No.' Alf was feeling a bit silly now.

She told him to describe the man, which was difficult, and asked whether he had an accent.

'Not from here, he wasn't. From down South, I think.'

At the end they said he'd been very helpful and if he remembered anything else to let them know.

When he got home his father was at the table, marking, but as soon as he saw Alf he jumped up.

'I had a call from the police. What have you been up to?'

He hadn't seen his father so distraught since Jesse had left home.

It was unexpected. He thought he could do it without Dad knowing. His father was waiting for an answer.

'I told them about a man I met in Arkengarthdale last Sunday.'

'What man?'

'He was carrying a shotgun, in the woods, near where that man was murdered. They asked if anyone had seen him.'

'You didn't tell me.'

'It wasn't important. I was eating my sandwiches and he asked what I was doing and to sling my hook.'

'And he had a gun?'

'Yes, he had a shotgun slung over his shoulder, that's all. Anyway, what did the police want?'

'They want to talk to you again – tomorrow.'

Eventually, Alf was able to calm his father down and set about preparing their tea. He'd seen a recipe for chicken thighs baked with lemon and garlic that he was going to try. He thought he'd serve it with rice and courgettes.

Nina had guessed correctly; Phil was coming in "to help them with their enquiries".

'To be fair,' argued Ruby, 'we do need to know a bit more about this bunker place and whether it was locked or not, who had a key and whether he'd visited it prior to the first of July.'

Nina didn't answer. There was nothing she could do. Hazel appeared and began updating Ruby on progress.

'You're not listening, are you Nina?' her colleague said with a grin.

'Of course not, Hazel.'

She began by telling Ruby that a lad from Bishop Auckland had been in the woods in Arkengarthdale on Sunday the twenty-fifth, where Webb had seen the gunman. He met a man with a shotgun who seemed keen for the kid to get on his bike – literally.

'Description?' asked the researcher.

'Southern accent.'

Nina pretended to use her keyboard.

'So was this after Webb was murdered?' Ruby was referring to a file. "He died not more than three weeks ago but not less than a day or two." No, not necessarily,' she concluded.

'He would've had to have kept Webb alive for nearly a week if he murdered him after the sighting.' Hazel looked across at Nina, who kept typing. 'We need to get this lad to do an ID. Get a photo sent over to Bishop Auckland as soon as our suspect arrives.'

Nina listened, tapping nonsense into her computer. She hoped Phil would take her advice and admit to owning a gun because forensics could easily eliminate him once they showed that his wasn't the one that shot Webb. Once Hazel left the office she asked Ruby whether they had the forensics for the lead shot that killed Webb.

'Yes, it's been sent to the lab already so they'll have a profile when they find a potential match.'

As soon as Ruby went home, Nina called Mills.

'Listen, Phil has been brought in for questioning.'

She waited while her friend expressed shock, indignation and apprehension.

'I've told him to admit to owning a gun. The lead shot from the crime scene has already been sent off. It's probably at your lab, can you find out?'

'Yes, of course.'

'If they compare it with his ammunition it will prove it wasn't him, won't it?'

'Not necessarily, not if it's come from the same supplier.'

'But how will they know?'

'From the trace metals – it's like a fingerprint in each manufacturer's supply of lead.'

Nina thought about it. 'So if they're not from the same suppliers they will have different fingerprints?'

'Yes, at least sufficiently different to prove the point. How long will they keep him, Nina?'

'Depends.'

The silence hung between them. Nina wanted to reassure her friend but Mills wasn't stupid.

'I'll keep you updated,' she said before finishing the call.

She had no intention of leaving the building before she knew the outcome of Phil's interview and rang Nige to warn him she'd be late home. He was busy making the tea.

'No problem,' he said when he heard why she was calling. 'Stay as long as you need to and let me know what happens to Phil.'

Hazel did her best to put Phil Freedman at ease but he seemed restless and had difficulty concentrating. After an hour she sent someone off to fetch a cup of tea. She wished she could pop out for a cigarette, but knew the sooner she finished the interview the sooner she could go home and have a cooling shower. The tiny room was airless and claustrophobic. She looked across the table at Freedman, who was still staring at the floor. His left leg was jiggling up and down. After an eternity her colleague returned with two plastic cups of dark brown liquid. Freedman shook his head, pointing at his untouched cup of water. The audio recording was initiated and Hazel took a deep breath.

'Shall we go through it again?' She tried to sound friendly but was getting frustrated. 'You said you'd been given the key by the National Park officer on Tuesday the twenty-seventh of June.'

'I don't know the date but I think it might have been on the Tuesday – early in the week,' he muttered.

Hazel sighed. 'Good. And did you visit the bunker during that week?'

'Not until Saturday when I... when it...' He was shaking visibly.

'When you found Mr Webb. Exactly.'

He picked up the cup of water in front of him with both hands and sipped before replacing it carefully down on the table. His head lowered a fraction.

'Now this is very important, so please concentrate,' Hazel began. 'Was the bunker locked when you arrived on Saturday?'

He mumbled something.

'Can you speak up, please?'

He raised his head. His face was pale and sweat glistened on his forehead. He shouted, 'I don't know!'

'But *you* had the key. Did you have to use the key to open it on Saturday?'

He looked confused by her question and sighed loudly. 'No. I helped open the top but it wasn't locked.'

'How do you explain that?'

He seemed puzzled. He wiped moisture from his upper lip and dried his hand on his jeans.

She tried again. 'How do you explain the bunker being open when it was locked on the Tuesday?'

He shrugged.

'Do you see that there's a discrepancy in your account? The bunker is locked on Tuesday but it's open on Saturday. You have the key but you say that you didn't visit the bunker during the week.'

He nodded, as if agreeing with her statement.

'Are you agreeing with me, Mr Freedman?'

'Yes.'

'Good. Now I have another question. Do you own a shotgun?'

She waited.

'Well, Mr Freedman?'

He looked up and stared at her. 'Yes I have a gun.' His voice was clear now.

'Is it in your residence?'

He nodded.

'Is that a yes?'

'Yes.'

'We will need to collect that from you for forensic testing.'

He took another shaky drink from the paper cup before straightening up in the chair. Suddenly he was animated.

'Am I being accused? Do you really think I could have killed him? Why would I do that? It's ridiculous! I didn't know him.'

Hazel watched the colour drain from his face, his fists clenched before slamming them down on the table.

'Answer me!' he shouted. 'How am I supposed to have done that to a man?'

He was shaking uncontrollably as he tried to stand. He leaned on the table to steady himself but his legs seemed to collapse under him and he half fell against the chair. The chair skidded back to the wall and he slumped against it, sliding gently to the floor.

'Get help!' Hazel yelled and her colleague made for the door.

A minute later a uniformed officer arrived, put him in the recovery position and checked his pulse.

'What's been going on?' he asked Hazel. 'He's obviously not well. What did you do to him?'

'Nothing.' She went over to the audio device. 'Interview terminated at six twenty-five.'

'Mills? It's Nige. Sorry it's late. Nina told me to call you. She's at the hospital with Phil. No, he's ok – well, not really, but he's in good hands. He collapsed while he was being interviewed so they re-admitted him. Nina says it was Hazel's fault but I think she was a bit emotional.'

'Should I go over?'

'No, Nina says he's been sedated and she's on her way home. I just wanted to let you know.'

'You were going to the clinic with him tomorrow, weren't you?'

'Yes. Nina thinks they'll transfer him over there now that it's clear he's not coping.'

'Poor Phil.'

'Yes. She says it makes it worse because Hazel is convinced he's unhinged and could have…'

'Shot that man? No!'

There was silence at the other end.

'We know that but to them he's under stress and acting out of character,' he said eventually.

'Nina said they'll want to compare his ammunition with the lead shot at the scene. They'll be searching the cottage while he's away.'

'Probably.'

'It's not fair. While he's ill he can't defend himself from these accusations.'

'Nina says it's all because he had the key to the bunker so only he could have put the body there.'

There it was again, the worrying thing that Mills couldn't get out of her head. The bunker was definitely unlocked when they arrived on Saturday. She told Nige and he was his usual logical self.

'That just means one of two things: either Phil unlocked the bunker and deposited the body, which would be pretty stupid considering he had the only key, or it was never locked in the first place, which means anyone could have accessed it.'

Try as she would, Mills could not remember whether the padlock was locked before they left. She tried to visualise what had happened. She could see Dave getting the new padlock from his car and waving it as he went back to fit it. So they hadn't been there. Perhaps he hadn't shut it properly before they went off to the pub.

'I'm going to message Dave,' she told Nige. 'He might be able to recall whether the padlock snapped shut properly. After all, it may have been faulty. And I'll visit Phil tomorrow afternoon if he's still in the hospital.'

'Then I'll see you there,' Nige said.

Alf's father insisted on being around when the police came to see his son, so he arranged to be home at lunch time. Before the officer arrived he did his best to reassure Alf that what he was doing was a public duty and he was proud of him. But when DS Fuller arrived he still demanded to know why his son was being asked more questions. The officer explained politely that they simply wanted him to look at some photographs and tell her if he recognised the man that he'd reported seeing.

Alf's heart pounded as he sat at the dining table. Neither spoke but he thought his father looked stressed. He guessed he'd been in similar situations with Jesse before he left home. Alf could remember occasions when uniformed officers came knocking. The woman sat down opposite them and spent a few minutes setting up her laptop while his father made her a cup of tea.

'I've some photographs on here of people we believe might be the man you saw with the shotgun. I'd like you to look at them and tell me if you see a likeness.'

Alf took a deep breath. He'd been thinking what if the photographs weren't of the man he saw but of Shane or Jesse? What if his father saw them and asked why the police had their photos?

She turned the laptop round and pressed a few keys until three pictures came up on the screen. Alf's first reaction was relief – they weren't familiar faces.

'Take your time.' The woman encouraged him with a smile.

None of the photographs looked like the man who'd shouted at him. Alf was good with faces. He could've drawn it for them if they'd asked.

'No, it's definitely not any of them,' he answered. 'Sorry.'

'Never mind,' said DS Fuller, packing her laptop away. 'It's helpful to know we can rule them out.'

His father came back with a tray and the woman apologised for having to leave.

'Was it any help?' he asked Alf when she'd gone.

'No,' said Alf. 'But I could've drawn the man's face if she'd asked.'

'Why don't you do that, son?'

So as soon as his father had gone back to work, Alf started on some sketches. The man had looked rather like the newsreader that was sometimes on the local news, except he had more hair, and after a few attempts Alf felt he had a pretty good likeness. The man with the gun had shouted at him so the face was quite angry looking but that's how he'd seen him. He scanned the picture into his computer and emailed it to DS Fuller.

Phil was still sedated when Mills arrived and they wouldn't let her see him. Nige was already in the cafeteria and fetched another tea and they shared a packet of shortbread biscuits. Neither of them spoke for a while. The nurse had said that only close relatives were allowed to visit at the moment and she asked Nige whether they should get in touch with Phil's parents.

'He told me not to bother them when I suggested it but that was before he came here. I wouldn't know where to reach them.'

Mills wasn't sure whether she had their address somewhere. She'd never met them although she thought they lived in the Midlands somewhere but there was no reason why she would have their phone number.

'We might find their contact details back at the cottage,' she said. 'I could drop in except I don't have a key.'

'Ah, well I can help you there.'

He produced a key from his pocket and pushed it across the table.

'I said I'd look after the place while he was at the clinic. He only had one key so I got this one cut. I haven't tried it yet but it should fit.'

'I wonder if he'll go to the clinic now he's collapsed.'

'Not today, that's for sure. They told Nina that he's got to be up and about before he leaves here.'

He looked at his watch. 'I'd better be getting back. I've got to send our External Examiner the final archaeology results before the meeting next week.'

'Don't you have to pick the children up from school, it's nearly three o' clock.'

'No, Nina said she would go.' He laughed. 'Apparently she's got nothing to do this afternoon.'

'Well, I hope you have better luck with *your* final exam results. I'm waiting to hear from Sara Pendleton today. She was going to see the Head yesterday to complain about Dr Cuthbert. I'm keeping well away.'

Nige grinned. 'I'll look out for the fireworks from the Forensics Department office then.'

Mills sat and checked her phone after he left. There was no message from Sara and nothing that required her to be at the university. She'd done her duty at Yardley Forensics the day before so she felt entitled to a few hours off. If she wasn't allowed to see Phil she would help him by visiting his cottage instead. She had the excuse that she was looking for his parents' phone number but there was something else she was looking for, if the police hadn't already found it.

Chapter 15

Nina had been right. While Mills was doing her usual consultancy work at Yardley Forensics that week, she'd seen the lead shot from the victim found in the bunker. Tim had been asked to fingerprint the lead using elements such as silver, cadmium, arsenic, antimony and copper. It was a fairly standard test which could be used to check whether a batch of bullets or cartridges matched the murder weapon. They were running the samples while she was there, so the police must have the results by now.

Mills let herself into Phil's cottage and stood in the hall while her eyes became accustomed to the dark. The place was a mess but no worse than it had been before. She cleared plates and mugs from the sitting room and carried them through to the kitchen. Flies buzzed round the open bin stuffed with empty tins and food trays. She opened the window and tied the neck of the plastic bin bag before hauling it outside. There was a metal dustbin at the side of the house but that was nearly full. She pushed the bag inside, balanced the lid over it and put a heavy stone on top.

Back inside she boiled the kettle and poured hot water into the sink, adding some cold and a large squirt of washing-up liquid. While the dishes soaked she began a meticulous search of the cottage, pretending to herself, and anyone who asked, that she was tidying up. The shotgun wasn't in the kitchen cupboards or under the sink and there was nowhere in the hall to put it. It wasn't downstairs. She climbed the steep staircase and into the bathroom – she would clean that as soon as she'd finished looking. Just the two bedrooms left. The front one was literally empty so if it was here it must be in Phil's room.

A crumpled bed with nothing underneath. No wardrobe, just a large Victorian chest of drawers. She pulled the top drawer open gingerly and felt around under a jumble of underwear and socks. The next drawer held a couple of sweaters. The bottom drawer contained two pairs of trousers, a hoodie and a pile of papers. She stood up and looked round one last time then went back downstairs. In the hall, hanging on a peg was an anorak. She picked it up to search underneath and was about to hang it back up but stopped. It was heavy, very heavy. She inspected the pockets and found a box-shaped bulge. A hidden pocket contained a plastic box of twenty shotgun cartridges. She hesitated, held it for a minute while she decided what to do. Finally, after careful consideration, she removed three and replaced the box inside the jacket pocket.

Back at home Mills called Yardley Forensics and asked to speak to Tim. He'd helped occasionally with pieces of her university work and it was fine if he came in at the weekends to do jobs for her. She would pay him from her research grant and Brenda would turn a blind eye.

'Tim? I'm glad I caught you. I've got some urgent samples and I wondered if you are free this weekend?'

He wasn't doing anything important on Sunday, he said, and Mills knew he was saving to get married so the money was always welcome.

'That's brilliant, Tim. I'll see you at nine?'

She looked at the cartridges lined up on the table. She was certain it would only take a few hours to dissolve and analyse the lead in the same way that

Tim had used for the shot from the murder victim. By Saturday evening she would know if Phil's ammunition matched it. What she would do then she had no idea. She was wondering whether she should have taken the entire box of cartridges when the landline made her jump. She lunged at it.

'Yes?'

'Mills? It's Fiona. Weren't you were coming down here this evening.' She sounded confused.

'No, I changed my mind.'

'That's what your father said must have happened. I don't understand.'

'The conference was cancelled,' she lied.

'Cancelled?'

'Yes, unexpectedly. And Phil's been taken ill so I want to be up here. Sorry, I should've called.'

'No, it's all right. It's just… well, Hugh booked a table and I said we can't go without…'

'No, no don't do that! You should definitely go. It's where Dad proposed, isn't it?'

'It is Mills but I don't think…'

'Just do it. Have a good time. Enjoy the weekend. Dad's made a real effort. It may all turn out to be for the best.'

Fiona sounded even more perplexed when the call ended. Mills hoped the weekend wasn't going to be a disaster for her poor father.

Friday nights were usually chaotic but this evening Nina looked around with a sense of achievement. All three children were ready for bed as she'd promised a short DVD if they were bathed and in their pyjamas by seven. Toys had been tidied away and Rosie had joined the boys for tea as it was fish fingers and she preferred that to the cottage pie Nina had cooked for supper. She turned on the television and started the film. In half an hour it would all be quiet and she could enjoy a peaceful meal with her husband – when he finally arrived home.

The call on her mobile was from Hazel.

'Nina, sorry to bother you but I need your advice.'

'What's that?'

'I've got a picture of the man we're looking for.'

'A photofit?'

'No, it's not. It's a drawing by a lad who met him in the woods.'

Nina was thinking quickly. If Hazel didn't know the man, it couldn't be Phil.

'How can I help?' she asked, relaxing.

'Who could we ask in the Arkengarthdale area who might be able to identify him?'

'The pub would be a good bet if he's local. They're very helpful in the "Red Lion".'

'Ok, I'll get someone down there first thing.' Nina could hear her sigh. 'Although it might have to be me.'

'It's not a picture of Phil then?' asked Nina.

Her colleague ignored her. 'Must go. See you Monday.'

Not until Monday? thought Nina. So she was still off the case, which meant Phil continued to be "someone of interest".

Five minutes later Nige arrived home and the DVD was forgotten. The boys got over-excited as usual and she demanded he take them upstairs to clean their teeth and get into bed. Rosie followed, leaving Nina to finish preparing their meal.

'How was Phil?' she asked her husband when he re-appeared ten minutes later.

'Sedated. They didn't let us see him.'

She told him about Hazel's call. 'So it sounds as though they have someone for the shooting,' she added, handing him a plate of cottage pie and cabbage.

'Does that mean they won't be bothering Phil again? He should be transferring to the clinic as soon as he's well enough, and getting treatment, not being harassed by your lot.'

'I hope so. We'll ring the hospital and see if he can have visitors.'

'You could go you know, in your official capacity.'

'I can't do that, Nige.'

'Just a suggestion. He's got no-one else to bring his pyjamas and grapes.'

Later that evening, Mills rang to ask if they'd heard if Phil was still sedated. Nina had to admit she knew less than she did and Mills re-iterated Nige's plea for her to use her role as a police officer to find out what was happening to their friend. Finally she gave in and rang the hospital.

'Good evening. I'm Detective Sergeant Nina Featherstone,' she announced, hoping her nerviness wasn't audible. 'I wanted to know what plans are in place for your patient Mr Phil Freedman.'

The person at the other end was talking to someone and Nina began to wonder if she was being ignored. She waited for several minutes.

'Are you still there?' the woman asked. 'I'm sorry about that. I've just checked and they say that he will be transferred to Catterick tomorrow if they can get transport.'

'Would that be to the PTSD clinic?'

'I don't know. Is that where he's going?'

'I expect so. Thank you, that's helpful.'

She put the phone down and grinned at Nige. 'They're moving him tomorrow if they can get transport.'

'That's a relief. Can we visit him there?'

'I would think that having support from friends would be part of his treatment, wouldn't you?'

'I don't know what it will involve. Maybe he needs to get away from us all. I can't imagine what the treatment will consist of. After all, isn't it designed for the armed services, not osteoarchaeologists.'

'I told you, it's for anyone associated with armed combat and he's worked with members of the forces in various places abroad when there have been disasters.'

'I guess so. I just hope it helps. Will he have to stay long?'

Nina sighed. 'I don't know, Nige. We'll find out more tomorrow.'

She cleared the dishes away and began tidying up. It was possible they wouldn't be able to see Phil at the clinic. She'd been wondering whether they should contact his parents. Relatives, next-of-kin, could talk to the professionals, learn about the treatment their son was having and find out if he was improving.

'How can we contact Phil's mother and father?' she called from the kitchen.

'Don't know. He doesn't see them much.' Nige appeared in the doorway. 'In fact, when he was here, he said that he hasn't seen them since he's been back.'

'And he was abroad all that time.'

'Which means he hasn't seen them for eight years.'

'I suppose he kept in touch with them though.'

Nige shrugged. 'I don't think they're close.'

'That's awful.'

'It is, so now perhaps you understand why I want us to spend time in Wales with my family. Half of my cousins haven't even met Rosie, never mind the boys.'

'I know. I suppose it's different for me. Apart from my uncle and aunt that came to visit my parents, I haven't met any of my relatives – they're all back in India.'

'Are you saying we should go to see them too?'

'No, not at the moment, Nige. It will be a big enough adventure getting to Wales with the kids.'

Hazel's son never surfaced until mid-day on a Saturday, so she left him a note telling him not to expect her back until later and it would be a takeaway for tea. It was the weekend so she decided that jeans and a casual shirt would be acceptable despite it being official business. Armed with the very detailed sketch, she set off for the Dales, stopping to pick up a coffee at Scotch Corner Services.

In Hazel's opinion the "Red Lion" was in the middle of nowhere. She couldn't understand how anyone could live in such isolation. She parked in front of the tiny pub and knocked on the door several times until it was opened by the landlady. She shielded her eyes from the sun to study the picture.

'That's Jeff Bradby,' she said immediately.

'Are you sure?' Hazel asked. 'Take your time.'

'I don't need time – it's the spitting image of Jeff Bradby.'

'And he is?'

'They run the bed and breakfast up the road.'

Hazel got directions and drove a couple of miles up the dale before turning off to Whaw. A sign outside the B&B indicated there were no vacancies.

'I'm sorry, we're full for the next three weeks.' The woman was smiling politely.

Hazel flashed her ID and asked to go inside. She followed her into the kitchen and refused her offer of a hot drink.

'I expect you're here about Mr Webb,' the woman said.

'Why would you think that?' Hazel asked.

'Because of what happened to him up there in that bunker place and with him staying here.'

'No. I'm here because of this.' She produced the sketch of Jeff Bradby. 'Do you know this man?'

The woman stared at the paper for about fifteen seconds before looking up at Hazel then back at the sketch.

'Who is it supposed to be?' she asked irritably.

'Jeff Bradby.'

The woman studied it again. 'Why?' she demanded.

'What relation is he of yours?' Hazel asked, ignoring her and getting her notepad out.

'My husband.'

'Is it a likeness?'

'Yes but why…?'

'Is he here?'

'He's in the shed.'

'Out there?' She made for the door to the garden before Mrs Bradby could go and warn him. Hazel didn't know whether he might make a dash for it. She could sense that his wife was following close behind.

'Jeff Bradby?'

He was working on a metal hinge and had a screwdriver in his hand. 'Yes,' he replied without looking up.

'Could you put the screwdriver down please?'

That got his attention. He automatically put it on the bench and wiped his forehead with the bottom of his T-shirt.

'What can I do for you?' he asked.

'I'm DS Fuller, I'd like to ask you some questions.'

Fortunately he didn't make a run for it or try to push her out the way. In fact he seemed happy to oblige.

'I'll make a pot of tea,' offered his wife as they settled at the kitchen table.

Hazel went through all the usual preliminary questions before explaining why she wanted to speak to him.

'I believe you have a shotgun, Mr Bradby?'

'Yes, it's for the rabbits.'

'And you carry it with you when you go out – into the woods, for example?'

He looked worried. 'I might do. There are rabbits in the woods.'

'Were you carrying it in the woods last Sunday?'

'I don't know.'

'Please try and think, Mr Bradby.'

'I can't.'

'He often goes off with it,' his wife interrupted. 'Is that against the law?'

'Do you remember if he was carrying it last Sunday?' insisted Hazel.

'It's quite possible, he often does. Is he in trouble?'

'Last Sunday, a boy on a bicycle was confronted by a man matching your husband's description, carrying a shotgun.'

'Oh, Jeff. What have you done?'

He was sweating. 'I did see a lad in the woods last Sunday. I thought he was up to no good. I told him to get lost but I didn't threaten him with the gun.'

Hazel made some notes and Mrs Bradby put a mug of tea in front of her.

'Would you like a biscuit?' she offered.

'No, Mrs Bradby, I would not like a biscuit. I just want to complete this interview, if you don't mind.'

The woman sat down quickly.

'Mr Bradby, can you explain what were you doing with the gun in the woods?'

'I said – rabbiting.' He looked across at his wife, who stared back at him.

'Are you sure about that?' Hazel was certain he was lying. 'Do you eat a lot of rabbit?'

'He does shoot rabbits that come in the garden,' Mrs Bradby said. 'But we don't eat them.'

'Well, if we don't get to the bottom of it, I'll have to ask you to attend for a formal interview.'

The couple were looking anxiously at each other and then he spoke, 'The reason I was short with the lad was because he was close to where the traps are placed.'

'Traps?'

'Yes, what traps?' his wife asked.

He looked at her. 'It's just a little side-line. I keep an eye out for them.'

'Who are *they*?' Hazel asked.

'People responsible for culling the badgers. They set traps down in the wood and I just have to let them know when they've caught one. There's nothing to it.'

'Do you have contact details for these people?' she asked, thinking they could at least confirm his story.

He gave her a mobile phone number but explained he hadn't spoken to them for over a week now. The traps had gone and they hadn't been in touch since. She asked for his gun and any ammunition he had and went off, planning to speak to the badger cullers as soon as possible. It could be a coincidence but the victim was an animal welfare officer.

As Mrs Bradby saw her out of the front door, Hazel asked if she'd known about her husband's "sideline". She said no quite vigorously, explaining that she didn't hold with killing badgers even if it was an official cull. That was probably why he hadn't told her what he was doing.

'One other thing: I think you reported that Mr Webb met a man in the woods on the first night he was staying with you?'

'Yes. I said it was probably a poacher or gamekeeper.'

'Could it have been your husband?'

She thought for a moment. 'No, definitely not, he sat watching television all evening. I remember because I'd wanted him to give Mr Webb a lift back from the pub.'

'Well, if you remember anything at all…'

'There was one thing. The day after Mr Webb disappeared a man came to my back door. He was quite wild looking and it gave me a turn.'

'Who was he?'

'He said he came from the cottage up the road.'

'Did he have a name?'

'Pete or Paul, no it was Phil, that's right. He said he was called Phil.'

Hazel thanked her and left.

As soon as she found a mobile signal, Hazel stopped. She opened her notebook and scribbled down the name Phil then tried the phone number Bradby had given her. There was no response. She tried ringing again several times during the morning as she delivered the firearm and ammunition to

Forensics and went back to the office. She asked the on-call researcher to find out about the badger cull in Arkengarthdale and settled down to write up what she had so far. By the time she got home Liam had left for his mate's house and would get something to eat there.

Thanks son, Hazel thought.

She made a scratch meal with the left-overs she found in the fridge before settling down in front of the television with a bottle of red. She was woken by her mobile.

'You asked about a badger cull in Arkengarthdale?' the voice said.

'Yes thanks.' She sat up.

'There's nothing officially planned for that area.'

'Are you sure?'

'Certain. It's not a dairy farming area so there's no point.'

Chapter 16

Alf had been monitoring the news about the man found in the nuclear bunker ever since he'd given his sketch to DS Fuller. At first there was little in the news reports but the local papers soon began to produce snippets and even the regional news on the television gave details of his life. Alf had compiled a file on his laptop that grew by the day. His name was Christopher Webb but he was known as Chris. He'd been using a different name because he was working undercover as Len Hardy. He wasn't married but he had a partner called Linda Bailey and she had a daughter called Katie. He lived in Sunderland and worked as a welfare officer. That was what had really caught Alf's attention, animal welfare and the fact that he had been found dead in the nuclear bunker that Grandad had worked in. He'd looked up animal welfare officer and it said that they protect wildlife. It specifically included badgers and when he looked that up there were horrible reports about criminals that bait badgers with dogs.

Alf was convinced that Shane was involved in a badger-baiting ring but he had no idea what to do. He couldn't talk to Dad because he'd be onto the police straight away, no messing. The other puzzle was the man he met in the woods. Was he connected to Shane, he wondered, and if so, how to find out?

When his father had knocked gently on his door, he'd guiltily closed the screen before inviting him in. That was what his dad was like, careful with him to the point of politeness.

'Just to say that I'm off to bed,' he said, putting his head round the door. 'I'm going to see Grandad again tomorrow. I don't suppose you want to come?'

Dad had been delighted when Alf offered to go with him to visit Grandad. He felt a bit of a fraud when the old man appeared so excited to see him again. They went through a repeat of the last visit, ending up in the same pub for lunch. Grandad reminisced about the past and described the old friends he used to meet there. Alf took the opportunity to quiz him about the nuclear bunker.

'Did you go there until it was closed up?' he asked.

He'd calculated that Shane wouldn't have been born then but there was something he wanted to find out.

'Yes, until sixty-one.'

'So you couldn't go down after that?'

The old man was cutting up a roast potato. Without looking up, he said 'Maybe.'

'You mean you could?'

He lifted his head and waved his knife. 'Not officially.' He grinned mischievously.

Alf watched and waited.

The old man was enjoying the moment. He put down his knife and fork and leaned across the table. 'We had our way,' he said with a wink. 'But it wasn't official.'

'I would've loved to go down into that bunker,' Alf said, deliberately egging him on.

'I took my lad down a few times,' the old man admitted, taking up his cutlery and attacking his lunch again.

'Shane's been down there?'

'Yes, he thought it was a grand place to explore when he was a youngster.'

So Shane would have known about the place, which meant he could have visited it more recently. The thought disturbed him and for the rest of the day he was struggling with a very difficult decision.

Mills had arrived at Yardley Forensics on Sunday morning at exactly nine o'clock. Tim's car was already in the empty car park and she was soon handing him the three cartridges she'd taken from Phil's jacket. She put on clean white coveralls and followed him into the preparation room where she watched him extract a small number of lead shot pellets from each of the cartridges, weighing them before dropping them into beakers of acid on a hotplate. It would be a while before they were ready for analysis, he told her.

They went to the tea room for a coffee and chatted about the work that Tim had been doing. He remarked that he had been fingerprinting samples of lead shot in the previous week and there was another parcel due in on Monday morning. He didn't know the details but it would be more cartridges for lead analysis. Mills said she would take her coffee to the office and catch up on her emails but as soon as her computer was fired up she looked at the sample register online.

The cartridges sent in the week were from the crime scene at the bunker. She went to the analytical results and printed out a copy. Next she looked at samples due in and found the request for a further batch of cartridges. This time the paperwork included Hazel Fuller's authorisation. Mills wondered if these came from Phil's ammunition box. She assumed they would arrive the next day to be tested immediately. In that case she would make sure she was around to check the results.

Back in the laboratory Tim said it would be several hours before her samples were actually analysed, although he would be setting up the instrument now. She offered to go into the centre of Harrogate to fetch something to eat. He liked a chicken salad sandwich and she knew where she could find one and a decent cappuccino for him.

As she wandered slowly towards town she thought about what it would mean if Phil's lead shot matched that from the victim. It would simply be a coincidence that the killer and Phil bought ammunition from the same supplier, not an unlikely hypothesis. However, what if Tim notices a similarity between the two sets of samples and asks where hers came from? Now she was becoming anxious about what she'd done. She was so distracted she went past the café and had to retrace her steps. Sensibly the barista offered her a cardboard holder for the coffees and she walked back, balancing them in one hand with bags of food in the other.

'I was thinking,' Mills began as they ate their brunch. 'If you give me the raw data on a memory stick, I can calculate it myself.'

Tim looked puzzled. She usually told him to save her the effort by producing the results for her.

'It'll mean you can get off sooner,' she suggested.

She thought he'd be pleased but he didn't look it.

'But the same day rate, of course. You won't lose out.'

He gave her a relieved smile.

So three hours later, Mills was seated at her desk when Tim said goodbye. Now she could sit quietly and work on the numbers he'd given her. The spreadsheet contained many columns of figures but she knew the operations required to produce the final values. After half an hour she had a set of numbers in front of her. Five trace metals in the lead: silver, cadmium, arsenic, antimony and copper. Just five numbers. She wrote them down in a column on the paper in front of her, one below another: a, b, c, d, e. With heart racing she found the electronic file with the report that went off to the police earlier in the week. She scrolled to the end of the report where the five metals and their numbers were listed. She filled the second column and stared. There was no mistaking the similarity. Phil's ammunition matched the lead shot from the victim perfectly.

'Sorry, it's a "pay as you go" phone – impossible to trace.'

Hazel was having a frustrating morning. She'd asked Ruby to come in despite it being Sunday. Now it seemed the number Bradby had given her was unobtainable and untraceable. His explanation of the badger cull was sounding more implausible by the minute. She needed to speak to him again as soon as possible to find out why he was patrolling the woods with a gun at all hours. It would be preferable if the interview was on their home turf so she rang her colleague for support.

'Nina! Sorry to wake you up,' she joked.

'I bet I was awake long before you were this morning.'

Hazel asked if she would come in to Northallerton police station for an hour or two so they could speak to Mr Bradby again and clear up a few issues. Reluctantly Nina agreed, provided it was after lunch.

'Perfect. It will take that long to pick him up and ferry him down here. I'll let you know when he's on his way.'

Hazel asked local uniform to collect Mr Bradby and bring him over. She completed her reports and tidied up her desk until, finally, Nina appeared.

'Nice lunch?' Hazel enquired, sarcastically.

'I've brought you a roast beef sandwich and a piece of apple pie. I couldn't stop halfway through cooking it, could I?'

'You're a star!' said Hazel, unwrapping the greaseproof paper and tucking in.

'So what's going on?' asked Nina.

Between mouthfuls Hazel explained that Bradby's story about a badger cull wasn't holding water.

'With Webb being an animal welfare officer I began to wonder about a connection,' she said, wiping crumbs from the corner of her mouth. 'Excellent beef, by the way. I thought cows were sacred to your lot.'

Her friend was always teasing about her upbringing.

'Just eat it!' Nina commanded.

'Anyway, he's due in the next half hour so we should get a plan sorted.'

Jeff Bradby looked anxiously around as he was escorted to the interview room. When asked if he knew why he had been brought in he shook his head dejectedly. Hazel turned on the recorder and did the preliminaries before they began the interview that they'd planned carefully. The preparation was useful but it didn't provide the results they'd hoped for. The man had been asked to keep an eye on the metal cage that was baited and left in the wood where it wouldn't be noticed. He'd been promised five hundred pounds if he spotted a badger in the trap and rang the number he'd been given.

'So did you find a badger any time?'

'No.'

'Are you sure?'

'Yes.'

'Five hundred pounds seems a lot of money for what you were required to do,' Nina suggested.

'I had to check it regularly. I was down there day after day.'

Hazel raised an eyebrow; it wasn't what his wife had said.

When she asked him to describe the man that had given him the job, he couldn't remember.

'It was in the pub on a Friday night. He asked if I'd do it and when I agreed, he gave me a card with the number on. That was the last time I saw him.'

'Can you please try to describe him?' asked Nina.

'Medium height.'

'Beard, moustache, clean shaven, hair colour, eye colour?' Hazel insisted.

He shook his head. 'I can't really recall him.'

'What about an accent. Was he local?'

He considered for a minute. 'Not Yorkshire. He might've been a Geordie. I'm not good with accents round here.'

However they persevered he genuinely seemed unable to tell them anything else about his dubious employer and they arranged for him to be taken back to Whaw.

'I think he's telling the truth,' Nina concluded.

'You always do. You see the good in everyone.'

'I think he's too stupid to be lying. Presumably this contact that he met in the pub was out to catch a badger for a different reason to culling.'

'Badger-baiting?'

'Yes.'

Nina didn't tell Hazel that she was planning to visit Phil Freedman when she left her. She didn't like using her position as a police officer, especially as she wasn't on the case, but it was the only way she was allowed to see him. It was worrying her that he had no-one looking out for him and Nige had convinced her she was doing the right thing.

The clinic was bright and welcoming and they'd allocated Phil a small room to himself, although strictly on a temporary basis. They made it clear they expected him to become a day patient as soon as possible. He was sitting in an armchair facing the window and looked round slowly when she knocked on the open door. Nina thought he seemed tired and withdrawn. It didn't help that he was unshaven and dressed in shorts and a T-shirt that was too big for him.

She offered to bring him his own clothes to wear, his wash things, books to read, whatever he needed. He seemed uninterested. She said she would bring pyjamas and a dressing gown, if he had one. He just shrugged and asked why bother? He said he would be leaving soon, and he couldn't understand why he was there anyway.

When the staff had asked Nina about contacting a relative, she'd offered to find a phone number for Phil's parents. But when she raised the question with him, he was suddenly alert and adamant he didn't want them involved. Apparently his father had Alzheimer's and his mother had to care for him, which took all her physical and emotional strength. He didn't want to add to her anxieties. It was an admirable sentiment, thought Nina, but didn't help his condition.

After half an hour Phil looked all in. He smiled wanly as she said goodbye and she sensed he was still confused by his situation. When she was leaving, she advised the staff that Phil's parents were too frail to be of any support, so they asked if he had any close friends. It was then she told them that Mills was his girlfriend.

'Well, she's a girl and she's his friend,' she argued later when Nige queried her white lie.

He asked if she'd informed Mills of her role and that was when she tried to ring her friend but there was no answer.

Mills did what she always did when she wanted to work something out. She walked up onto the moorland above Mossy Bank and sat on the large stone at the curve of the track. She could see Laurel Cottage down below and the farm buildings on the other side of the dale. A tractor was moving round and round a field across the way, cutting grass for hay and silage. A grouse rattled across the track a few yards away and then silence.

She knew Phil wasn't capable of killing anyone but a prosecution lawyer could use the matching lead shot to convince a jury that he murdered the man. Together with the fact he held the key to the bunker it would be difficult not to come to a verdict of guilty. If the box of ammunition in Phil's jacket had already been found by the police, he would certainly be the prime suspect, particularly in his vulnerable state of mind.

Back in the cottage, an hour later, she sat in the garden and tried to read. It was a relief when she heard the landline ringing indoors and she picked it up just in time as it went to voicemail.

'Millie!'

It was her father. He wanted to thank her. He'd had a super weekend with Fiona and Flora.

'So are you back together?' she asked.

'Yes – on a trial basis, Fiona says. Apparently I have to mend my ways if I want it to be permanent.'

'Quite so. Has she given you a list of performance indicators?'

'What?'

'Nothing. I think it's great that she's back.'

They had clearly made up for now and Mills told her father that she was glad to be of help.

'It taught me something, Millie. You showed me that you have to act if you want things to go your way. I'd forgotten that, so thank you for reminding me.'

'Glad to be of service. Give my love to Fiona and Flora.'

After the conversation had ended, Mills wandered back to her seat in the garden. *You have to act if you want things to go your way.* That's what he'd said and he was right. She locked the back door, picked up her keys and the spare key to Phil's cottage.

Mills was back at the laboratory first thing on Monday. She was curious about the origin of the ammunition arriving for analysis that morning and she didn't have to wait long before the parcel arrived by specialist courier. She signed for it and placed it carefully on her desk. She had received so many parcels for forensic analysis but none had seemed so important. The paper stated that the ammunition had been taken from a Jeffrey Bradby. The name didn't mean anything to her. Was he another suspect? If so there were two possible outcomes of the test Tim was about to perform: either the lead would match the killer's or it wouldn't. Without a match Mr Bradby would probably be in the clear but if it matched, he would be in the same position as Phil.

The box of cartridges from Phil's cottage was now in her handbag under her desk. The ones she knew matched the killer's. She'd been back to remove the box, to avoid the police discovering it if they came back to search his place again. However, it would be so simple to exchange his cartridges with the ones in the parcel on her desk, making Bradby's lead shot a match. With another suspect to concentrate on, Phil might avoid suspicion all together. Nina's phone call had been late in the evening and what she had said only confirmed her resolve to protect Phil. When Nina was asked to name his closest friend, she'd thought of Mills. That meant something didn't it? She was determined to ensure he got better and was left alone by the police.

Chapter 17

'Nina, I've got the forensics on Mr Bradby's ammunition.'

'I know, Ruby told me. It doesn't match the crime scene. But thanks for calling to let me know, Mills. I guess he's no longer a suspect.'

It had been a fleeting temptation but Mills knew she'd been right to leave Phil's box where it was and sent Bradby's ammunition to Tim for analysis.

'What about Phil? Is he still a suspect?' she asked.

When Tim had told Mills the results, she almost wished she had exchanged Bradby's samples for Phil's cartridges. If she had, he wouldn't be under suspicion now.

'I hope not, Mills. Have you been to see him yet?'

She was embarrassed to admit she hadn't.

'You must go today,' her friend insisted. 'I'm really worried that they want to discharge him and he can't go back to that dreadful hovel he lives in.'

'It's not so bad.'

'Mills, how can you say that! He needs to be looked after. Fed and rested while he gets treatment as a day patient.'

Mills knew what her friend was suggesting and it annoyed her. 'Are you offering?' she asked.

'You know we don't have the space – not like you do.'

She was serious apparently. That really did send her into a panic.

'I told Phil I would take him some clean clothes. Can you do that as you have his key?' her friend asked.

How could she refuse? She agreed to go to the clinic with a change of clothes and to find out when he had to leave. She was about to finish the call when something occurred to her.

'One thing Nina, will Forensics be looking for Phil's ammunition to analyse too?'

'I don't know but I expect they'll want to do a thorough search again if he is the only potential suspect they have.'

The fact that his ammunition matched that on the victim was weighing on her mind. It had seemed a simple thing to hide it but now she wondered whether she'd made a big mistake and as she drove over to Arkengarthdale she resolved to replace the box in the jacket hanging in the hall. If the police wanted the cartridges analysed, so be it. Already she was worrying that Tim might notice how exactly the shot that she asked him to look at matched the samples he'd received from the police only a few days before.

It was a beautiful summer evening by the time she reached Phil's cottage and she stopped to watch a curlew circling overhead before entering the dark interior. To her relief it was undisturbed, so she assumed there had been no further police search. She rifled through the jacket hanging in the hall and stuffed the box of ammunition in the inside pocket. She'd been stupid to take it, particularly now she realised it had her fingerprints all over it. She went upstairs to find a bag and began stuffing personal items into an empty rucksack she found in the corner of the bedroom. She felt quite uncomfortable selecting underwear and pyjamas for him. She picked out a pair of jeans and a sweatshirt for no particular reason except she'd seen him wearing them.

Throughout the journey to the clinic she rehearsed what she would say. Nina wanted her to look after him but he probably wouldn't want her to do that. She could arrange for him to have someone come in to cook and clean for him or he could stay in a B&B – she'd seen one nearby. Yes, that would be the perfect solution. She was going to tell Nina but stopped halfway through dialling. It would be better to present it to her as a *fait accompli*.

Mills thought the staff at the clinic were really nice, considering she wasn't supposed to be there at dinner time. Phil was in his room, sitting by the window with a meal in front of him. She apologised for interrupting but he told her he wasn't hungry anyway. She said he should eat but he didn't reply.

'I've brought you some things: pyjamas, washing stuff, clothes – I don't know whether they're right though. I can always go back and get something else that you need.'

She gabbled on, filling the silence. Phil looked out of the window.

When she stopped talking, he said, 'Thank you,' politely.

Then, as she went to leave, he turned and called her back.

He grabbed her hand. 'I saw them carrying a man's body through the woods.'

'You were dreaming.'

'But it was so real.'

'Nightmares, they can be.'

She stood waiting until he let go and turned back to the window again.

After a few minutes without speaking, she went along the corridor to find a member of staff. A friendly young woman greeted her and told her how nice it was to meet her.

'I understand that it's difficult,' she began.

Yes it is, thought Mills. Very difficult.

But the woman had continued speaking and Mills picked up the words '...ready to be discharged.'

'Did you say tomorrow?'

'Yes. The doctor will have been round by about eleven but if he'd like to stay for his lunch, maybe pick him up about one o' clock?'

Mills froze. Unable to think of a suitable response, she simply nodded. 'Ok, one o' clock.'

Back in Phil's room, she explained the arrangement to him.

'So, I'll come to pick you up at one, ok?'

A shrug. A nod. And with that she left. She'd been totally out of her depth. Nina would've known what to do but then Nina would take him home if she had a spare room.

There were a few tears on the drive home. More than a few glasses of wine during the evening. Little sleep and up at five, on the internet, noting down the phone numbers of B&Bs in the area.

Her DI was looking pretty fed up by the time Hazel had briefed him on the Bradby situation. The suspect was either stupid or extremely clever. Whichever it was, they were no nearer finding out who had shot Chris Webb. Bradby's story about the trap in the wood suggested someone wanted a badger for dog-fighting. It wasn't unheard of in the region but unusual to find it in the Dales. Bradby's assertion that he only knew the contact's phone number was suspicious but unless he volunteered any further information they had reached a dead end. They had to let him go.

Back in the office, Ruby gave her the final report from Forensics.

'Anything helpful?' Hazel asked, as she opened the file.

Ruby thought for a moment. 'The only identifiable fingerprints at the bunker belong to Phil Freedman and Dr Sanderson. No surprises there. The lead shot from Mr Bradby doesn't match the ammunition used to kill the victim.'

'We'll eliminate him from the case then, although we still need to find the guy that employed him to watch the badger trap.'

'D'you want me to pull out the files on badger-baiting cases in the area?'

'Yes, and find out what's happened to Mr Freedman. I think we'll need to search his place again... and properly this time. Have we had any intel from Linda Bailey's family liaison officer?'

'Nothing useful. Are you still interested in her ex?'

'Jason?' Hazel hesitated. 'I guess I could pay him another visit, just to keep in touch.'

'One other thing. There was an anonymous call to Crime Stoppers yesterday evening. A man gave the name of someone who knew about the bunker and played there as a kid. He wouldn't say why we would be interested in the guy. He rang off before we could find out.'

'Make a note of the name but don't waste time getting details now, it's probably just someone with a grudge.'

'I haven't much to do on the case.'

'No? Well then, I suggest you get more background on Phil Freedman and his friends. Let's get a picture of what makes Mr Freedman tick.'

She left the room, letting the door bang noisily. Ruby sighed. That's going to prove awkward, she thought, considering his closest friends seem to be Nina Featherstone and Mills Sanderson.

Knowing that Freedman had been abroad for many years, Ruby decided to get the shorter task out of the way first and began searching for names connected with badger-baiting in the area. There hadn't been much activity recently but she pulled out the information on some old cases, although there was nothing close to Arkengarthdale. However, there were a couple of well-known rings involved in fighting with dogs or foxes towards Bishop Auckland and she added the names to the list, including one that drew her attention. A seventeen year old who had received a warning for attending a dog fight in Teesside ten years previously was called Armstrong. It was the same surname that was given in the anonymous call to Crime Stoppers. After a bit of work she was able to put a note on Hazel's desk with the contact details for both men.

Mills was ringing her sixth B&B when Nige arrived in the office. She was in the middle of saying that their guest would need rest and, once again, the owner was explaining that she liked the house to be vacated after breakfast. Basically, they were either fully booked or wanted their guests to be out during the day. She had another five numbers to try but when she put the phone down, Nige asked her what she was doing.

'Is that what I think it is?' he asked. 'Are you trying to find somewhere for Phil to stay?'

'Yes.' Mills was defensive.

'But I thought he was going to yours.'

'Did you?'

'I'd rather he stays with us than ends up in a guest house.' Nige was indignant.

'You don't have a room for him,' Mills pointed out.

'We can sleep on the sofa.'

'Don't be ridiculous.' Mills was punching in the next number on the list.

'Stop! What are you doing, Mills? Why can't you put him up?'

She put the phone down. 'I don't know what he needs. I'm not a psychologist or psychiatrist or whatever... counsellor, I mean. I can't be there all the time, can I? And what if he becomes, you know, unpredictable?' The lump in her throat was choking her.

'You're not scared of him?' Nige looked horrified.

'Of course not,' she lied.

'So you think a room in a B&B is a better alternative?' He sighed loudly and shook his head. 'I'll call Nina, she won't turn him away.'

'I'm not turning him away, Nige. I'm just not a suitable person to do it.' Tears were welling up.

'None of us are, Mills, are we? All he needs is a bed, food and someone to talk to. The clinic will do the rest. It might mean ferrying him to Catterick and back for his sessions but it's easier now it's out of term-time, isn't it? We can help with the taxi service and spend some time with him as well. We can sort out a rota. What d'you say?'

She wiped away the wetness round her eyes and smiled at him. She supposed it would not be so bad if they helped her.

'I'm picking him up this afternoon but I haven't sorted out the spare room.' She used it as a study and the unmade bed was covered in books and papers.

'I don't have anything important on today. Why don't I collect him and bring him over. You go and get ready for his arrival.'

'Isn't it your Examiners' meeting tomorrow?'

'Yes but this is far more important. Get moving or you won't have time to clean the house to Phil's high standards,' he said with a laugh.

Mills went home via the supermarket and loaded her trolley with fruit and vegetables, healthy snacks and yoghurt. Then she went round again, this time choosing chocolate biscuits, crisps, popcorn, doughnuts and ice-cream. When feeling depressed *she* didn't want to eat wholesome food, did she?

As soon as she reached Laurel Cottage and had packed the groceries away, she vacuumed round and made up the spare room. Piles of papers were shoved under the bed and windows thrown open throughout the house. Nige wasn't due to deliver Phil for another hour or two so she made a quick mug of tea and opened the chocolate biscuits; she needed something to nibble while she became more and more anxious about the next few days and possibly weeks, she supposed.

Nige rang to say they would be with her by four, so there was just time to cook the sausages. She figured she could get away with bangers, oven chips and beans for the first night. After that it would require more organisation. She was just turning the sausages when there was a hammering at the door and Nige called through the letterbox. He was carrying the rucksack with Phil's few belongings and took it straight upstairs.

Phil stood awkwardly in the hall. Mills eased past him and shut the front door.

'You know it's not necessary,' he said, looking at the floor.

'What?'

'I can go back to the cottage. I'm sure you'd prefer it and I would.'

Mills didn't know how to reply. Fortunately Nige came thundering down the stairs and declared himself parched.

'Tea?' Mills offered.

'Got anything cold?' he asked.

'Only beer.'

'That'll be just fine.'

She looked at Phil and then at Nige.

'Just a soft drink for me,' Phil said, as if reading her thoughts. 'They've got me on this medication that's not really...'

'Tea it is,' Mills said, staring at Nige. 'I've made something to eat. Can you stay?' She was still looking at Nige.

He consulted his watch. 'Yes, no problem.'

They ate outside in the warm afternoon. It was comfort food, followed by chocolate ice-cream and tea to drink.

'I suppose I should go soon,' Nige said, checking the time again. He seemed reluctant to leave.

'I imagine Nina will be wondering where you are.' Mills was sorry to see him go.

So finally she and Phil were alone, sitting in the late afternoon sun with nothing to say. And they remained there for what seemed like an age but it was probably only a few minutes. Eventually Mills got up to clear the dishes away.

'I can help,' Phil said.

She washed and he dried. She put the dishes away.

'How long are you expecting this to last?' he asked as she sorted the cutlery in the drawer.

'What d'you mean, you staying here?'

'Yes.'

'As long as it takes.'

He laughed. '*That* long?'

She laughed and finally she could see the old Phil, briefly. It didn't last. He wandered into the sitting room and stretched out on the sofa. Soon he was fast asleep and she fetched a book, not wanting to disturb him by putting the television on.

At half past seven he woke up and said he was turning in. She asked if he had everything he needed and he said yes. Soon the movement above ceased and she assumed he was asleep. Nina rang to ask how things were and Mills said fine.

'Nige said he was ok,' her friend said.

'Yes. I just don't know how it will work on a day-to-day basis.'

'It'll be fine.'

That's easy for you to say, thought Mills, wondering what time she should wake him up and when she would get into work the next day.

As it turned out, she needn't have worried. Just as it was getting light she was woken by shouts. At first she panicked, thinking someone had broken in, but soon realising it was her guest, she ran in without thinking and found Phil struggling with his bedding. She pulled open the curtains and asked if he was all right. His face was covered with sweat and he had an expression that Mills could only describe as panic on his face.

'I'll make some tea,' she said and went downstairs.

About ten minutes later she heard footsteps and Phil appeared in his pyjamas.

'I'm sorry for waking you,' he said.

'No problem.'

She handed him a mug of tea and they sat together in the kitchen without conversation, listening to the rain beating on the window.

It was actually easier than Mills had imagined it would be and when she left for work Phil reassured her that he would be resting around the house all day. She promised to make a lasagne when she got back, definitely no later than five, maybe even four, but definitely no later than five. Despite relaxing a little, she was relieved to be in the car and back into her usual routine. The rain had stopped and it was promising to be a beautiful day. The roads were quieter now the school holidays were approaching and the car park was almost empty. Those staff and students remaining had taken to wearing shorts and sandals round the campus, always a sign that the vacation had started.

'How's Phil?' Nige was already behind his desk, going through a pile of papers.

'You're in early,' Mills said, deliberately changing the subject.

He didn't look up. 'Examiners' meeting at ten.'

'Good luck with that.'

'I'm not expecting any fireworks – unlike yours.'

Mills was about to answer when he continued.

'That girl Sara was here this morning in tears. She said she'd be in the cafeteria until lunch time if you wanted to see her.'

If she was honest, she didn't want to see Sara but she'd sent a couple of emails asking for a meeting which Mills had ignored so far.

'Did she say what it was about?'

'Don't you know?'

'I can guess.'

'Well, you guessed right. She isn't happy with the outcome of the meeting with your Head.'

Mills went straight to the cafeteria, where Sara was sitting alone with an empty mug in front of her.

'I came to your office but you weren't in,' she complained.

'No,' said Mills. 'Can I get you a drink?'

She shook her head.

Mills fetched a coffee and sat down opposite her, apologising for not replying to the emails.

'I wanted to tell you what happened last Thursday after we talked,' Sara began. 'I went to see the Head but he said I had to make an appointment.'

'Well, he is a busy man.' Mills sipped her scalding hot drink.

'Yeah, right. He put me off so when I saw him on Friday he had Colin... Dr Cuthbert with him.'

'I see.'

'He... Colin... denied everything of course, the scumbag.'

Her voice was getting louder as she became more emotional and Mills looked round to see who might be listening. A sole male student sat the other end of the room.

'But you told them about the email he'd sent you with the model answers?'

'Yes. He said it was fake.'

'What did Professor Cole say?'

'He took Colin's word over mine of course. He said I was lucky to get a degree at all and that by rights he should have me disciplined but as it was a first offence he was being lenient!'

Mills was worried that she was going to burst into tears – but quite the reverse – the student was growing more and more furious. Before she could find a way to empathise and calm her down, Sara started again.

'I've seen the disciplinary procedure and I've decided that it's the way forward. There's a panel that has to listen to the evidence and judge what has happened. I'm happy to subject myself to that; it will be much fairer than what Cole says.'

Mills took several more sips before responding. The girl had a point. A hearing would probably include people from outside the department so, hopefully, Professor Cole wouldn't be able to influence the outcome.

'But you'll have to get the Head to instigate the disciplinary action in the first place,' Mills reasoned.

'Not necessarily. I read the rules and I got my friend to check. It doesn't have to be the Head of Department. Any member of staff can, if they have due cause, it says. So I thought you could, Dr Sanderson.'

Chapter 18

Hazel picked up the note from Ruby first thing in the morning and immediately rang the numbers she'd left. No reply from one but the other picked up.

'Yes?' The voice was gruff and hostile.

'Mr Armstrong?' Hazel asked. 'Mr *Shane* Armstrong?'

'Who's asking?'

'My name is DS Hazel Fuller…'

The phone went dead.

'Doesn't want to speak to me, apparently,' she told Ruby. 'I think I might need to make a visit. I can drop in on the way to Jason's.'

Ruby wasn't sure why her colleague was meeting Linda Bailey's ex-husband again, apart from the fact she'd been impressed by his house and his manner. She suspected it wasn't entirely police business. She'd noticed that Hazel had touched up her roots the night before and she couldn't wait for Nina to arrive so she could share the gossip.

Ruby was too polite to challenge her but, if she had, Hazel might even have blushed. Jason had suggested they meet in a nearby hotel because, he said, his mother had friends round which might have proved awkward. She popped into the cloakroom on the way out to refresh her makeup and check that her straps weren't peeking out from her low necked blouse.

Before setting off she punched the Armstrong's postcode into the car's navigation system and turned on the radio. It was a nice day for a drive to Berwick via Bishop Auckland and good to be out of the office. Nina was a good mate but her faith in Phil Freedman was becoming increasingly awkward as it looked as though he was the only suspect with access to the bunker, who owned a gun and was clearly mentally unbalanced. Hopefully his involvement could be confirmed once the forensics came in on the ammunition they'd located in his cottage.

Visiting the Armstrong family was a bit of a formality since it was based solely on the anonymous call and the fact the son had been involved in watching a dog fight. She planned a quick in and out to confirm they hadn't been anywhere near Arkengarthdale and the bunker where Webb's body was found. She was glad of the satnav as she turned first left off the main road and then right through a tangle of roads until she had no idea where she was, only that she was three hundred yards from her destination.

She was in a narrow road, clearly designed before cars were invented. Vehicles were parked on both sides of the street, leaving only enough room for a single car to manoeuvre between. The row of terraces was tightly packed and she turned off the radio to concentrate on looking for number fifty-eight. None of the houses were particularly well-maintained but fifty-eight was almost the worst. She eased into a space further up the road and walked back, through the gate that was hanging on one hinge and up the weed-covered path to the peeling front door. She knocked and waited.

She was about to knock again when a voice called from close by and Hazel spotted a man in his vest leaning from an upper window next door.

'You won't find him in, love,' he called. 'Not at this time. Try the bookies down the street!'

He pointed from where she had come. Irritated, she was tempted to give it a miss but she could see the sign on the corner and marched down ready to do battle. The door was open and inside the shop two figures were hunched over a newspaper.

'Mr Armstrong?'

Both men turned round and stared.

'Shane and Jesse Armstrong?'

'He's Shane,' said the older man pointing at his companion.

'So I guess you're not Jesse?'

They both laughed and continued to stare at her.

She introduced herself and showed them her ID. She thought that would wipe the smile off their faces.

'I'd like to have a quick chat with you Shane, just a formality. And where is Jesse by the way?' she added.

'Not around.'

'On holiday?'

'Yes, something like that.'

She asked if he'd prefer to go back to his house but he chose to stay in the betting shop and so they found a quiet corner – or rather his mate did – so they could talk without him overhearing. When she asked, he told her he'd never been to Arkengarthdale, he didn't know a Chris Webb and what did she mean "a nuclear bunker"? And what was "Tan Hill"? It was clear he'd never visited the Dales or wanted to.

'And what about your son, Jesse?' Hazel asked. 'I understand he was found at a dog fight when he was a teenager.'

The man looked solemnly at her. 'That was an aberration. He was young but he's mended his ways.'

'When is he back from holiday?' Hazel asked, shutting her notebook.

Shane scratched his stubbly chin. 'I'm not sure. He might be staying away for a while.'

His mate had turned back to the newspaper and Shane's attention was drawn to it.

'Is that all?' he asked without moving his head.

'For now,' Hazel replied and left them discussing whether to back a horse called "Sweet Mischief".

Mills wished Nige was available to advise her over the university's disciplinary rules. She'd read the document and it sounded very complicated. The invigilator could raise the issue of cheating with the student if they suspected it at the time. A full report had to be made to the Registry before the meeting of an Investigating Committee and the student had a right to reply. The Investigating Committee sounded very formal, being appointed by the Vice Chancellor and chaired by the Head of another Faculty. There was a special panel that members could be drawn from to sit on the Committee but it appeared that no-one from the department would be involved.

Importantly, Mills discovered that the original report of the cheating had to be prepared by the invigilator and so it would fall on her if Sara insisted on proceeding with the case.

The only member of her own department who had to be present at the hearing would be Professor Cole as both the Head of Department and the Chair of the Board of Examiners. He had the right to call witnesses, as did the student, who could also appear in person. Mills was pretty sure that Sara would want to take up that offer. However, the committee had the option of dismissing a case before it got to that stage and Mills hoped that would happen when they saw the evidence.

It struck her that Sara would be taking an enormous risk because the penalty for cheating administered by the committee was to award zero marks for the paper, which would result in an overall fail of the year. She might be offered the opportunity to re-sit but in Mills' opinion that wouldn't go well. She sent a message to Sara pointing out the key points and offering to write a report that, in her opinion, she had had prior access to the model answers. Sara could then write her explanation of how she had come by them, if she so wished. But Mills warned her that the price for bringing Dr Cuthbert to justice could be that she would fail her degree.

She'd had enough of university politics and was keen to know whether any more ammunition had been received for analysis at the forensics lab. It would seem odd to ring Tim with a direct question so she decide to drive down there for an hour or two, remembering she'd promised not to be home late. She hadn't thought about Phil all morning and wondered if she should ring but decided that it might seem a bit over-anxious.

Normally Mills felt herself relaxing as she drove into the industrial estate and parked in front of the Yardley Forensics building, particularly when the ancient car belonging to her boss was already there. But today she feared Phil's box of ammunition might have arrived for analysis and it would not go unnoticed. Mills climbed the stairs slowly and peered into the office. Brenda's door was closed but her own desk was piled high with packages. As soon as she went inside, the inner office door opened and Brenda was grinning at her.

'Mills, I'm glad you're here! A mound of post arrived this morning and I'm trying to sort out the

VAT. Can you go through them with Tim and Donna for me?'

'Yep.'

She was already looking at the delivery advice documents, trying to second-guess which were important. There were three small packages and one box. Had they sent the entire box of cartridges, less the three she'd removed, or had they sent a few examples?

'Are you all right, Mills?' Brenda was staring at her from the doorway. 'Feeling ok?'

She pulled herself together. 'Yes, of course. I'll take them down and get them logged in.'

She gathered everything up in her arms and struggled out into the corridor. Glyn was in his office, staring at his computer monitor. He looked up when she went in and greeted her in an unusually friendly manner. She deposited the packages on his desk and began opening the padded envelopes to remove the samples, carefully sealed in plastic bags. First one: hair. The second one: paint flakes. The third: more paint. Just the parcel was left. They must have sent the whole box, thought Mills.

'Box containing shotgun cartridges to be sampled with a minimum of three examples and analysed in triplicate for five element fingerprint,' Mills read out.

The samples were given the lab's reference number before Mills carried the bags down the corridor to their preparation area and then looked for the analysts. Tim was busy making up solutions in the lab but she found Donna in the tea room on her break. Mills told her about the samples, all of which would require considerable work to detect trace chemicals: drugs in the hair, lead isotopes in the paint and a whole suite of heavy metals in the lead shot. Tim would have to analyse the paint and the lead shot but Mills hoped, if Donna prepared the samples, he wouldn't see that the cartridges looked identical to the ones she'd asked him to analyse. They were rather a distinctive purple.

'That's fine,' said Donna, rinsing her mug under the tap and placing it in the cupboard. 'I'll take them down to the lab now.'

'Perhaps make a start on the lead shot first? And can you ask Tim to pop down here so I can discuss the analysis?' Mills asked, hoping to distract him from seeing the samples Donna was about to unpack. She put the kettle on and waited.

'Tea?' she asked when he arrived.

'Please.'

'Busy?'

'Yeah, the instrument's playing up and I've got the engineer arriving in a few minutes.'

'In that case I won't keep you. I just wanted to let you know some paint flakes arrived this morning and some lead shot.'

She'd deliberately avoided saying anything about cartridges. Donna would have removed the lead shot from the purple cases by the time Tim had finished with the engineer and need never know that he was analysing more of the same ammunition. Relieved, she returned to her office with her tea and settled down to catch up with her emails. It was only when Brenda emerged from the office carrying her bag and said she was off, that Mills looked at the time and knew she wouldn't be back home before six.

And soon she realised that she'd been over-optimistic. The road out of Harrogate was more busy than usual and she became increasingly frustrated as the traffic crept forward slowly. She put her foot down but her progress was interrupted again on the Reeth road when she joined a queue of cars crawling along behind a tractor. Finally, at a quarter to seven she drew up outside Laurel Cottage.

'Sorry I'm late,' she called as she swung the front door shut behind her.

There was no reply and no sign of Phil in the sitting room or the kitchen. She called up the stairs but there was silence. She could detect the smell of food cooking and assumed that Muriel was having a barbecue next door. But when she went through to the back door, she saw the smoke was coming from her own garden. Phil had his back to her, leaning over the rusty old contraption that served as a barbecue.

'Hi!' she called and joined him outside.

He turned round as if she'd caught him doing something he shouldn't. 'I found these sausages,' he said. 'I thought I ought to cook something. I didn't know what time…'

'Sorry. I should've rung. The traffic… you know.'

'No problem,' said Phil. 'They're nearly ready. And there are potatoes in foil here.'

'Sounds great, I'll get some beers.'

Mills went to the fridge. There was just one bottle left although there'd been six that morning. She grabbed her last bottle of wine and went back out.

'I thought I'd have wine,' she said, handing him the last beer bottle.

She found a half-used bag of salad leaves and divided it between two plates. They sat in the sun and ate without talking. When Phil finished his beer she brought him another glass and they finished the wine together.

'We'll have to go into town for supplies tomorrow,' she said, draining the bottle into his empty glass.

He looked at her but said nothing.

'I went down to the lab today. Brenda says hello.'

'How is the old girl?'

'Same as always, except she's bought new clothes, ones that fit her. By the way, they sent your cartridges in today for analysis,' she added casually.

She waited for his response.

He shrugged. 'Why did they do that?'

'To see if they match the crime scene.'

He laughed but she could see that it bothered him. He soon excused himself and went to his room, leaving her to wash up and sit brooding over what would happen when they found that his ammunition was a match.

Hazel had intended to stay for an hour or so but the hotel had a beautiful garden with comfortable seating and tables with umbrellas if you wanted to be in the shade. She didn't want to be shaded. She sat in the full sun and enjoyed the warmth on her bare arms and legs. Jason suggested a spot of lunch and she'd enjoyed a large warm chicken salad followed by cheese and fruit. He asked if she was allowed to have a glass of wine and she said it wouldn't harm. So they sat and chatted about this and that. He didn't ask why she wanted to speak to him again and she didn't say but inevitably the conversation drifted to his marriage and Linda.

'You know her father is a gamekeeper on a big estate in Northumberland?' he said, stretching across to top her glass up.

'Really?'

'Yes, she was brought up in one of the estate cottages. Out with her father checking the traps and doing whatever they do. She used to be out beating and shooting. A regular Annie Oakley.'

Hazel didn't know who this Annie person was but wanted to know more about his ex-wife's use of guns.

'Did she have a gun when you were with her?'

'I don't know. I don't think so but she used to go and stay with her parents regularly and I'm sure she was out shooting then. Probably she had access to one.'

Hazel wondered if he was deliberately introducing the connection to raise her suspicions.

'Well, I don't imagine she would want to dispose of her boyfriend, even if she had the means.' She sipped her wine, hoping her remark sounded sufficiently dismissive. She didn't want him to think she was taken in by his innuendo.

'I wonder. She had a terrible temper. I told you she could be quite a bully. That's why we split up.'

'I thought she had the restraining order taken out on *you*.'

'Well, that's how she made it appear but she always started it. I was just defending myself.'

Fortunately the silence that followed was broken by a waiter appearing to ask if they wanted afternoon tea. It was already after three.

'Stay for a cup of tea,' urged Jason. 'They do superb cakes.'

It would be good to have something to soak up the wine, thought Hazel.

'Just a cup, then I must be going.'

When she left he asked if they could meet again – he'd so enjoyed her company. She said she wasn't sure but he was persuasive and she finally agreed to meet for a drink on the following Tuesday evening, when Liam had judo practice.

As she drove home she went over their meeting. He was good looking, charming and entertaining. They'd had a really nice afternoon at a very pleasant venue. She was well aware he had sewn a seed of doubt in her mind regarding the domestic abuse charge, which was probably exactly what he meant to do. Perhaps he'd carefully planned the whole event to convince her and now she needed to talk to Linda just to be sure.

Chapter 19

When Nige asked how Phil was getting on, Mills wasn't sure how to answer. She'd been woken by him crying out twice in the night and this morning his door had been firmly closed. She'd wondered how he'd be with no alcohol in the house and was nervous of what she'd find when she went home.

'Not too bad,' she replied.

'Really?'

'As good as can be expected.'

'Well, it's his clinic tomorrow. Do you want me to take him?'

She nodded. 'I think a change of company might do him good.'

Their discussion of Phil's treatment was interrupted by a phone call from Sara Pendleton. She was determined to go ahead with the disciplinary procedure and nothing Mills said would alter her decision. When the call ended Mills put her head in her hands.

'Bad news?' Nige asked.

'Just the worst. I'm about to jeopardise Sara Pendleton's chance of getting even a third class degree.'

Mills started work on the report required from her as the examination invigilator. She showed it to Nige when she'd finished and he agreed it was clear and unbiased. The form had to go the Faculty Head, and her Head of Department. She sent a copy to Sara for information.

Before Nige went to lunch, Mills told him about the lead shot that was being tested at Yardley Forensics. She hoped he would pass on the information to Nina without her having to explain how she already knew that Phil's matched the crime scene.

'Does Phil know?' he asked.

'I told him what was happening but I didn't give him the results. It doesn't mean anything, does it? There could be hundreds of boxes of the same ammunition sold in the Dales.'

'Yes,' agreed Nige. 'It's just a coincidence. Can I bring you anything from the cafeteria?'

Mills was alone when Professor Cole marched in without knocking and told her exactly what he thought of her. He listed all the things wrong with her report, from the fact that Sara Pendleton was not her responsibility – she was Cuthbert's tutee – through to Mills being only a half-time member of staff in his department and that situation could easily be changed. She tried to explain it was Sara who had persuaded her to raise the issue but he wasn't listening. Before he left he informed her that Dr Cuthbert was already in possession of her document and would have questions.

Nige noticed she was upset when he returned and tried to be supportive but Mills could tell he thought she had been misguided. She was planning to avoid any further conflict by leaving for home when she received a call from the Faculty Head's office. Could she be available for a meeting at four?

The afternoon dragged and Mills begged Nige to stay in the office in case Colin Cuthbert made an appearance. An hour later Mills suggested they adjourn to the cafeteria to pass the time. They rehearsed what she would say to the Faculty Head about Sara Pendleton.

'Will you tell him about her and Cuthbert?' Nige asked.

'No. I'm just sticking to the facts. All I can say is that her examination performance greatly exceeded expectations and she somehow successfully answered a question that had a component missing. Therefore I suspect she was cheating.'

'They might dismiss it as speculation.'

'Then it's up to Sara what she does with that. She wants to admit to it but explain why and how it happened.'

'And get revenge on Colin Cuthbert?'

'When you put it like that, yes, to get revenge.'

'Talk of the devil,' Nige said under his breath.

He was looking past her towards the door. Mills turned to see Dr Cuthbert chatting to a male student while they headed to the counter. As she turned back round Nige groaned.

'Dr Sanderson, fancy seeing you here!' Cuthbert called.

He made his way towards them as he instructed the student to bring him a coffee. He stopped and rested his podgy hands on the table.

'The Head gave me a copy of your report,' he began. 'Perhaps you'd like to tell me why you've got it in for my tutee?'

'I haven't,' Mills replied, looking at Nige.

'Well it certainly looks that way. She was awarded a lower second fair and square. I don't know what you plan to achieve doing this now. It's too late, darling.' He looked across at Nige. 'You'd best be finding some more work for your friend here, Featherstone. I don't think the Head will have a role for her next term.'

He went across to join the student on a table at the opposite end of the hall. Nige didn't speak for a minute.

'That went well,' he said finally, with a grin.

'It's not funny. Worst case scenario: I lose my half post in Forensics and Sara loses her degree.'

'Best case: you keep your job and Cuthbert loses his.'

'That's not going to happen.'

At ten minutes to four, Mills went off to see the Faculty Head as requested. He was in a meeting and she hung about in the corridor outside his office until the door opened suddenly. Professor Cole emerged, red-faced, and brushed past her as he stormed down the corridor. She remained outside, wondering what reception awaited her. It was several minutes before she was invited in.

She needn't have worried. Professor Lynam was very business-like in his manner, asked pertinent questions and allowed her to answer fully. She admitted that she'd spoken to the student about the accusation and had listened to her explanation of events that led to her cheating.

'You mean she's admitting it?' He was clearly surprised.

'Yes, I believe she wants to have the opportunity to answer the charges.'

'Does she fully understand the ramifications if she's found guilty?'

'She does.'

He went through the formalities in detail and Mills confirmed that she understood the procedure. She added that Sara had wanted her to take the accusation forward. He then told her that Professor Cole was very unhappy with the situation.

She said, 'I know.'

'It's not the first time that you and he have had, shall we say, a difference of opinion, is it?'

It certainly was not. Last time she had revealed that Professor Green, a senior scientist in the department, was interpreting forensic evidence wrongly and he had chosen to retire after an acrimonious dispute.

'But I was proved right last time,' she argued.

'Well, whatever your history, we must concentrate on the facts here. I will let you know whether the panel want to have a formal meeting in due course. Meanwhile, can you please advise Miss Pendleton that she may forfeit her degree if the decision goes against her?'

'I think she'll want to submit her own justification of her actions.'

'That's all to the good. We want to be fair to everyone concerned here.'

Mills hoped that didn't mean taking the side of Dr Cuthbert. The meeting ended and she left, unsure exactly how the process would play out. Whatever happened, she knew already she hadn't done herself any favours in the Forensics Department.

There was no smell of cooking and no sign of Phil when Mills got home. She made a mug of tea and sat in the garden, waiting. She went indoors and looked in the freezer. She pulled out a pack of fishcakes and turned on the oven. Thinking she'd have a quick shower, she went upstairs and was about to go into the bathroom when she noticed Phil's door was not quite shut and inside was in darkness. Gingerly she pushed the door wider. Phil was lying on the bed in his underpants, apparently fast asleep. She pulled the door closed and tiptoed past.

Once she had showered and dressed, Mills went downstairs to prepare the meal, not that it involved very much. She shoved the fishcakes in the oven, emptied a pack of salad leaves into a bowl and hoped Phil wasn't hungry. After the allotted cooking time, she went back upstairs and knocked loudly on his door. There was no sound. She went in and called his name until finally he rolled over and stared at her.

'Dinner's ready.'

He mumbled that he'd be down in a minute and ten minutes later he appeared. At least he was dressed and had possibly splashed his face. The stubble on his chin was more pronounced and he had definitely not brushed his hair. She took their plates outside and they ate without speaking. It was very different to their meal the evening before.

'So what have you been doing today?' she asked finally, unable to bear the silence any longer.

He shrugged.

'But you've not been up there all day?' She didn't mean it to come out so judgementally. 'I mean, were you tired?'

'Yes.'

He either meant he had been in bed all day or he'd been tired. Either way, it wasn't a good sign.

'It's your clinic appointment tomorrow, isn't it?'

'Is it?'

'I thought you could come with me to uni and Nige can take you from there. It saves him coming all the way over here. But it means leaving by eight,' she warned.

He sighed then nodded. 'I'll be in my room if you need me,' he said, and that was the last she saw of him until the next day.

After she'd washed the dishes she rang Nige to tell him about her plan to bring Phil over in the morning.

'I thought it would be good for him to get out and spend a bit of time on campus but now I wonder if he'll be able to cope – he seems very down.'

Nige approved of her plan since it saved him time and he had to get a few things done before he could take Phil off to Catterick.

'Don't go yet, Mills, Nina wants a quick word.'

He handed her over to his wife.

'Mills, I've got a question for you.'

'Oh yes?'

'Yes. How come you knew about Phil's ammo matching the crime scene before Ruby did?' she asked accusingly.

Mills had to think fast. 'I don't know…' She played for time, 'I was at the lab, I think. I must have seen the results there.'

'Oh.'

Her friend seemed satisfied with her answer.

'Does that mean he's still under suspicion, Nina?'

'It certainly does. Hazel seems quite convinced, from what Ruby tells me, and my DI is planning to contact the CPS for advice.'

Mills cursed. 'How long before they…'

'Arrest him? Your guess is as good as mine.'

'What if he's unfit?'

'That's a two-edged sword, Mills. If he's mentally unstable it would make him a more likely suspect, don't you think?'

Mills had to agree. Nothing they could do was going to help his case.

'Well let's hope his clinic appointment helps,' was all Nina could offer.

Mills described Phil's nightmares and how he'd cooked for her previously but had now spent the entire day in bed. She told Nina to communicate it all to Nige so he could pass the information on to the clinic. They couldn't rely on Phil doing so.

DS Fuller had been in a good mood when she arrived in the office that afternoon. She'd smiled at Ruby and asked, very politely, if she could have the files relating to Linda Bailey, *if she had time*. That was a first. As it happened, Ruby had looked out anything she could find on Chris Webb's partner, which amounted to three incidents of domestic abuse by her then husband, Jason.

Hazel went very quiet as she leafed through the file. She spent ages looking through the photographs.

'He must've been a right thug,' Ruby commented after a while.

'Mmm.'

'Did you interview him?'

'Yes.'

'And?'

Hazel looked up. 'Nothing. He seemed perfectly normal.'

'Just goes to show. D'you think he could've attacked her new partner out of jealousy?'

'I think I should talk to her – there may have been extenuating circumstances.'

'You think?'

Ruby pressed "print" and collected the sheets from the printer. 'Results of forensics on Freedman's shotgun pellets,' she said, passing them over to Hazel.

Hazel asked, 'What's it say?'

'A match to the crime scene.'

'Right. I think we might have a case. I'll go and see Mitch. He'll contact the CPS. Meanwhile I want to have a word with Linda Bailey.'

'Why?'

'Just to tie up some loose ends, Ruby.'

Hazel had to admit that she and Linda Bailey had started off on the wrong foot when they'd first met. When the woman had phoned in to say her partner was missing, she'd not taken her seriously. It had only been a few days and he worked away from home most of the time, for goodness sake. So when she rang the bell this time Hazel wasn't expecting a warm welcome.

'Oh, it's you. Is there some news?'

'Just a few questions. Can I come in?'

'I've got to pick up Katie in twenty minutes…'

'It won't take long.'

The flat was as she remembered it, clean, tidy and homely. Had Jason lived here with her? Probably not. She guessed Linda came here after the marriage failed.

'So what did you want?'

They'd moved into the living area and Hazel had taken a seat on the sofa. She laid the files on the table and opened one of them. She watched the young woman's face when she spotted the photographs inside.

'Why have you brought those?' she asked angrily.

'I was checking all aspects of the case and I was given these files.'

'You think Jason might be involved in Chris's death?' She looked horrified.

It gave Hazel the excuse she needed. 'Do you want to tell me about what happened?'

'He's a bully and a control freak. He didn't like me going out after Katie was born and got jealous when friends came over.' She indicated the open file. 'That's what happened if I stepped out of line.'

'Was there any provocation? A row perhaps. Maybe you riled him a bit.'

'Riled him? Would you dare *rile* someone who uses his fists like that?'

'I just wondered whether…'

'Look, I don't know what you're trying to say but I can assure you I did not do anything to provoke his attacks – quite the reverse in fact. Tiptoeing around him to avoid confrontation, it nearly drove me mad! Now, if you don't mind, I'd like to collect my daughter from nursery.'

'I just want to explore all avenues. Please sit down. One last question: do you have, or have you ever owned, a gun?'

Linda looked puzzled. 'No.'

'Are you sure?'

'Yes, I'm sure. What is this about?'

'Do any members of your family own a gun?'

'Yes, of course. My dad's a gamekeeper.'

'Have you ever used his gun?'

She sighed. 'About ten years ago, when I was helping him with the shoots. Yes, of course, but not since then.'

Hazel picked up the files and rose to go.

'Can I ask if you ever see your ex-husband now?'

'Certainly not, he's not to come anywhere near me or my daughter.'

'Isn't that a bit harsh?'

She looked at Hazel with an expression of disbelief then shrugged. 'Sorry, I've got to run – if you've nothing to tell me about Chris's murder?'

Hazel stood in the street watching Linda disappear round the corner. Impossibly she believed both their accounts, knowing one of them must be lying, and she didn't want it to be Jason.

Alf had been scanning local radio stations and newspapers on the internet, as well as social media, searching for any mention of the nuclear bunker murder. It had gone incredibly quiet since the initial discovery of a body and his anonymous call to Crime Stoppers hadn't produced the result he'd expected. Two days had passed and there were no reports of a man helping the police with their enquiries. It gnawed away at him until he could stand it no longer.

Shane's landline rang for just a few seconds before he picked up. He sounded disappointed when Alf announced himself.

'What d'you want?'

'I wondered if you had any more work for me.' Alf had planned this.

'No.'

'Have you stopped working down there?'

'Yes, we have, so I don't need you.'

'Is that because of the murder?'

'What d'you mean?'

There had been a pause, just a fraction of a second but enough to raise Alf's suspicions. It gave him confidence. 'I mean the animal welfare officer.'

'Don't know anything about that.'

'No? That's odd. They found the body in the nuclear bunker your dad used to work in.'

'Don't know what you're on about, son. I'm busy so if that's all?' He slammed the phone down.

Alf sat on the edge of his bed, pulse racing. He had no proof but his instinct was that Shane had something to hide. If he was innocent, the police would prove it – if not, he didn't want to hide a crime, even though he was partly involved himself. In fact he'd probably be charged with aiding Shane to trap a badger. If he contacted DS Fuller now, his father would be bound to find out and he would be even more upset if he eventually discovered it from the police. On the other hand, if he told his father how he knew Shane was trapping badgers, he'd have to explain his involvement. But it wasn't being involved in Shane's criminal activities that caused him concern. He was tortured that Dad would know he'd been lying to him about where he'd been going in the past. He lay on his bed and stared at the ceiling. When Roy called "goodnight" as he went passed on his way to bed, Alf replied faintly and turned his face into his pillow.

Chapter 20

Hazel and Ruby joined the others in the conference room for the morning briefing. Mitch wanted to share with everyone the forensics from the bunker.

'They've had serious problems pumping out the water,' he reported. 'First they had to get a generator set up and then, just when it was clearing, it rained overnight and the water level rose again. Anyway, it's empty now, not that it's revealed anything much to help us.' He picked up a file and opened it, removing a single page. 'The only item found in the mud below water level was a biro. It's a short white ballpoint pen with a lid on. It has some writing on but difficult to decipher. They think it says "Chisholm". Ruby, see if you can find out where or what "Chisholm" is.'

Hazel asked, 'Is that all they found?'

'They located blood on the ladder and the DNA proves it's from the victim.'

'So he wasn't shot where he was found?'

'We don't think so. It suggests he was taken there after he was killed.'

Hazel asked, 'Carried down the ladder or dropped?'

'Not dropped,' Mitch replied. 'Fractures, or lack of them, suggest he was gently lowered into the bunker. It must've taken two people to manage that, don't you think?'

Everyone agreed.

'So now we're looking for an accomplice as well as the suspect.'

'The suspect?' Ruby asked.

'Phil Freedman. He had access to the bunker, a gun that uses the same ammunition as found at the scene and he discovered the body.'

'And the accomplice?' she asked.

'Someone close to him… so close they're willing to help him hide a body.'

Someone asked what his motive might be.

Hazel spoke up. 'He's being treated for post traumatic stress disorder. There doesn't have to be a reason for what he did.'

Mitch thanked the team and ordered Hazel to send a car round to fetch the suspect. Before he left, he asked Ruby to list Freedman's close friends and call them in for questioning.

Once again Mills had been woken several times in the night by Phil's anguished cries. She'd learned not to go in to him but left him to wake from his nightmares alone. So she came round very gradually when the sound of the back door opening woke her at half-past five in the morning. Moments later the smell of tobacco smoke drifted into her bedroom from the garden below. She felt for her slippers and grabbed a sweatshirt before stumbling downstairs.

'Want a cup of tea?' she asked, sitting down next to him.

'Yes, that would be cool.'

She sighed. He was beginning to sound like a teenager, as well as acting like one. Fine. She went inside and put the kettle on. She took his mug out to him and went upstairs to shower. Back in her bedroom she stared at the mirror and told herself it would be fine. He'd go to the clinic and they'd sort him out and it would all… be… fine.

They left for uni at seven-thirty. There seemed no point in sitting around waiting for eight o'clock. The roads were quiet and the car park was empty. She took him to the cafeteria where they drank coffee until Mills was sure Nige would be in the office.

'Here we are,' she said, leading the way.

Nige took her to one side. 'Quickly,' he said. 'Nina says there's a warrant out for him. She said we should go straight to the clinic.'

They'd disappeared out of the door before Mills fully comprehended what he meant. She tried calling Nina, unsuccessfully. She turned on her computer, hoping there would be a message from her friend. There was only an email from Sara Pendleton with a copy of her submission to the panel considering her case, so Mills distracted herself by reading it through.

The student had made a good job of her defence and she'd left nothing out, not even how when her tutor had invited her to dinner, she was the only guest. How she'd been flattered by his attention and soon been drawn into a relationship that lasted all year. It had been entirely his idea to provide the model answers to the exam questions – they just arrived in her inbox. If it was accepted as true, Dr Cuthbert's reputation would be in shreds. Mills was tempted to suggest minor changes to spellings and grammar but decided that Sara's submission was more believable in its raw form.

At ten twenty-two she received a phone call from DS Hazel Fuller. She was required for interview as soon as possible. They could send a car.

'That won't necessary,' she said. 'I'll drive over straight away.'

If it meant clearing Phil's name, she would be there as soon as possible, she thought, gathering her things and leaving the office. As she came to the entrance hall she heard a familiar voice and coming round the corner found Colin Cuthbert in conversation with the Head. They stopped as she approached and she could feel them watching her leave the building. The sooner the panel met to hear Sara's case the better as far as she was concerned. She just wanted it to be over, whatever the outcome.

The weather reflected her mood. The sky had clouded over and it had begun to drizzle with rain. The windscreen wipers smeared tiny insect bodies across her view and she cursed as she tried to clear it with jets of soapy water. She'd been instructed to go to the police station in Northallerton. Mills found a 'pay and display' in town and ran the short distance in the rain.

She'd expected another brief chat about how she and Phil had found the body. By now the forensics from the scene would have been available and maybe some new clue had been found that they thought she could help with. She assumed she'd be sent to an office somewhere in the building but when she announced herself at reception she was told to wait there until someone appeared from headquarters down the road. It seemed a long wait and, when she saw it was Hazel Fuller coming in from the street, Mills wasn't particularly relieved.

There was no familiar greeting from DS Fuller. 'Follow me please, it's not far.'

Mills had to walk fast to keep up before being ushered into a small room containing a table and two chairs.

'Sit down, please.'

She obeyed.

'I expect you know why you're here?'

Mills shook her head. If this was how Hazel wanted to play it...

'You were with Phil Freedman when he found Chris Webb's body in the Tan Hill bunker on the first of July.'

Was it that long ago? Nearly two weeks? 'Yes, that's correct.'

'You and Phil Freedman, you're close?'

'We're friends.'

'Not more than that, Mills?'

'No.'

Hazel was a colleague of Nina's and Mills knew that they were mates, so she'd always wanted to like the woman but there was something about her that Mills couldn't get past. Possibly it was just her professionalism that got in the way of them being friends.

Hazel was raising her voice, 'I repeat, weren't you once an item?'

'Once, yes, before he went abroad.'

'So you *are* close.'

'You could say that, I suppose.'

Hazel's phone pinged and she looked down at it for a few seconds then up at Mills.

'Do you know where he is at present?'

She thought for a second. 'Not at present, no.' It was true.

'He's not at his address.'

'Isn't he?'

'Has he moved?'

'I don't think so.' Mills took long breaths to steady herself.

'Mills, I'm worried about your friend.'

She wished Hazel would stop using her name.

'I'm worried that he's in a lot of trouble. There's evidence that puts him as our main suspect in a murder. The problem is that he would have needed help in moving the body to where it was found. I'm looking for a good mate who would have helped him out.'

She tried hard not to look away from Hazel's searching stare. After several seconds the phone pinged again and she looked away.

Mills knew her voice sounded too emotional. 'If he was the murderer, he'd be daft to take the body to the bunker when he knew we'd be going there soon after with someone from the National Park.'

'But he's not rational, is he Mills? He has come back from war zones and plane crashes full of bodies and is suffering from mental problems, isn't he?'

She was right but she was wrong to suspect him. 'What are you saying? He killed this man, and I helped him carry the body over the moor to the bunker and tipped him in?'

'Something like that.'

'Well, it's nonsense. Can I go now?' She felt angry but she knew she just sounded irritable as she rose to leave.

'Not yet. We want to find your friend and when we do, I may need to speak to you again.'

She sat down again. 'So I have to stay here?'

Hazel smiled. 'Of course not, Mills. Just don't be too far away in case we need you again today.'

She picked up her phone and escorted her to the front door before disappearing out and up the road in the rain. Mills assumed she was heading back to headquarters and followed her. As she walked past the old prison and into Alverton Court, Mills messaged her friend.

'I'm waiting to see DS Featherstone,' she told the receptionist in the police headquarters.

They arranged to meet in a small café towards the end of town once Nina was free. Mills was already seated in a quiet corner finishing her second cup of coffee when her friend came through the door, shaking her umbrella. They waited until the girl had taken their orders before catching up.

'Did Nige get him off to the clinic?' Nina asked.

'Yes, but Hazel asked me where he was living…'

Nina held up her hand to stop her. 'Don't tell me. The less I know about what you and Nige are saying, the better. I'll tell you what I know.' She sighed. 'The CPS has told Mitch he can proceed with the case against Phil, on the basis of the matching ammo and knowledge of the hiding place.'

'Is it definite that the body was moved, like Hazel said?'

Her voice was hushed. 'Yes, no doubt. There would have been more blood if he'd been shot at the scene and there were traces on the ladder which suggested the body was carried down there quite carefully. There would've been more broken bones if he'd been thrown down.'

'Is that why they think there was an accomplice.'

'Yes.'

'Hazel more or less accused me.'

Nina shook her head despondently. 'That doesn't surprise me. If not you, they'll be roping Nige in.'

Their drinks arrived and it was a few minutes before Nina spoke again.

'Does Hazel know where Phil is staying?'

'No, she asked…'

'Whoa, don't tell me. Just answer me yes or no, ok?'

'Ok.'

'Does she know that Nige has taken him to Catterick?'

'No, I don't think so.'

Nina looked thoughtful. 'I wonder.'

'What?'

'Nothing, I'm thinking how we might buy him a bit of time.'

Afterwards Nina walked with Mills to the car, sheltering her with an umbrella, and told her to get back to work. If Hazel wanted to speak to her again she would just have to wait for Mills to drive back. Mills asked what she would be doing in the afternoon.

'I might go for a little drive myself.' But she would say no more.

Hazel was at her desk typing up her report while she waited for Ruby to bring her a sandwich. As soon as she returned, Hazel would ask her to get permission to access Freedman's phone records, including where he was now. Meanwhile, she and Mitch would have to decide what to do about Nina's husband. Nigel Featherstone appeared to be Freedman's best male friend and was next in line for an interview.

'They didn't have chicken, so I got tuna. Hope you don't mind.'

Hazel pulled a face.

'You can have my egg if you like.'

'Thanks.'

Ruby handed her the packet with a bag of crisps, which Hazel examined carefully. 'They're cheese and onion.'

'Yes, that's all they had.'

Hazel carried on typing, leaving her lunch untouched.

Ruby stood waiting. 'Can I ask you something?'

'Mmm.' Hazel didn't look up.

'It's about the other day, when you went to see Mr Bailey.'

Hazel looked up almost guiltily. 'What?'

'You said you saw someone in a betting shop?'

Her colleague smiled. 'Oh yes, Shane Armstrong and his equally unpleasant pal.'

'It's just that the biro they found near the body, it had "Chisholm" on it and there's a chain of betting shops called "Chisholm's" so I wondered…'

'Can't remember what the shop was called but if it's a chain the pen could've come from anywhere. Probably left from when it was operating as a nuclear bunker – or whatever it was.' She went back to her typing.

Ruby knew when Hazel wasn't interested. She went to her desk and checked the internet. Her colleague might be proved right. The bookmakers started in the 1950s so the pen could have been there from when the bunker was operational. She took her sandwich to the kitchen and ate it while she made two mugs of tea. Back in the office Hazel still hadn't touched her lunch. She put the mug on her colleague's desk and sat down again.

'I need a check on Freedman's phone. No-one seems to know where he is. Quick as you can. And have you seen Nina today?'

'She was around first thing but I haven't seen her since.'

There was no response from Hazel. She was busy making a call. 'Hi Mitch, Freedman's gone missing.

Ruby's getting a triangulation check done but we need to alert the region to look out for him. He could be dangerous. Let me know when you receive this call.'

She jumped up and announced she was going to find the DCI. 'Let me know if Nina turns up, I need to talk to her.'

Nige was sitting in the clinic's visitors' area working on his laptop. He'd anticipated spending several hours waiting for Phil to finish his treatment and had come prepared. He was hoping to finish his project report before the family holiday and there was only one more week before they were off to Wales. His attention was distracted by a familiar voice and he looked up to find his wife entering the room followed by the receptionist.

'I'll see if he's around but he sometimes takes an early lunch break.' She went down the corridor.

'Hi, what's the matter?' Nige asked as Nina sat down beside him.

'Nothing, I thought I'd have a word with someone about Phil's mental health, that's all.'

'Is that as a friend or a copper?'

'Both. He really needs help, doesn't he? I mean one or two hours a week isn't going to speed his recovery is it?'

He wanted to know more but the woman was coming back and Nina was already on her feet.

'Would you like to come this way?' she asked.

Nige watched his wife disappear from view, apprehensively. He timed her – she was away exactly twenty-four minutes. When she returned she was looking pleased with herself.

He asked, 'What *have* you done?' He imagined the worst.

'You don't need to wait. They've found a bed for him. He'll be staying here for a few days.'

'Why? Has he got worse? What's happened?'

'Nothing has happened. They realise he is a danger to himself and needs constant care for now. I'm going back to work. See you later.'

Nige tried to explain to Mills when he got back to the office but he wasn't sure what had happened himself.

'I suppose it's worked out rather well, quite by chance,' he said.

Mills shook her head in disbelief. 'By chance? Dr Featherstone, you can be very dim sometimes. It's good someone in your family has a brain.'

She explained that she thought Nina had been very clever because it would be unlikely that someone diagnosed as suffering from a mental health problem would be arrested and taken away from where they were being cared for.

'At least it buys him a bit of time,' agreed Nige.

'And us. I'm sure that you and I are being lined up as Phil's accomplices.'

Chapter 21

Alf's father had sat at the table after tea preparing end of term reports for his pupils until late every evening that week. Alf had wanted to wait until the end of term before talking to him but this thing couldn't wait, it was driving him mad. So he came home early on the Friday and made a shepherd's pie using an old cookery book he'd found in a bookcase. There were hand-written recipes on scraps of paper folded inside and ideas cut out of newspapers and magazines. One was for shepherd's pie made with left-overs from the Sunday joint. Well they didn't have lamb for Sunday lunch so he'd asked at the meat counter in Sainsbury's and the woman told him he needed minced lamb for a true shepherd's pie.

'I never knew that if it was made with beef it's called cottage pie,' he told his father as he brought it out of the oven.

The potato topping was satisfyingly browned and the thick gravy was oozing through the edges.

'I thought we'd have broad beans with it,' he called.

'A regular Jamie Oliver, aren't we now!'

Roy was pushing his pile of papers to the end of the table and put out the mats. He came in to fetch the cutlery and hesitated as he spotted the recipe book. He leafed through it, stopping at the hand-written notes and read them in silence.

Finally he said, 'Your Mum was a brilliant cook. You must get it from her.'

He took the knives and forks from the drawer and went back into the dining room.

Roy was clearly enjoying his meal but Alf had difficulty swallowing. The next few hours, maybe even days, were going to be difficult, very difficult.

'Dad, I want to tell you something.'

'What's that, son?'

'Promise not to say anything until I've finished?'

Roy put down his knife and fork and paid attention.

Alf began by admitting that he'd not been going out with friends on those Saturday nights but helping Shane, in order to get some pocket money.

His father waited for him to finish talking and was about to speak but Alf stopped him.

'I'm afraid there's more,' he said.

He went on to explain what Shane was doing in Arkengarthdale. Roy was looking more and more alarmed. Alf decided that was enough. He didn't need to mention his fear that Shane might have had something to do with the welfare officer's death. His dad wasn't stupid though and could, eventually, make the connection.

Neither of them finished the meal. Lamb mince was left congealing on their plates as Alf sat waiting for his father's reaction. At first there was confusion, then anger and finally despair.

Alf asked, 'What d'you think I should do?'

'Tell the truth. It's always best to tell the truth, son.'

'But who to?'

'What he's doing is wrong, as well as being illegal. You need to let him know that you know that.'

'What good will that do?'

'The main thing is to stop him. He knows that if he's caught it'll be serious. Do you think Jesse is involved?' It was an afterthought.

'Yes.'

They talked around the situation for over an hour. Alf thought his father would be on to the police immediately but he seemed anxious to protect Jesse, who had clearly been led astray, yet again, by that evil man. Eventually it occurred to Alf that his father wanted to protect him as well as his half-brother. He went to his room to think things through and make a call.

'What d'you want now?' Shane snapped when he heard who was calling.

'I'm going to tell the truth about what you're doing.'

'Listen, son, I told you before, I'll tell your dad what you've been up to if you breathe a word.'

'Too late. He knows.'

Alf terminated the call and ignored it when Shane tried calling him back. He left the phone ringing and went downstairs.

'You said before that we must tell the truth. I think I should tell the police, even if it means I'm part of it.'

His father nodded, as if admitting defeat. 'Yes. It's the right thing to do.' There was a weak smile of encouragement.

Alf went back upstairs to send DS Fuller a message implicating Shane in the crime of badger-trapping. He didn't mention that he suspected Shane of being mixed up in the death of the animal welfare officer, even to him that sounded too far-fetched. He hesitated before pressing the "send" button. Back downstairs he said it was done and now they just had to wait. His father gave him an awkward hug and said they should make a hot drink. Alf noticed his breath smelled of whisky.

Ruby was in the office by ten o'clock knowing that her colleague wouldn't arrive early on a Saturday. It wasn't her turn to provide research cover but Hazel had asked her as a special favour because she planned to bring Phil Freedman in and charge him with the murder of Chris Webb. Ruby hoped they could find some uniformed officers to drive him all the way to their nearest custody suite, which was now in Harrogate. Her job would be to gather all the intel and provide a motive, although Hazel said he was just a bit mental. She'd told her it wasn't acceptable to use such a term but her colleague said she didn't care about political correctness.

Ruby was busy texting Nina with an update when Hazel burst in. She quickly finished the sentence *going to charge him today* and sent it.

'Bloody traffic.'

Ruby knew it was more likely that Hazel had overslept after a heavy night with the Australian red. She offered to make coffee and left her colleague to settle in. By the time she returned, the printer was producing a pile of papers.

'Can you deal with these, Ruby? I need to get on with more important stuff.'

'What are they?'

'Reports for the file, searches, forensics and all the boring paperwork. They're mainly emails.'

Five minutes later she threw a file marked "Freedman" onto Ruby's desk and left the room. Inside were records of interviews and statements collected by the DS. The papers from the printer were mainly emails containing forensic results and contacts with official sources. Ruby began sorting them into the file. Typically she had to separate out several messages unrelated to Phil Freedman that had sneaked into the pile. One particularly caught her eye because it mentioned that name again: Shane Armstrong. It was from the lad that had drawn the likeness of Jeff Bradby.

As soon as Hazel's paperwork was sorted, and despite the DS's lack of interest, Ruby began a new file on the Armstrongs: their previous brushes with the law over dog-fighting and the "interview" in the betting shop down the road from his house. She checked Armstrong's address and found there was a branch of Chisholm bookmakers in the same road. She saw no reason why she shouldn't discuss this with Nina since it had nothing to do with Phil Freedman. When she rang, her colleague was just going out to the supermarket.

'It's ok, Ruby,' said Nina. 'Nige knows what we need. He can take Rosie.'

Her husband pulled a face and took the plastic bags off her. 'Come on, Rosie,' he called. 'We've got the short straw.'

Nina passed him the list and waved them off. 'Sorry, you were saying?'

Ruby explained the contents of the email. 'This lad seems quite reliable. From what he says, he's implicating himself in this badger-trapping offence. I assume that Shane Armstrong is the man who set Jeff Bradby up to keep an eye on the trap in the woods.'

'Sounds a reasonable assumption but that doesn't mean …'

'I wouldn't connect the cases either,' Ruby answered, 'except for the pen found at the murder scene. It comes from the same chain of bookmakers that Armstrong uses.'

'Bit tenuous.'

'I know but when you add in the fact that the victim was an animal welfare officer.'

'Tell me about the pen. There may be something that can provide forensics.'

'It's a cheap disposable ballpoint pen, white with black writing on the side. It says "Chisholm" and something else that's been worn away.'

'Bookmakers, I guess.'

'Probably.'

'What colour is the ink?'

'I have no idea. Black I suppose. That's the colour of the lid. We have no idea how long it's been there – the bookmakers has been going since the fifties. That's before the bunker was closed down.'

'Get onto Chisholm's and find out when they started producing advertising pens.'

'I've tried. No-one seems to know, not categorically.'

Nina suggested Ruby rang Mills to ask if it was possible to find out the age of a pen, so she did, without saying why she was asking.

Mills told her that there were many ways inks could be used to date documents but a pen was a pen. Dating a pen was another thing altogether. Biros were invented a long time ago, maybe in the sixties or earlier but Ruby already knew that. She let Nina know that she was no further forward.

When Nige came back from the shops he asked what Ruby wanted. Nina knew she should be careful to keep police business to herself but had found in the past that it helped to talk about stuff if she didn't divulge too much.

'Ok, so here's a puzzle for you,' she said. 'You find a white biro with a black lid and an advertising logo on the side. You want to know how old it is.

Was it manufactured recently or fifty years ago? What do you do?'

'Look up how long they've been making them.'

'Since 1950.'

'Ask the company that printed the logo.'

'Don't know who it is.'

'Ask the company whose logo it is.'

'They don't know when they ordered them.'

'In that case I don't know either.'

They unpacked the shopping and made lunch. It was while they were waiting for the kids to finish eating that Nige suddenly sat up.

'Did you say the pen had a lid?'

'Yes, a black one.'

'The colour is unimportant. Does the lid have a hole in?'

'Why?'

Nige was busy on his smartphone.

'I thought so. The hole in the lids of biros was introduced in the eighties after a child choked to death. Mind you, that doesn't narrow it down much. Hardly recent is it?'

However, to his surprise, Nina seemed impressed with his deductions. She smiled at him, reached for her mobile and typed quickly.

Ruby was puzzled by the message she received from Nina asking her to check if the biro lid had a hole in it. It took three phone calls and a wait of several hours but finally she had the answer, as well as a photograph. The lid did indeed have a hole in it. Meanwhile she'd ascertained the significance of this. It meant the pen had been manufactured in the 1980s or later and therefore had not been dropped while the bunker was operational. Of course it could have belonged to the victim but she hoped it was the killer's. She was looking forward to giving Hazel the news.

However, the DS was in a right mood when she finally re-appeared later that afternoon.

'Freedman's in a sodding clinic claiming he's got post-traumatic stress disorder. They say he's not fit to be interviewed and I wasn't allowed to see him.'

'So he won't be going anywhere, will he?' Ruby offered.

Hazel didn't answer but went to her desk and turned on the computer.

'Have you got that file, Ruby?'

'Yes, all sorted. And I found this email…'

She explained it concerned Armstrong and that the message came from the lad who had sketched Bradby for her. She told Hazel about the pen and the bookies and how the hole meant it must be newer than 1980, but her colleague wasn't listening. She was pounding away on her keyboard, presumably updating Mitch on why she couldn't arrest and charge Phil Freedman. Sometimes Hazel Fuller could be a right wazzock, thought Ruby, preparing to leave. But before she did, she sent an email to the lad, thanking him for the information.

'I'm off then,' she said when she'd shut her computer down.

There was no answer.

She stood, scraping her chair noisily. 'Hazel, it's late, I'm going home.'

Her colleague looked up. 'Ok.'

'I just want to say,' Ruby began. 'I just want to say that Shane Armstrong appears to be someone we should be looking at.'

'You think so?'

'Yes, I do. It's all in the file on your desk marked "Armstrong".' She pointed at it. 'He has a strong motive to keep Chris Webb quiet and the pen found in the bunker could have belonged to him.'

'Could it?'

'I'm just saying.'

Hazel didn't answer, so Ruby picked up her bag. As she made for the door, she glanced back and smiled to herself. Hazel had picked up the file and was opening it.

When Alf's mobile pinged and he read Ruby's acknowledgement, somehow he felt calmer. The police had seen his message and there was nothing he could do to change that. He went downstairs to tell his father.

'You've done the right thing, lad.'

Roy had plastic supermarket bags in his hand. He was on his way to the shops. Alf assured him there was nothing he needed, except for the things on the list.

'What's harissa and why do you need it?' his father asked.

'It's a paste,' Alf replied. 'I need it for a chicken recipe.'

'Sounds like we're in for a treat then.'

When, an hour later, there was a hammering on the door, Alf assumed his father had his hands full and couldn't get the key in the lock. But when he opened it, Shane pushed past him and stood squarely in the hallway with his arms folded.

'Who have you been talking to?' he began.

Alf waited, his heart racing.

'What have you been saying? Do you want to get him into trouble?'

'Who?'

'Jesse, of course. What exactly are you accusing him of?'

'Nothing, I don't know.' He hadn't expected to see Shane face to face. He hadn't thought about what to say to him.

'If you repeat your lies to anyone, you'll get Jesse into a whole load of trouble. Is that what you want? Your own brother?'

'He's not my brother.'

'You have the same mother, God bless her.'

Alf rubbed his forehead. This was unfair. He hadn't accused Jesse of anything. It was Shane he suspected of harming the wildlife guy. To his relief he heard the gate bang and his father appeared, loaded down with shopping.

'I thought I recognised the van, Shane. What brings you here?'

He always treated him civilly if he did have to speak to him, which was rarely. It was for Jesse's sake, he told Alf. His half-brother would always be part of their family, after all.

'I had some business with Alf here,' Shane said, standing his ground.

'So I heard. I can't say I was happy to know what you've been up to.'

'It's not your business, Roy. It's between me and Alf.'

'Not if it's police business.'

'Well it's no-one's business but mine and Jesse's. If you want to get *him* into trouble, you're going the right way about it.'

'I'd like you to leave my house. You're not welcome, you already know that.' Roy calmly opened the front door wide and stood waiting.

'If you see Jesse, just tell him he should come home.'

'He's always welcome here,' Roy answered.

Shane was about to respond but seemed to think better of it and marched out. Roy surprised Alf by slamming the door loudly behind him.

'I managed to find your harissa.' It was all he said before carrying the shopping bags into the kitchen.

Alf helped him unpack the groceries before starting to prepare the chicken thighs while his father went off to mow the lawn. Cooking was the one thing that absorbed Alf completely. Whether he was chopping vegetables, browning meat or mixing spices, he felt relaxed and even happy. He particularly liked reproducing the dishes from his mother's hand-written recipes that his father so enjoyed. That was why he was making the chicken dish for him. Alf felt that if he could spend the rest of his life working in a kitchen, he would be happy.

His contemplation was interrupted by a text from DS Fuller asking if he had a photograph of Shane Armstrong that he could send her. Puzzled, he finished preparing the meal so it was ready to go in the oven later and went to his room. There he looked out a photograph that he'd taken at Jesse's twenty-first birthday party. Alf had been given a camera the previous Christmas and had taken loads of pictures for a few months before the novelty wore off. That was six years ago but it was a good likeness of Shane. He emailed it to DS Fuller with a message saying that Shane was the man on the left and he hoped it would be good enough. Good enough for what? He had no idea why she wanted it and didn't like to ask.

Jesse's phone went straight to voicemail. Alf hesitated then told him to call. He was always welcome in their house, he said, wondering if his dad had really meant it.

Hazel laughed when she received Alf's message. He was such a polite lad, similar in age to her son and yet so different. She packed up, switched everything off, picked up a print-out of the photograph, and drove to Arkengarthdale. If Jeff Bradby recognised the man as the one he met in the pub who offered him five hundred pounds to check the traps for badgers, *then* she would take an interest in Shane Armstrong but only if he did.

When the door of the B&B opened, Hazel was met with a wonderful smell of baking. She realised that she'd not eaten since early morning and hoped she would be offered something to keep her going until she got home. Mrs Bradby didn't seem pleased to see her.

'I'm very sorry to bother you at this time on a Saturday evening and I appreciate it may be inconvenient...' Hazel hoped she sounded sufficiently ingratiating to the wretched woman.

'I was about to serve out our dinner,' she said but at the same time she opened the door wider and stepped back to allow Hazel into the hall.

'It won't take long. If your husband is here, I just want to show him this photo.'

The woman tried to look at it as Hazel waved it in front of her but she whipped it away. 'Is he in?'

'He's in the kitchen, through here.'

Hazel followed her to where Jeff Bradby sat at the table reading the paper. When he saw her he jumped up.

'Do sit down, Mr Bradby. I just want to show you this.'

She placed the photo down carefully in front of him. He folded the newspaper as he stared.

'Do you recognise the man in this photo?'

He picked it up and examined it carefully.

'Is he the man you met in the pub that offered to pay you to check the trap?' she asked.

'Yes, I think it is.' He continued to stare at it.

'Are you sure?'

'Yes, I recognise the long hair.'

'Long hair?' Hazel grabbed the photo and examined it. 'I meant the man on the left,' she said, showing it to him again.

'No. Not him. It was that young man.'

'You're certain?'

'Yes.'

She thanked the couple for their help and left. As soon as she was in her car she tried to make a call but of course there was no signal. She waited until her phone pinged into life at Reeth and stopped on the green.

'One very quick question, Alf. Who is the young man in the photograph with long hair?'

Chapter 22

'It's just an initial enquiry,' began DI Mitch Turner, 'but we are very interested in Armstrong and his son. They've got previous for dog-fighting and it looks as though they've been wandering about in Arkengarthdale trying to catch a badger to bait.'

'I'm going straight up to Bishop Auckland to interview the father now,' Hazel explained to the rest of the team. 'A traffic patrol spotted his van travelling west on the A66 and took him in last night. He's been in the cells overnight. He says he doesn't know where his son is but he thinks he's gone abroad. Ruby, can you follow that up?'

Nina watched her colleagues, waiting and hoping to get a sense of whether Phil was now off the hook. But nothing was said. They dispersed on their various tasks and she sauntered back to the office.

'Is this a serious lead?' she asked Ruby.

'Sure is.' The researcher was already at her desk, turning on her computer and searching through her notebook. 'This guy has motive, opportunity and form.'

'So he's a definite possibility for the murder of Chris Webb?'

'I think so, but Hazel's not convinced yet.'

'Perhaps she will be when she meets him.'

Ruby gave her an encouraging smile as she left. Outside Nina sent messages to Nige and Mills, letting them know that a possible suspect was being interviewed. It wasn't long before her friend was on the phone wanting to know more.

'You know the score, Mills. I can't tell you any more than that. Someone has been picked up who was operating illegally in the woods around the time the victim went missing. He has a possible motive and a bit of a reputation although he hasn't been charged before. That's all I can say, probably more than I should.'

'Can I tell Phil?'

'Yes of course.' If that meant that Mills would visit him at the clinic, it was worth the indiscretion.

Mills looked across at Nige. 'That's got to be promising, hasn't it?'

He nodded encouragingly. 'Although don't make any promises to him, will you.'

Mills grabbed her bag and made for the door. As she walked quickly down the corridor she saw Professor Cole coming towards her. She kept going but he called out.

'A moment, Dr Sanderson.'

She stopped, expecting sharp words from her Head of Department.

'I haven't seen a project proposal from you for the coming year yet. They should all have been in last week but there are a few of you that have failed to provide them by the deadline. Tomorrow please, so they can be discussed at the Faculty meeting on Friday when the funding is sorted out. Otherwise there will be no funds. It is particularly important in your case because we need to be assured that your project is relevant to the Forensics Department as well as for Archaeology.'

He strode on, presumably to chivvy other tardy academics. Mills hurried to the car park and checked her watch. There was time to see Phil and get back to the office to cobble together an acceptable proposal in an afternoon – she hoped.

Her last visit to Catterick had not been a success and she was anxious about how Phil might be with her. He'd talked about his nightmares, and seeing dead bodies. No wonder he flipped when he came across the body in the bunker. He must've been wondering what was real and what was in his mind. Anyway, hopefully she'd be able to give him the good news that someone else had been arrested and Hazel would be interrogating him thoroughly, no doubt.

The staff at the clinic seemed pleased to see her, suggesting that Phil would welcome a visitor. To her relief, they met in a day room, where two other people were sitting chatting in the corner.

'You look well,' she said, genuinely surprised at how much better he seemed.

'Good days and bad days,' he said.

'Well, it's a good day today because Nina told me that the police have someone else on their radar so hopefully they won't be bothering you now.'

'That's something I guess.'

Mills was surprised at his lack of enthusiasm but she supposed he had other things on his mind.

'Are you sleeping better?' she asked, thinking that it probably explained his more relaxed appearance.

'I am.'

'No more nightmares?'

'Not so bad.'

Something occurred to Mills but she wasn't sure if she should say anything. Unable to ignore it, she began carefully and very quietly.

'Before, at your cottage, did you find it easier to sleep when you were in the woods?'

He thought about it. 'At first, yes, I think so. But then, one night, it was worse so I stopped.'

He looked all right so she continued.

'Was that the one you told me about? When you saw... you know...'

'I thought it was a man's body being carried, as if it was on a stretcher. It was so real it freaked me out. I guess it was just a flashback. They say that happens.'

'I wonder if it *was* a dream, Phil. I wonder if what you saw actually happened and that was Chris Webb being carried away to be left in the bunker.'

He looked at her as if the reality was more difficult to comprehend than a flashback.

'You think?'

'I do,' said Mills.

She didn't know whether it was a good thing or bad to remind him of the incident. She wanted to ask if he could describe the men or the body but she kept quiet and decided to change the subject.

'I've got to write a grant proposal this afternoon,' she said. 'No pressure. It's got to be half forensics and half archaeology. I thought I could do something with isotopes.'

'Sounds challenging.' He seemed genuinely interested.

'Not really. It's about using isotopes to identify where people originate from.' She avoided mentioning bones.

She remembered the lunch at "Tan Hill Inn" the first time they'd visited the bunker. She'd told Dave all about her ideas but Phil hadn't seemed very interested.

'That's a good cross-discipline subject. Using archaeological techniques for modern forensics is always exciting. I could put you in touch with some people working in that area.'

It was the first time Phil had shown enthusiasm for anything she was doing.

They talked for a long time about the science behind her project and he gave her some names of people at universities in Switzerland and France who might be useful contacts. She made notes and scribbled ideas down until she noticed that Phil had begun to look weary.

'I'd better go and start writing this proposal I suppose but thanks for all the ideas, it's been a great help.'

She meant it. He'd kick-started her own enthusiasm for the subject again and she was keen to get writing. As she left, she wanted to try one last idea.

'It's about getting a dog, Phil. I thought that if I got a lurcher, you could train it while you're staying with me to recuperate.'

She didn't wait for an answer but jumped up and left before he could say no.

As soon as she was back in the department she rang Nina and told her about Phil seeing a body being carried through the woods.

'That actually makes some sense, Mills. They're interviewing a guy who was active in that woodland area at the time. It's possibly where Webb was shot. Forensics said the body had been moved. Did you say Phil saw two men?'

'Yes, he said it was like they were carrying a stretcher. That's why he thought it was a flashback.'

Nina assured her she would pass the information on to Ruby and did so immediately. They were alone in the office, waiting for Mitch and Hazel to return from interviewing Armstrong. Ruby told Nina she'd received a message from Hazel to find where Jesse

Armstrong was. His father said he'd left the country but wasn't sure where, possibly Spain.

'So the two of them could have killed Webb and moved the body to the bunker that night or maybe later,' Nina said.

'Would your friend remember which night he saw them?'

'I'm not sure. Probably not. He's not very well.'

'Shame. They could've moved him any time during that week.'

Ruby went back to her searches and Nina dealt with paperwork for more mundane cases that were being passed to her while Hazel did the important stuff. Finally, at five past four, the door burst open and Hazel appeared.

'Any luck with Jesse Armstrong's whereabouts?' she asked Ruby.

'Not so far. None of the usual routes have come up with anything. Was he going on holiday or just absconding?'

'No idea. Dad is suggesting that he's been acting suspiciously, so he wasn't surprised when he disappeared. He's denying any involvement himself but doesn't quite do so for his son.'

'Is he trying to cast suspicion on his son because it diverts it from him, hoping his son won't be found?' asked Nina.

'Not sure he's that clever,' Hazel said, sitting down at her desk. 'He's certainly got good reason to want to get rid of an animal welfare officer, that's for sure. He denied any knowledge of the bunker but, thanks to Ruby, we know that an Armstrong was in the Royal Observer Corps during the cold war and worked down there. It turns out it was Shane Armstrong's father. I think the son, Jesse, is the key to this. Whether he shot Webb or he assisted his father, either way he's scarpered and keeping his head down.'

'I'll keep looking for any evidence that he's left the country,' Ruby said.

Hazel picked up the phone and dialled. 'DS Hazel Fuller… Yes, hi… Yes, Shane Armstrong… Look, when you implement the search can you look for a passport belonging to a Jesse Armstrong? If you find it, call me immediately. Thanks.'

She smiled across at Ruby, 'There you are. Don't say I never give you a hand.'

Ruby winked at Nina.

Hazel then turned to her other colleague. 'It looks as though your friend is off the hook for the moment, Nina.'

'I don't think you ever really had him on the hook, did you, Hazel?'

Her friend looked at her sharply.

'I'm only teasing, Hazel. But I'm glad he can recuperate in peace.'

She immediately sent a message to Mills giving her the good news.

Roy had gone to bed but Alf was still trawling through the internet to see if there was any mention of Shane Armstrong being arrested for the murder of Chris Webb. He drew a blank and wondered if nothing had come of his allegations. Initially he thought the radiator was making the knocking sound and ignored it but the central heating hadn't been switched on for months and it was getting louder. He went to the window and looked out onto the garden. There was nothing to see but as he turned he glimpsed something moving and a torch light. He ran downstairs, unlocked the back door and went outside.

'Alf, it's me, Jesse!'

He peered around and caught sight of the outline of a figure in the dimness.

'Come here then,' he called, wondering what to expect.

His half-brother stepped into the light from the kitchen doorway. He usually dressed quite well with the latest trainers and jackets but he looked a mess. His long hair, normally tied back, was plastered over his face and his jeans were muddy and torn.

'What are you doing here?' Alf asked.

'Can I come in?'

He didn't wait for an answer but brushed past him. Alf followed him and locked the door but not before he'd glanced round the garden to ensure Jesse was alone.

'Can I have a glass of water, please?'

This wasn't like Jesse. He was usually full of bluster. Alf gave him a drink and asked if he wanted something to eat. He looked as though he needed a hot meal and Alf went to the fridge.

'I can put some chicken in the microwave,' he offered and Jesse nodded. He made a mug of tea for them both while they waited for the food to heat up.

Footsteps on the stairs and Roy appeared in his dressing gown, hair ruffled from sleep.

'I wondered what the noise was... Jesse! What are you doing here?' He didn't sound angry, just surprised.

Alf waited, hoping his half-brother would supply an answer.

'I needed somewhere to stay,' he muttered, avoiding Roy's gaze.

'That's all right. We've always got room for you, son.'

The microwave pinged and Alf fetched the plate and cutlery.

Roy stood watching Jesse eat. He seemed to be enjoying his meal and Alf was pleased. When the plate was clean, Jesse leaned back and smiled. 'That was special,' he said. 'Mum used to make that. She called it her special chicken.'

Roy patted his shoulder. It was something they had together, Alf thought. He could hardly remember the mother that he shared with Jesse. His half-brother was thirteen when she died and he must have so many memories tucked away. He wasn't jealous but it would've been nice if he'd talked to him about her.

They made up the bed in the spare room at the front of the house. Alf preferred the smaller bedroom overlooking the garden so had never moved into what had been Jesse's bedroom. He left Roy talking to his half-brother, hoping he would explain why he'd come. It could be because the police had actually arrested Shane. Finally his father came to tell him that Jesse was asking for their help.

'I told him he could stay here as long as he wanted to.'

'Is he in trouble?'

'No, I don't think so. He just needed to get away from Shane for a bit. He didn't say why but I assume it's related to this badger business.'

'Are the police involved?' asked Alf.

'He didn't give me any details. He just wanted to get away. He'll probably feel more like talking in the morning.'

'If he's still here.'

'What d'you mean?'

'In the past he only ever appeared when he needed money. He'll be off again as soon as he can.'

'That's a bit harsh, son.'

'Well, just be careful where you leave your wallet.'

Next morning, when Alf went downstairs to make breakfast, his father was already seated at the dining table talking to Jesse. They were deep in conversation but stopped abruptly when Alf went in.

'Don't mind me,' he said. 'I'll make scrambled eggs on toast.'

He left them to it and went into the kitchen. When he carried their breakfasts in he was surprised to see his father with his arm round Jesse's shoulders. He put the plates down in front of them. Both looked as if they'd been crying. He was about to leave them when his father called out.

'Stay here, lad. Jesse wants to explain something.'

Alf will never forget the next few minutes. Jesse, his big older brother was in tears. He could hardly speak but he wanted to tell Alf what he'd just told Roy. How his father had asked him to go to Arkengarthdale with him and he'd refused at first.

'That was when I called to get you to go, but you said no.'

Alf remembered the call. It was when Jesse taunted him for not telling his dad that he was working with Shane.

'Your leg was bad.'

'Sort of. I used it as an excuse. I didn't want to get involved, not again. I want to do something better than that.'

Alf caught his father nodding approvingly and thought him a fool for being taken in by Jesse.

'Tell him what happened when you did go with him, son.'

Jesse leaned forward, his head in his hands. 'There was a man. He'd been shot in the head. Dad said it was an accident and it was best just to find somewhere no-one would find him. I didn't want to but he said we'd both be put away for life if they found the body.'

'You could've refused,' Alf said. He was angry that Jesse was expecting sympathy from them but aware that he could have been in the same situation himself.

'I should've.' His voice was muffled as he sank lower towards the table.

'Why didn't you?' Alf shouted. Would he have behaved the same way?

'Hey.' Roy told him to sit down and listen. 'Carry on, Jesse.'

'Ok, so I helped him carry the guy to the van and then we drove until we reached the place where they found him.'

'In the bunker?' asked Alf, finding the conversation surreal.

Jesse leaned his head on the table and sobbed quietly.

His father was incredibly calm. 'I've suggested to Jesse that we go to the police station this morning.'

'What about school, your class?'

'This is more important, Alf. Jesse and I will go this morning to explain the situation, won't we?'

The lowered head nodded.

Alf reckoned he would run off before they got through the doors.

'So eat your egg and have a cup of tea before we go,' Roy urged. 'It'll probably be a long morning.'

Upstairs, out of earshot, Alf expressed his concerns to his father but Roy was adamant.

'You forget, Jesse was with me for nine years before he moved out. He's a good lad at heart but his father's influence has had a detrimental effect on him. This is his chance to put it all behind him.'

Chapter 23

Nina and Hazel drove over to Bishop Auckland together. The local force had detained Jesse Armstrong at the station for interview and were waiting for them to arrive. Nina was now convinced that the son had helped Shane Armstrong move the body and she told Hazel about what Phil had seen in the woods. Her colleague said little on the journey but was ready with her questions once they were there. As usual she didn't pull any punches with Jesse Armstrong.

'How do we know it wasn't you that had the gun?' she began. 'You help your dad out with his "business" don't you? You haven't had a proper job as far as I can see.'

'I've got part-time kitchen work.'

Hazel ignored him and was flipping through the file. 'Tell me about this wonderful sport of badger-baiting. Is it more fun than dog-fighting?'

'I didn't want anything to do with it. I wouldn't go with him. That's why he took Alf.'

'Now you're trying to implicate your brother?'

Nina was watching the lad. He shifted in his seat and sighed. 'No. I told him I had a bad leg so he asked Alf, that's all.'

'And did you have a bad leg?'

'No.'

'So how come you were with your dad that night when you moved the body?'

'Alf wouldn't go on the Tuesday, so he said I had to.'

'You could have said no.'

'You don't know my dad. He wouldn't take no for an answer. He threatened to… well, I had to go.'

'He threatened you?' It was Nina's turn.

'Yes.'

'With violence?'

He nodded.

So they asked him to go through exactly what happened that night and once he began there was no stopping him. At first his voice was low – almost inaudible – but after he was asked to speak up he lifted his chin and stared at the opposite wall. He described carrying the body to the van and bundling it in the back. It was damp and muddy from being left in the woods. He said it was like a nightmare, it was unreal. Hazel made a quick note for forensics to go over Shane's van. Jesse couldn't remember where they drove to but they stopped at the side of the road. His father made him help carry the body across the moorland; it was heavy and awkward and he kept stumbling. His dad was swearing at him. He left Jesse alone with the corpse while he went back for tools to open the padlock. But when he came back and tried it, the bunker wasn't locked. His father was laughing, he remembered. Jesse stopped to take a sip of water.

'How could you see what you were doing?' Nina asked.

'Head torches. He went down the ladder first and took his feet. I had to lower it down.' His face was screwed up in disgust. 'My clothes were covered in his blood.'

'What did you do with them?' asked Hazel.

'Put them in the washing machine.'

She made a note to get a list of clothing from him for forensic examination.

Nina suggested they had a short break and offered Jesse a coffee or tea.

Roy was waiting outside while Jesse was being questioned. Hours went by. Eventually they sent a young man in uniform to tell him that Jesse would be held for the time being until they had the full picture.

Nina and Hazel didn't get back to Northallerton until late afternoon and there was still plenty to do.

'Do you believe him?' Ruby asked when they gave her Jesse Armstrong's account.

'I do,' replied Nina. 'He didn't have to come in and it all makes sense.'

'So the father will be charged?'

'Both of them.' Hazel was definite. 'It will be up to the courts to decide. The forensics will show whether Jesse is telling the truth.' She was looking at the time. 'Now I've really got to go.'

She drove home wondering if she should be going out that evening. The house was quiet, Liam had already gone to judo, leaving a note to say he'd be back late. Nothing new there then. She went upstairs and showered, chose jeans and a simple shirt, redid her makeup and brushed her hair. No perfume, no jewellery and no fancy underwear. She was back in the car in less than an hour and on her way to Berwick, wondering why she was bothering. Jason Bailey was certainly not worth it but she just couldn't resist the opportunity to tell him so.

She was nearly an hour late and the front door swung open as she parked in the drive. He ushered her inside, remarking how nice she looked. She assumed they would be going out to a pub or a restaurant but she could smell cooking and he was opening a bottle of wine.

'Mum will be down in a minute,' he said with a smile. 'We thought it would be nice to cook for you.'

What? The three of them having dinner? This was not what she'd envisioned at all. She took the wine glass and perched on the bar stool.

Mother came downstairs as Jason was refilling their glasses. She was smartly dressed in beige trousers and a silky top, Hazel noted, and her hair and makeup was impeccable but she was old, definitely over seventy, maybe eighty. Hazel wasn't good at guessing ages, particularly women's.

'Hello, you must be Hazel. I've heard so much about you. A detective sergeant. That's so clever of you.'

'Hi.' She ignored the woman's patronising manner and smiled at her.

Mother insisted they move into the lounge where the seating was more comfortable. It meant Jason kept disappearing to check on the food and Hazel had to maintain polite conversation with his mother. The nosy woman kept asking about her private life and Hazel found herself telling her about Liam and how his father wasn't around. Mother expressed the view that a child needed a father and Hazel said that Liam's father was someone you wouldn't want anywhere near your children.

Unfortunately the conversation turned to Jason's family and how that deceitful girl, Linda, had behaved so badly and had alienated Jason from her only grandchild. Hazel had finished her second glass of red and had eaten nothing all day. She didn't hold back. She decided to tell the woman what she thought of her son's behaviour, sparing no details.

'I've seen the photographs, Mrs Bailey, and I can assure you she wasn't making any of it up.'

'I'm sure you're exaggerating, dear.'

Was she really unaware of the circumstances of why her son was excluded from his family? Had he hidden the truth from her or was she simply ignoring it?'

'What's that, Mum?'

Jason had appeared with a bottle and went to top up Hazel's glass. She stopped him.

'We were talking about why you can't visit your daughter,' Hazel said, looking at him defiantly. 'Your mother doesn't seem to understand.'

'We don't want to talk about that,' he said with a smile. 'Dinner will be ready soon.'

Hazel had meant to challenge him with his police record alone. To explain to him that there was no way she would touch him with a bargepole and she'd told Linda to contact her personally if he went anywhere near her or Katie in future. However, it was more difficult with Mother in the room.

'I've changed my mind,' she said, getting up and handing him her empty glass. 'I've got work to do and I don't want to waste my time with someone who beats up their wife.'

'I've explained that it wasn't my fault.' He was still Mr Cool, smiling benignly.

'I've seen the evidence. I've spoken to Linda and, believe me, it *was* your fault and you're not to go near them while I'm around. I've told Linda to let me know if she sees you within a mile of her or Katie. Do you understand?'

His countenance changed. He looked furious but was glancing at his mother. She was rigid, perhaps with embarrassment or maybe she really didn't know what he was capable of – or maybe she did. Hazel wasn't going to wait to find out. She went into the kitchen, grabbed her bag and left, slamming the door behind her. As she backed out of the drive the front door flew open and Jason stood shouting obscenities at her. She gesticulated at him and left.

Mills had known there was a chance she would be called as a witness when the panel met to discuss Sara Pendleton's cheating. The message had come the evening before and she had worried about it overnight. Now on the journey in, with the windscreen wipers beating against the lashing rain, she felt the weather matched her mood perfectly.

Nige commented that she looked very efficient, meaning she had "dressed up" for the occasion. She'd felt it warranted a skirt and that meant tights and heels and a shirt. She sat around trying to keep tidy until eleven o' clock when the panel convened. There were seats outside the Board Room and there she met Sara, looking equally smart in a very nice trouser suit.

'My mum bought it for me for job interviews,' she confided.

Mills wondered what job prospects Sara might have after the hearing. They sat side by side waiting until eventually Mills was called in. The Faculty Head smiled and thanked her for attending. She looked across the table as she took her seat and Professor Cole glowered at her. They went through her submission and at the end asked if she had any comments she wished to add. For example did she know anything about Dr Cuthbert's involvement in the case?

Mills was taken aback. She looked at Professor Cole, who had said nothing throughout the discussion, but he was looking down at his papers. In her written submission she'd stuck to the information she could provide as the examination invigilator but she knew Sara had given chapter and verse on her relationship with Cuthbert. She decided to keep it as brief as possible.

'I know that Sara has provided you with details of how she came to have the model answers for the examination. I don't have any information of my own related to that.'

They smiled and nodded, thanked her for coming and let her go.

'Please ask Miss Pendleton to come in now,' the Head of Faculty called after her.

Outside Sara looked tense. 'Can I come and see you after?' she asked as she went in.

Mills went back to the office and reported events to Nige. It was nearly half an hour before there was a gentle tapping on the office door. Nige got up and opened it, gave Mills a wave and disappeared, indicating he was off for a coffee.

'How did it go?' Mills asked.

Sara sat down and breathed out heavily. 'Well – I think.'

'How's that?'

'They believed me. They said it wasn't right but they could understand how I might have been persuaded to do what I did.'

Mills wanted to know what would happen to her marks.

'I've got to re-sit the exam. It's effectively a fail.'

'Oh, Sara!'

'No, it's all right.'

Mills was thinking that the girl couldn't pass another exam. It was a shame but perhaps it was the right outcome. Then she realised she would have to set a new question for the re-sit, everyone would.

'Marie says she'll tutor me over the summer. I've got nearly two months,' Sara said.

'Marie will?' Her friend was the brightest girl in the group. It would be hard work but if she was willing…

'Yeah. We were going backpacking together but she messaged me saying it's more important to get me a pass. Look!'

She waved her phone at Mills as proof.

'She's a good friend.'

Sara looked at her phone with a smile. 'She is.'

Mills wondered what would happen to Colin Cuthbert but Nige re-appeared and, anyway, it wasn't something to discuss with a student.

'So, a busy summer for you, Sara. If you want me to mark questions from past papers, I can do that if they're from my course. I'll be here nearly all summer.'

Sara thanked Mills profusely and left looking as if she'd already been given a degree. Mills admired her for embracing the challenge of the re-sit and genuinely hoped she succeeded in gaining a degree, finally.

'Re-sits?' Nige asked.

'Yes. She seems genuinely keen to revise over the summer. I hope she sticks at it.'

'And what's this about being here all summer? Aren't you having a holiday?'

To be honest, Mills hadn't even thought about it. She had no plans except for the two-day conference in Rome.

'No, I was thinking of getting a dog.' It just came out and she surprised herself when she said it.

'Really?'

'Yes, I've seen a lurcher at the re-homing centre. Harris he's called. He's beautiful.'

'Rosie keeps on to us to get a dog but we haven't got the room – or the time. Talking of which, I'm off. I'm going to see Phil today aren't I?'

'That's what Nina said.'

When he was gone Mills went to the website of the re-homing centre in a panic in case Harris had found a new owner. His picture was there but they may not have updated the information. She rang the number and read the description while she waited for someone to answer. *Harris is a playful boy who gets along well with most other dogs although he can be a little worried by some. Harris can initially be a little wary of people but with a tasty treat and a scratch he comes around quickly and is your best friend. With a little training, he will make an excellent family pet.*

When the woman answered, Mills made an effort to sound sensible and reliable. Her first encounter had been such a disaster that she was nervous of the reception she might be given. But no, they would love for her to come over and talk about Harris, now that she had decided that she would like to offer him a home. Mills asked if she could come that afternoon and it was arranged for three o'clock.

She went to the cafeteria to have a quick snack before setting off. It was nearly empty at this time of year when undergraduates had left and lecturers, particularly in her faculty, were off on field-work. She picked up a salad and a cold drink, paid and made for a table by the window. Outside there were figures sunbathing on the lawn and a few lads playing football.

'May I sit here?'

Mills looked up at the Head of Department's assistant. 'Of course.'

She moved her tray out of the way and Emma sat down.

'It's quiet, isn't it?' she said. 'I prefer it like this.'

'I guess you're glad when it's the end of term,' Mills said.

'Aren't we all?'

There was an awkward silence.

Emma coughed. 'I wondered if you'd heard the panel's conclusions.'

'Sara told me about the re-sit.'

She nodded. She sipped her drink, placed the mug down carefully again and leaned forward. 'Dr Cuthbert has been suspended.'

Mills was taken aback. She hadn't thought that would be the consequence of the panel's deliberations.

'It won't be for long, of course,' Emma continued.

Mills was relieved and was about to say so when she continued.

'The decision will be made quite soon, whether he is to be dismissed or not.'

'I didn't realise. I mean I didn't think…'

'I thought you'd want to know.'

All Mills could think was how she could get away from the building without having to meet him.

'I'm sorry to rush off,' she said. 'I've to see someone.' About a dog, she thought.

Alf was sweating in the hot kitchen as he pulled a tray of scones out of the oven. He'd been occupying himself by picking recipes out of his mother's cookbook. He'd sent a text to his father but had heard nothing all day. The work surface was covered in cakes and biscuits but he'd run out of sugar now so he switched off the stove and began tackling the washing up. Despite his efforts there was nothing for tea because he hadn't wanted to leave the house in case Dad returned with Jesse. There were sausages in the freezer and he hauled them out, putting them on the window sill to thaw out. He was pulling the apron off over his head when he heard the door bang.

'Dad?'

His father came in slowly and dropped into his armchair. He appeared exhausted and, for the first time, Alf thought he looked really old.

'Is there a cup of tea, son?' he asked.

Alf went, without speaking, into the kitchen and prepared a mug for both of them. He piled ginger biscuits onto a plate and carried them in.

'What's this?'

'Biscuits.'

His father snapped a piece off one and put it in his mouth. He called something to Alf in the kitchen but he couldn't hear what he said. When he carried the tea in to him, his father repeated, 'Your Mum used to make these.'

'I know. It's her recipe.'

He'd been taken aback when he tasted the raw mixture from the bowl. It was a sensation he recognised, the raw ginger powder on his tongue. He must've been allowed to lick the mixture from the spoon when she was making them.

'Have you been there all day?' Alf asked as they sat together sharing the biscuits.

He nodded. 'They've kept Jesse for more questioning. He'll be on remand until the court decides whether he will be released on bail.'

'Will they do that?'

'They wouldn't say. I told the solicitor I would offer to help if I could. He told me Jesse was assisting the police and that there is a good chance he could be granted bail. If he is there'll be conditions, maybe a curfew. I said he'll come and stay with us.'

'Here?'

'Yes, it's what Stella would have wanted. He is her son too, Alf.'

It was getting late. 'Did you want me to cook something?'

'No, those biscuits were fine.'

Alf went to the kitchen and returned with slices of lemon cake.

'Did you know that Jesse had a job in a restaurant in town? I don't know where but it's just a menial thing, washing up or preparing vegetables I think. That will stop for now of course but it's good to know he was making a go of it.'

'That'll be why Shane asked me to help him.'

'He's a good lad at heart. If he can stay with us until the trial he'll be all right.'

Chapter 24

Hazel had arrived too late for Mitch's briefing. He'd specifically called the team in to congratulate them on the arrests for Chris Webb's murder.

'Wasn't really down to us,' muttered Ruby to Nina. 'Jesse Armstrong's half-brother is the one he should be thanking.'

'Have they *both* been charged?' asked Hazel.

'Yes and they'll be remanded until their court appearance,' said Ruby.

'Shane Armstrong denies having anything to do with it, which means he's letting Jesse take the blame,' said Hazel. 'But Forensics found blood in the back of his van and on his clothing as well as the boy's. It's a good bet that it'll be a match with Webb's and that will put him right at the scene.'

'Well, I hope the son gets bail,' Nina said. 'He was clearly forced to help his father under duress.'

'True. Armstrong sounds like a right bully.' Hazel knew about bullies. Liam's father had been one. And Jason Bailey was another. She'd gone from his house to his ex-wife's last night – to apologise. It wasn't something she would share with her colleagues but she was upset that she'd disbelieved Linda's description of Jason's behaviour. She told her how easily taken in she'd been herself. They'd shared a pizza and a glass or two of plonk. She was lucky to have driven home without incident. It had left her feeling sorry for herself and she'd finished the evening with a nightcap, or maybe more than one, before bed. Hence her late arrival.

It was time for another apology, or at least a reconciliation.

'How's your friend?' she asked Nina.

Her colleague seemed surprised by the question.

'Oh, he's... well, he's in the clinic in Catterick getting treatment. But you knew that.'

'Is he any better?'

'Yes, he is. Nige saw him yesterday and they say he'll be discharged soon. He'll still be under their care but as a day patient.'

'That's good.'

'Yes, it is.'

Hoping that they were now mates again, Hazel asked, 'So when are we going to have a proper girls' night out?'

Nina laughed. With three kids she wasn't up to clubbing these days. '...and we're going away as soon as the kids break up this week.'

'Still going camping in Wales?' Ruby asked with a grin.

'Funny you should ask. Apparently one of Nige's uncles has a large house in Snowdonia which will be empty when we're there because he and his wife are visiting their daughter in Australia. So we're going to stay there, fortunately. I say fortunately – I did threaten to stay at home if camping was the only option!' she admitted.

'I bet the kids would've loved it though.'

'There's a large garden so they can camp out there if they like.'

Phil was sitting by the open patio doors when Mills arrived to pick him up from the clinic. It would be a few minutes while they sorted out his medication, so they sat in the sunshine and she told him about her trip to see Harris.

'I can't pick him up yet, though. They have to come and see the cottage and that could take up to ten days to arrange. I can't wait.'

He agreed that the dog sounded like an ideal pet for her. Perhaps it really was too soon for him to consider a faithful companion, Mills thought.

They were surprised to hear Nige's unmistakeable Welsh accent drifting in from the corridor. A moment later he appeared looking pleased with himself.

'I'm glad I caught you before you left,' he said. 'I wanted to see you both as soon as possible.'

He perched on the edge of Phil's chair.

'I've talked to Nina and she's cool with it but she said I should run it past you.'

'What is it Nige?' Mills asked. He could be exasperating at times.

'So, my uncle and aunt are going to Australia and…'

It took him a while to get the story out but the key points appeared to be that he and the family were going to Wales for a fortnight and Nige wanted to spend some of the time 'wild camping' with his sons. Nina didn't want to camp so would stay in a house – a big house – with Rosie.

'That all sounds very nice, Nige, but why have you come all this way to tell us personally?' asked Mills.

'Because Nina thinks I shouldn't go camping at all but I said Phil would probably want to come with me and she knows you're the expert in survival and stuff.'

Mills looked at Phil.

'Sounds great,' he said with a grin.

She felt a twinge of disappointment and must have shown it.

'Nina says that you must come too, Mills, to keep her company,' Nige added.

'When?' she asked.

'We're leaving this Saturday. I'm afraid you'll have to drive yourselves but it's only a few hours to Snowdonia.'

Mills agreed it was a great idea and it would pass the long wait before the home visit from the adoption support volunteer. Suddenly the moment she'd been dreading, taking Phil back to his cottage, wasn't such a big issue after all.

'I'll get Nina to call you with the arrangements, Mills,' said Nige as he rushed off.

Soon Phil was climbing into the Mini and they set off to his cottage. In the car they discussed all the questions that Nige's offer had raised: Phil had a sleeping bag but would he need a tent? Did Nige have cooking equipment? They would need to bring provisions. He became quite animated as he listed the equipment they required if they were going to be completely independent. Mills expressed the view that Nige's idea of "wild camping" was probably less wild than Phil's.

The cottage in Arkengarthdale seemed even less welcoming than it had before. It was musty from having been shut up for weeks and there were signs of the police searches that had taken place: cupboard doors and drawers open, cushions lifted from the sofa. Mills looked at Phil.

'Do you really want to stay here? We'll be leaving in a couple of days. Why don't you come back to Laurel Cottage? I've got milk and bread and everything we need.'

He nodded reluctantly and started upstairs with his bag. 'I'll just get some clothes for the trip.'

On the journey over to Swaledale Phil apologised to her for the way he had behaved while he'd been unwell. Mills looked ahead as she manoeuvred the hairpin bend down to the ford and smiled. She told him she understood and it hadn't mattered, although it had, a lot. Back in the cottage she let Phil settle in while she rang her father to let him know she'd be away for a couple of weeks. It would be their wedding anniversary soon after she returned. She couldn't believe it was seven years, she said. The seventh wedding anniversary was wool, she told him.

'So that means a cashmere sweater, at least, for Fiona and don't forget!' she instructed him.

That evening, Mills made her pasta special. They drank a non-alcoholic raspberry cordial to celebrate the fact that Mills had been allocated a grant to pursue the isotope project she'd discussed with Phil.

'In that case, when we get back I'll introduce you to a professor I know at Nottingham University who can help you,' Phil offered. 'We could go down together; I haven't seen her for years.'

Mills had been right to believe that Phil just needed something to work on. Ok, so the bunker had been a disaster but hopefully, after a break with Nige and the boys, he'd be ready to get involved in forensic archaeology again.